Praise for Manda

HOW

"With her trademark wit and charm, Manda has penned a deeply romantic and emotionally satisfying story in *How to Romance a Rake*. Her heroine is plucky and tremendously appealing, and I cheered for her well-earned happily-ever-after."

—Vanessa Kelly, award-winning author
of *Sex and the Single Earl*

"Collins's second installment of the Ugly Duckling trilogy is both a lovely, sensitive romance and a taut thriller. Collins brings a dashing hero and a wounded wallflower together in the type of love story readers take to heart. With compassion and perception, she delves into the issues faced by those who survive physical and emotional trauma. Brava to Collins!"

—*RT Book Reviews,* 4 stars

"Absolutely delightful, *How to Romance a Rake*, the second book in talented author Manda Collins's Ugly Duckling series, is an emotion-packed, passionate historical romance."

—*Romance Junkies*, 5 stars, Blue Ribbon Review

"*How to Romance a Rake* is about two damaged pe unique bond. Manda C list, and I can't wait for

"*How to Romance a Rake* is a wonderful story in which a quiet and shy heroine triumphs over adversity, overcoming obstacles to win the heart of one of London's most eligible bachelors. It is the sort of story that warms the heart and reaffirms the notion that love conquers all. Books like *How to Romance a Rake* are why I read romance."   —*Romance Novel News*

"The passion sizzles in this book, and while Collins delves into deeply emotional issues, she also infuses her stories with plenty of humor along with a terrific secondary cast . . . If you haven't read Manda Collins yet, now's the perfect time to start. *How to Romance a Rake* is going straight to my keeper shelf. I highly recommend it!"   —*Romance Dish*

"Manda Collins's *How to Romance a Rake* is one of those rare books I enjoyed in pretty much every respect. There were too many exceptional elements to mention everything, but I was particularly blown away by the quality of the writing, the excellent humor, the integration of subplots, and the characters. I would not hesitate to recommend *How to Romance a Rake* to any reader of historical romance."   —*Historical Romance Critic*

HOW TO DANCE WITH A DUKE

"Sexy, thrilling, and romantic—whether she's writing of the mysteries of the heart or of the shady underworld of Egyptian relic smuggling, Manda Collins makes her Regency world a place any reader would want to dwell."   —*USA Today* bestselling author
Kieran Kramer

"A fast-paced, adventurous love story that will enthrall readers. Her dynamic characters, a murder, and passion combine with the perfect amount of lively repartee."

—*RT Book Reviews*

"If Manda Collins keeps writing novels like [this], she is sure to become a bestseller."

—*Romance Junkies,* Blue Ribbon Review

"A vivid reminder of why I love historical romances . . . an excellent debut by Manda Collins that has me desperate for the next book in this trilogy."

—*Night Owl Romance*, Top Pick

"Manda Collins is a sparkling new voice in romantic fiction. Her smart, witty storytelling will keep readers turning pages."

—Toni Blake

"A splendid read, well written and fun."

—*Romance Reader*

"Written with intelligence, wit, and compassion, *How to Dance with a Duke* is a book that should put Manda Collins on the radar of historical romance readers everywhere."

—*Romance Dish*

"A refreshing and fun debut spiced with just the right amount of mystery."

—Rakehell, Where Regency Lives

"Warmth, wit, and delicious chemistry shine through every page . . . With a heroine to root for and a hero to die for, *How to Dance with a Duke* is a romance to remember."

—Bestselling author Julie Anne Long

Also by Manda Collins

How to Dance with a Duke

How to Romance a Rake

How to Entice an Earl

Why Dukes Say I Do

Why Earls Fall In Love

Manda Collins

St. Martin's Paperbacks

This is a work of fiction. All of the characters, organizations, and events portrayed in this novel are either products of the author's imagination or are used fictitiously.

WHY EARLS FALL IN LOVE

Copyright © 2013 by Manda Collins.

All rights reserved.

For information address St. Martin's Press, 175 Fifth Avenue, New York, NY 10010.

ISBN: 978-1-250-02384-1

Printed in the United States of America

St. Martin's Paperbacks edition / February 2014

St. Martin's Paperbacks are published by St. Martin's Press, 175 Fifth Avenue, New York, NY 10010.

10 9 8 7 6 5 4 3 2 1

For Ramona Moorer Moody Driskell—
beloved wife, mother, sister, aunt. A
voracious reader who never gave up on me and
my writing dream. And the only person in
the world who still thought of me as "little."
Miss you, Mona.

Acknowledgments

As always, huge thanks to Editor Holly who is a rock star and deserves every bit of praise I can heap on her; Agent Holly who is always ready with a reassuring word when I need one; the awesome ladies of Kiss & Thrill, Rachel, Lena, Sarah, Krista, Amy, Sharon, Gwen, and Diana—love you guys! Lindsey, Janga, Julianne, Santa, and Terri—thanks for the hand holding, y'all, you're the best. Stephen Catbert, Tiny (sweet kitties) and Charlie (good dog) for keeping me company while I'm thinking about faraway worlds instead of treats and scratching, with only a minimum of complaints. And last but not least, my family, who put up with cancelled dinners, missed phone calls, and myriad other annoyances while I'm on deadline. Love you.

Prologue

"Put the knife down, your grace," Mrs. Georgina Mowbray said firmly, infusing every bit of military command she'd ever heard during her time following the drum into her voice.

She knew how absurd it was to try reasoning with a man who was clearly at the end of his rope—especially one like the Duke of Ormond who had undoubtedly been granted his every wish from childhood. Even so, she did try reason, hoping that the drunk, exhausted husband of her dear friend Perdita would not go through with his threat. "Killing your wife will not make you feel any better."

The only sign that Perdita felt genuine terror was the visible flutter of her pulse, only a hairsbreadth from the glinting blade at her throat.

Georgina, Perdita, and the young duchess's sister, Lady Isabella Wharton, had hoped to convince the duke—who was, admittedly, not the most reasonable of men—to allow his wife to leave his household and establish her own. Since Ormond spent most of his time indulging his love for hard living in places other than the ducal mansion in Mayfair, the ladies had hoped he'd not see the request for what it was—the first step in an attempt to disengage Perdita completely from her brute of a husband.

Unfortunately they'd allowed their hopes to overreach their common sense.

Of course Ormond had responded badly to their request, Georgie reflected, grateful to feel the weight of her small pistol through the fabric of her reticule. The ladies had been foolish beyond belief to think the man who had beaten his wife for wearing the *wrong* gown to a dinner party would possibly behave in a rational manner.

His next words only confirmed it. "She wouldn't be able to leave me if she was dead," the duke slurred. His lips twisted with resentment. "She was fine before the two of you got hold of her with your lies about me."

Georgina exchanged a speaking look with Isabella. Both women were glad that Ormond had no suspicions that Perdita herself had been the one to broach the subject to them, rather than the other way around. After so many years of enduring Ormond's cruelties, this week, Perdita had reached the point at which she no longer cared what her husband would do to retaliate against her for leaving. She only knew, she'd told her sister and Georgie, that if she did not leave now, she was unlikely to live for much longer.

If this was how Ormond behaved when he suspected

Perdita's friends of luring her away, Georgie cringed to imagine what his response might be should he discover the notion had been his wife's own.

She was grateful for her own position firmly in the middle class. She'd been somewhat self-conscious when the tonnish sisters had befriended her at a charity group's meeting, but once the three had discussed their similar situations—both Isabella and Georgie were widowed from men who had been quick to anger and free with their fists, while Perdita was still married to such a man—they'd formed an alliance. Since she'd been unable to confide in the friends she'd had among the other military wives who followed the drum, Georgina was enjoying, for the first time in her adult life, the relief of knowing that someone else in the world understood just what her life with her husband had been like.

Now, of course, Georgie realized that though her own situation had been difficult to endure, at least her husband hadn't been brought up to believe that his every decision was right and proper and that he could do whatever the bloody hell he liked. There was something to be said for the discipline of the military, which at least had meant that while her husband was doing his duty for king and country, he would not be focused on humiliating *her*. Poor Perdita never knew when and where the duke would strike.

"I would never leave you, darling," Perdita said, her calm demeanor belied by the slight hitch in her breath as Ormond's shaking hand pressed the blade ever closer. "You know I love you."

Her lips tightening, Georgie knew that her friend would not be able to maintain her placid pose for much longer. Catching Isabella's eye again, she glanced down at her left hand, curling all but her index finger inward, and lifting her thumb, making the shape of a gun. She watched Isabella's eyes widen as she realized what Georgie was saying.

The sisters had been slightly appalled when Georgina informed them of her habit of carrying the small pistol in her reticule, but once Georgie explained that she'd done so for her own protection in the peninsula, and it had simply become habit, the two women had reluctantly agreed that there were some occasions when having a pistol might be beneficial for a lady traveling alone in London.

Now, Georgie was grateful to her father, who'd insisted upon buying it for her when she married. Little had she suspected she'd be using it to protect a friend instead of herself. Though at this point, she was simply grateful to have it.

Nodding slightly at Georgie, Isabella began to speak—perhaps, it dawned on Georgie, to distract the duke while Georgie removed the pistol from her reticule.

"Ormond," she heard her friend say boldly, then perhaps realizing she sounded a bit too imperious, softened her tone. "Gervase," Isabella said, switching to the duke's Christian name, "we aren't here to take Perdita away from you. We simply wish for you to perhaps be a bit gentler with her."

"Why?" the duke demanded petulantly, his bloodshot eyes bright with suspicion. "She's not gentle with me. She scratched my face earlier. Damn her." He gripped Perdita tighter, and she whimpered.

Even as she closed her hand over the butt of the pistol, Georgina did not look away from the tableau before her. She did not wish to draw the duke's attention to her in any possible way. She could see the nail marks on his face, but she was not moved to any sort of pity for the duke. He had been trying to force himself upon his wife when she'd defended herself with her nails. It was hardly punishment at all for such a heinous act, Georgie reflected grimly, slipping her index finger onto the trigger.

Clearly disturbed by Ormond's growing unrest, Isabella spoke again. Georgie hoped he would keep his attention on her friend while she, herself, gripped the pistol against her side, still not letting the reticule drop from around it, needing the element of surprise that would come when she pulled the trigger. The way he held Perdita just now, it would be impossible to hit the duke without injuring Perdita in the process.

As if reading her friend's mind, Isabella spoke up, her tone imperious now as she addressed her brother-in-law. "You should be gentle with her because she might be carrying the next Duke of Ormond." Perdita hadn't said anything of the sort to either Georgie or her sister, but Ormond had no way of knowing that.

Moving as one, Georgina and Isabella stepped forward. Georgie felt the damp of sweat on her glove where she gripped the pistol.

"There, now," Isabella said, her voice placating, as if she were trying to soothe a skittish horse, "you don't wish to harm your heir, do you?"

But they'd no sooner stepped forward than it became clear Isabella's words had been woefully miscalculated. Rather than being transported with joy, Ormond instead became angry. "What? Is this true?" he asked, turning Perdita in his arms so that he could look her in the face. "You lied to me?" he demanded, the knife trapped between Perdita's arm and Ormond's fist while he began to shake her. "You lying bitch! You told me it wasn't possible!" he cried.

"No!" Isabella shouted, rushing forward to pull him away from her sister. "Stop it! Stop it!"

"Your grace," Georgina said in a hard voice, stepping forward as she jerked the pistol upward. "I warn you to stop that at once."

As she watched in horror, Georgie saw Isabella grasp the duke by the shoulders and attempt to forcibly pry him away from her sister. When she managed to hook her arm around his neck, cutting off his airway, the duke gave a muffled growl and shoved his body backward as if trying to dislodge his attacker.

Finally as they spun away from Perdita, Georgie saw she had a clear shot at the duke, and lifting her arm, she took aim and fired.

At almost the same time, the knife, which had been held between Perdita's body and Ormond's hand, fell to the floor, and must, as Georgie later learned, have been in the right position at the right time, because when the duke fell mere seconds later it was upon the same blade with which he'd threatened his wife.

That Georgina's bullet pierced his chest at the same moment was mere coincidence. Having watched the man threaten her friend, Georgie didn't much care which wound had done the trick.

The Duke of Ormond was dead, and she for one was glad of it.

One

It's extraordinarily ugly, isn't it?" Mrs. Georgina Mowbray asked her friend, and fellow army widow, Mrs. Lettice Stowe, as they stood before the latest painting to have taken Bath by storm in the fashionable Messrs. Oliver and McHenry Art Gallery in Clarges Street. "I do see that the artist has talent, but look at the expression on poor Cleopatra's face! She looks more like she's suffering from dyspepsia than the poisonous bite of an asp."

Lettice, who was rather less interested in art than Georgina, studied the painting, wrinkling her upturned nose in concentration. "I don't know," she said frowning, "I rather like it. It's so dramatic, the way she's draping herself across the chaise, her bosom exposed as the asp sinks its fangs into her. And who's to say that the bite of an asp doesn't feel like an attack of dyspepsia. You remember old Mrs. Lafferty whose husband was with the 23rd, who swore she was only suffering a bit of the ague when in fact she was having an apoplexy."

Georgina had to concede the point to her friend,

though she was fairly certain Mrs. Lafferty had been suffering from *both* the ague and apoplexy. But she didn't wish to quibble. Lettice was, after all, her only friend in Bath aside from her employer, Lady Russell, to whom Georgie served as lady's companion.

It had only been a few months since she'd come to the spa town and she missed her friends in London dreadfully. But unlike Isabella and Perdita, who were both the widows of noblemen, Georgie was the widow of a military officer who had been just as terrible at managing his finances as he had been at being a husband. And as a result, she needed to work to earn her keep.

Today, her employer was taking tea with her niece while Georgie enjoyed her afternoon off. She would never have expected that the life of a paid companion would be so fulfilling, but it was. Georgie appreciated order and her life following the army had taught her to appreciate the well-managed life. Especially when her relationship with her husband had been anything but reliable.

"Perhaps," Georgie allowed. "Though I do still think it's a remarkably ugly painting."

Shuddering, she asked, "Does it say who the artist is?"

"I'm afraid that would be me," said a male voice from behind them. A male voice she recognized." And I agree, it's a dreadful painting."

Georgina stifled a very unladylike curse before turning to greet the newcomer. Just as she'd known he would be, the Earl of Coniston stood behind them, one supercilious brow raised in amusement.

He had been betrothed to her friend Perdita for a few

short weeks earlier in the year, and during that time, Georgie had been forced to endure his company despite her dislike of him. He'd been good enough to Perdita—had even agreed to her dissolution of the betrothal without a fuss when she realized she wasn't ready to marry again so soon after her husband's death— but from what Georgie could tell, he was the very sort of dissolute, devil-may-care nobleman that she'd come to dislike during her time following the army. Especially given that the officers had often been handed their positions by dint of money and birth while the enlisted men under them were forced to do the real work.

And, perhaps sensing her dislike, Coniston, or Con as he was called by his friends, had found great delight in teasing her whenever they were in company together.

It was just Georgie's luck that he was her employer's favorite nephew, and would therefore be underfoot for her near future at the very least.

"Lord Coniston," she said, masking her dismay with a smile, "what a surprise to find you here."

"Not so surprising, surely, Mrs. Mowbray," her nemesis said with a grin. "After all, you must have penned the invitations for my aunt for her house party this week."

"I meant," she said, maintaining her poise, "this gallery, of course, not the city of Bath." It was just like him to deliberately misunderstand her.

Unchastened, he raised his brows. "Do you mean you think me such a cultureless fribble that I could not possibly have business in such a place? For shame, Mrs.

Mowbray. Surely, I have made a better impression upon you than that."

"As a matter of fact," Georgie began, before she was interrupted by Lettice. To her shame, Georgie had forgotten her friend was even there, such was the power of Coniston to overwhelm her good sense.

"Do introduce me to your friend, Georgina," Lettice said, her eyes alight with interest as she took in Coniston's good looks and Georgie's discomfort in his presence.

Reluctantly, Georgie said, "Lord Coniston, this is my friend Mrs. Lettice Stowe. We followed the drum together." Turning to Lettice, whose grin alerted Georgie to her amusement at the situation, she said, "Lettice, this is Lord Coniston, the nephew of my employer, Lady Russell."

She would have liked to find fault in Coniston's reception of her friend, but Georgie was forced to admit that his bow and expression of pleasure at making the acquaintance were all that was proper.

"What is it you dislike about this painting, my lord?" Lettice asked, returning them to their surroundings. "I should be interested to hear your opinion of it."

A dark curl brushed his brow, giving the earl a boyish air. "Where to begin, Mrs. Stowe?" he said gravely. "There are so many things wrong with it that I don't quite know which to condemn first. I will say, however, that it is obviously one of the artist's earlier works and doubtless he would prefer it to never be seen in public again.

"I have told the owners of the gallery to remove it many a time," he continued. "But they ignore my pleas to spare the good people of Bath from the horror of it."

Suddenly, a memory of her employer saying something about her nephew winkled its way into Georgie's consciousness. Closing her eyes, she bit her lip in frustration. Of course.

"It *is* yours, isn't it?" she asked the earl in a flat tone. He'd overheard her criticizing his work. He'd never let her hear the end of it.

To his credit, Coniston did not attempt to capitalize on her embarrassment. "It is indeed, I am sorry to say," he admitted. "I gave it to a friend as a joke years ago, and the beastly fellow sold it to this gallery. Every time I come to Bath I attempt to buy it back from the owners but they refuse, claiming it's one of their most popular display pieces."

Georgie couldn't help but sympathize with him. "How unfortunate," she said, looking once more at the hideous face of Cleopatra. "You have become a much better artist since you painted this," she added, thinking how mortified she would be if one of her sewing samplers, which were truly awful, were to be hung up next to someone else's neat and tiny stitching. "The landscape in your aunt's sitting room is particularly fine."

Coniston gave her a puzzled look, as if he weren't quite sure what to think of her when she was being generous with him. Georgie felt a tug of shame. Had she really been so difficult with him? she wondered.

"It's not so bad as all that," Lettice said, again reminding Georgie of her presence. "I was just telling Georgie that—"

But before she could finish, they were interrupted by another gentleman.

"There you are, old boy," the newcomer said, slightly out of breath. "The others are waiting. Let's get out of this mausoleum."

It was clear from the man's glance at Georgie and Lettice, and his quick dismissal, that he did not consider them worth his notice. Coniston, to his credit, looked embarrassed at his friend's bad manners.

"Ladies," he said, bowing to them, "I hope you find some more pleasing works of art to occupy the rest of your time here. I recommend the very fine Tintoretto in the corner."

And with a grin, he followed his friend from the anteroom of the gallery where Georgina and Lettice stood looking after him.

As soon as he was out of earshot, Lettice unfurled her fan and briskly plied it before her face. "Lord, Georgie, have you ever seen such a handsome man in your life? Why did you not tell me you were friends with him?"

"He's hardly a friend, Lettice," she responded with a laugh. "He is my employer's nephew. We met in London at the home of a mutual friend, but to be honest we are not on the best of terms."

"What do you mean?" Lettice demanded. "You seemed easy enough just now."

Georgie was silent for a moment as she tried to put into words her complicated feelings about Lord Coniston. He was friendly enough and had been kind to Perdita. But she found it difficult to admire a man who seemed to concern himself with nothing beyond the latest on-dit or the outcome of some much-talked-about prizefight. For better or for worse, she could not admire a man who was so lacking in seriousness.

"You were in the war, Lettice," Georgie tried to explain. "You saw how some of the aristocratic officers behaved."

At her friend's nod, she continued, "Lord Coniston reminds me of them. As if he has nothing more to concern himself with than the betting book or which opera dancer he's going to bed."

"And what," Lettice asked, with a frown, "is wrong with that? Goodness, Georgina, you behave as if the war is still going on. So what if Lord Coniston enjoys himself. Wouldn't you love to have enough funds to live as you pleased? It's not as if he's leading men into battle and compromising their safety."

It was nothing more than she'd told herself any number of times, and Georgie knew that Lettice was right on some level. "True enough," she said with a shrug. "I'm not sure why I am so hard on him. Perhaps I am a bit jealous of his freedom to do as he wishes."

"If you ask me," Lettice said with a sly look, "you need to loosen your stays a bit, so to speak. Let yourself have a bit of fun. You're no longer following the drum, keeping everything neat and tidy for that brute of a husband to come back to from the fighting. And it's time you remembered it."

It was an old argument, and one that Georgie did not wish to rehash again. One of the ways in which she'd learned to cope with the unpredictabilty of her husband's temper was to keep everything else in her life as predictable as possible. She lived her life by the ticking of the small heart-shaped watch pinned to the breast of her gown. And the one freedom she did appreciate was the one that allowed her to do so without reproach.

Looking down at her watch, she gasped. "Goodness, it's gone three! I promised Lady Russell I'd be back in time for tea."

"I thought it was your day off?" Lettice pouted, looking like a thwarted five-year-old.

Since Georgie didn't wish to explain again that she'd agreed to giving up a bit of her off day under no duress and that she, in fact, had offered to do it, she remained silent.

"I shall have to get back to Henrietta Street," she said, giving her friend a quick hug. "I'll see you at the Pump Room, tomorrow, all right?"

To Georgie's great relief, her friend didn't raise a fuss. But before they parted ways on the street outside the art gallery, the other woman said, "Just remember that your employer is not your friend, Georgina. She is your employer. It's just not possible for folks of their station and ours to be friends. Not true friends like we are."

It was an old argument, and rather than go into it for the umpteenth time, Georgie merely nodded and gave her friend another quick hug before hurrying down the street toward Lady Russell's town house.

She knew there was some sense in what Lettice said. But she'd learned from her friendship with Isabella and Perdita that not all members of the *ton* were supercilious and cutting. And if truth be told, Georgie trusted the sisters more than Lettice in some instances, because though Lettice was a good enough person, she had a tendency to look for the cloud in every silver lining. And if Georgie needed anything it was to be around people with a sunny outlook on life, given her own tendency toward seriousness.

No sooner had the thought crossed her mind, however, than she remembered the letter in her reticule. She had reason for her worries, she reminded herself.

The first had arrived a month or so ago. And knowing the hell Isabella had gone through after she'd received similar missives, Georgie was prepared for something terrible to befall her now that the second and third warning letters had arrived.

I know what you did last season.

The notes were unsigned. And she was quite sure if she compared her own letters with Isabella's that the handwriting would be identical.

Someone, she knew, was out to avenge the late Duke of Ormond's death. No matter how much of a brute he'd been. No matter that his death had been a matter of preventing him from murdering Perdita before their very eyes.

Whoever was behind the threatening letters, Georgie knew that they weren't interested in fairness or logic or justice. They wanted only revenge.

On that thought, her hand slipped down to feel the reassuring shape of the small pistol resting next to the notes in her reticule.

Let this person continue to threaten, she thought grimly. When they began their campaign to frighten her, Georgie decided, she'd be ready for them.

* * *

"Why are you here, Con?"

The Earl of Coniston turned with a sense of resignation to see his cousin, Mr. Philip Callow, bounding toward the door of their aunt, Lady Russell's, Henrietta Street town house. He was fond enough of his cousin, but Philip had never been much in the brains department.

"I should imagine," he said, tapping his riding crop against his boot, "for the same reason you are here, Philip. To celebrate Aunt Russell's birthday."

Indeed, if what his sister had told him was true, Aunt Russell had invited all of her nieces and nephews to Bath for a week for her birthday celebration. Of course the spa town was not nearly as fashionable as it once was, having been superseded in the *ton*'s affections by Brighton with its seaside bathing and lavish entertainments. There had been a bit of grumbling about the dullness of the locale, but as Aunt Russell was turning seventy and, moreover, had promised them all a sizable portion of her fortune upon her death, they each made the sojourn to Henrietta Street.

"I suppose that's right." Philip sighed. "I was hoping she'd decided to cut the rest of you out and leave the whole lot to me." He picked an invisible bit of fluff from his sleeve. "Weston is cutting up rough over my bill again."

Con was not surprised to hear it. It was unfashionable to pay one's bills in a timely manner, and if Philip was anything it was fashionable.

"Sorry to disappoint you," he said just as the door

was opened by his aunt's ancient butler, Rigsby, who ushered them both into the narrow house and instructed a footman to see to the valets and bags.

"The others are gathered in the drawing room," Rigsby said with a stiff bow, indicating that the two men should precede him.

But Con waved him off. "We'll find our own way, Rigsby. We don't stand on ceremony with family, after all."

In the absence of his parents, who were more involved with one another than their only son, he'd spent most of his holidays from school in Aunt Russell's house and was intimately acquainted with its layout. Even the secret passages that had been built into it by his long dead Uncle Russell's father.

"Wonderful," his aunt said as they entered the room, which seemed filled to the rafters with his cousins and their spouses. After a general round of greetings, knowing their duty, both men made their way to their aunt.

Lady Russell was ensconced in a comfortable wing chair near the fire, and Con was troubled to see that her foot was propped up on a stool. "Come and let me have a look at the two of you," she said brightly, inviting her hand to be kissed, a silent order with which both Con and Philip complied.

Con knew that to any outside observer, he and Philip were obviously related. Both of them bore the dark hair and blue eyes of the Callows, but there the resemblance ended. Whereas Con had grown into his frame some years ago, and bore his height and breadth of shoulder with confidence, Philip was rather more like the family name, that is, callow. Even so, standing side by side, they were a handsome pair and more than one set of female observers in the *ton* had remarked upon it.

"Philip, I believe you've grown," their aunt said, surveying the twenty-three-year-old with a keen eye.

To Con's amusement, the young man's ears reddened. "Aunt Russell," he said with an adolescent whine. "You shouldn't remark upon such things."

"But it's the truth, Phil," their cousin, Mr. Geoffrey Callow, chortled from his position at the mantel. "Have you got lifts in your shoes? I thought—" He broke off as his wife, none too gently, poked him in the ribs.

"Pay no attention to him, Philip," Elisabeth, Geoffrey's wife, said sweetly. "I think you're looking quite fine. Is that coat Weston?"

While Philip and the married couple discussed fashion, Con leaned forward to kiss his aunt's paper-thin cheek. Was it his imagination or did she seem more frail than she had the last time he'd seen her?

"Is it the gout again?" he asked, indicating her foot. "I thought the waters were supposed to be doing that some good."

"They were for a time," she said with a frown, "but I'm afraid even the foul-tasting waters of Bath fail to make a difference now."

"What does your physician say?" he asked. "Surely there is something to be done."

"He insists that she should change her diet," said Georgina Mowbray, stepping forward with a shawl, which she wrapped around Lady Russell's shoulders, despite the warmth of the fire. "I hope you will attempt to reason with her while you are here, my lord. She refuses to give up lobster patties no matter how I remind her of their effect on her foot."

"Mrs. Mowbray," Con said, giving the lady a slight bow. "How good to see you again so soon."

"What's this?" Lady Russell demanded, looking from one to the other. "You didn't tell me you'd seen Con lately, Georgina."

Giving Con a low curtsy, Mrs. Mowbray bowed her head and turned to Lady Russell. "Lord Coniston and I ran into one another in the art gallery earlier. I did not have time to tell you when I returned because the guests began to arrive."

Lady Russell's eyes brightened as she turned her gimlet gaze on Con. "I should have known you'd go to the gallery first," she told her nephew. "Were you able to get him to take that abomination of a painting down once and for all? I vow I have no notion of why he wishes to hang it there for all the world to see."

"Bath is hardly all the world," Con said wryly, "but I see your point." The Cleopatra painting was one of his earliest and lacked the skill and technique his work had become known for over the years. Now that the earl was considered to be one of England's most talented artists, the Cleopatra, despite its amateurish technique, was quite valuable and no amount of money would convince the owners to part with it. Much to Con's dismay.

"At least," he continued, "you display some of my better works so that I can rest easy knowing that the Cleopatra is not the only example of my talent to grace Bath."

"Is it usual for aristocrats to dabble in the arts?"

Mrs. Mowbray asked, her blond brows raised in curiosity. "I had thought—"

Con finished for her. "That it would be akin to being in trade? Oh, it is and many of my peers have let me know it. But since I haven't sold any of my paintings since my salad days it's not much of an issue anymore. I paint wholly for my own enjoyment now."

"Or mine," Lady Russell said with a grin, recalling to Con how long it had been since he'd seen her look really happy. He must credit Mrs. Mowbray with some of that, he knew.

"Which reminds me," Lady Russell said. "I should love to have a little portrait of my spaniel, Percy. He's such a little dear."

Con bit back a sigh; it would be the devil to get Percy, the most spoiled pet in three counties, to sit still long enough for a portrait, but since his aunt asked it, he would have to try.

"You shall have your work cut out for you, my lord," Mrs. Mowbray said with a rare smile. The effect was rather like watching a storm turn into a sunny day in the space of a breath. When Georgina Mowbray left off her usual, serious expression, she was a beauty. Con had suspected as much before, but had never really seen it for himself. How the devil did the woman not have a line of suitors leading out into Henrietta Street? he wondered. "Percy," she continued, breaking him out of his daze, "is as profligate as the Regent and as difficult to control as Byron at his most reckless. I wish you luck with him."

"Percy and I are acquainted, Mrs. Mowbray," Con replied with an exaggerated grimace. "I have little doubt painting his portrait will be as wretched as anything I've attempted. And that includes the time Uncle Russell made me empty the chamber pots for a week as punishment for frightening the chambermaid with a frog."

"Impudent boy!" his aunt chided, rapping him on the knuckles with her fan."I thought you were renowned for your charm. You do not speak to your legions of female admirers of chamber pots, I should think."

Con felt his ears redden. "Not so many as all that, Aunt," he said, trying not to sound like a green lad just up from the country. When a low feminine chuckle sounded from his aunt's companion he turned. "I suppose you find this amusing, Mrs. Mowbray?"

"To be perfectly honest, my lord," the widow responded. "I am enjoying the sight of someone besides myself being raked over the coals by Lady Russell. It is uncharitable, I suppose, but the truth."

Her wry humor gave Con, who had been puzzled by Mrs. Mowbray's friendship with Perdita and her sister Lady Isabella, some notion of what the sisters found in common with her besides an interest in charity. From what he could remember, the widow had followed the drum with her husband, who had been killed in the war. It was a rough life for a woman, he knew, and now that he'd glimpsed the beauty beneath the serious demeanor, he wondered if perhaps her usual manner wasn't something she used as a defense against unwanted attentions.

"Well, I like this," Lady Russell groused, though it was clear she was enjoying the repartee. "My nephew and my companion enjoying a laugh at my expense. I suppose it's to be expected at my age."

To Con's surprise, Mrs. Mowbray leaned down to hug his crotchety old aunt. And his aunt did not rebuff the show of affection. That she'd been able to break through his aunt's shell was another point in the widow's favor.

"You know we adore you, Lady Russell, but even you must admit that you have a certain fondness for exposing our vulnerabilities." Mrs. Mowbray smiled as she spoke the words and Con was amazed to see his aunt looking sheepish. "I pray you will remember what you're about this week, when there is so much at stake."

"At stake?" Con asked, wondering to which issue the lady referred. "I think the celebration of my aunt's birthday is hardly so fraught as that."

"Oh, do not be so nice," Lady Russell said with a dismissive wave. "You know quite well that the majority of people in this room are here to toady me into enlarging their bequests in my will. If I weren't so fond of them I'd be quite put out."

Looking about him, Con had to admit that his aunt was likely right. Some of these cousins he hadn't seen in the same room in years. But then again, his aunt hadn't celebrated her birthday in such a grand fashion in years. If ever.

"That's as may be," he conceded, "but it's not why I'm here."

"Of course you aren't, dear boy," his aunt said, patting him on the cheek. "You were always my favorite. And not just because you were the eldest. Mrs. Mowbray, you will not account for it," she said to her companion, "but Coniston was such a dear thing when he was a boy. He could sing like an angel and—"

"That's enough, Aunt," he said cutting her off before she could continue. What next? A recitation of his first pony ride? "I'm sure Mrs. Mowbray would rather not listen to tales about my childhood. We are, after all, here to celebrate you."

"Yes, we are," his uncle Rex said in his nasal voice as he approached their circle. "Hortense, I'm so glad you decided to have this little party. It's good to have the whole family back together again. Even if one could wish that you'd chosen a more entertaining spot. Bath is positively dull when compared with London."

While his uncle prosed on, Con felt Mrs. Mowbray's eyes on him, and when he looked up, she quickly glanced away. On impulse he reached out and touched her on the arm, indicating with a tilt of his head that they should move to the small window alcove on the far end of the room. Warily, his aunt's companion gave a brisk nod and made her way through the various clumps of Callow cousins to the window. Striding across the room behind her, Con was determined to put whatever it was that gave her a distrust of him behind them.

Because despite the affability he'd seen from her during their little chat with his aunt, there was something wary lurking behind Mrs. Mowbray's eyes. And he refused to spend the next week enduring covert glances of distrust from the woman.

Georgie fought down a wave of unease as she walked to the window overlooking the back garden. She knew

that outwardly she gave no evidence of being flustered—
she'd long ago mastered her expressions so that whatever
she felt inside was hidden from the outward observer—
but inside she worried that she'd done something that
would make the earl press his aunt to dismiss her. Or
that he'd learned somehow of the threats she'd been
receiving. Fear for his aunt's safety would certainly be
reason enough for him to wish her gone.

Reaching the window, she steeled herself to maintain her expression, and turned to face the earl. And
found him watching her.

Fleetingly she wondered if this was what it had been
like for Perdita to have all of his attention focused on
her.

Perdita had never really explained why they had broken their engagement but Georgie knew the reasons
for the dissolution were all on her side. If Coniston was
pining for her friend, however, Georgie couldn't see it.

"What is it you wished to discuss with me, my lord?"
she prompted, wanting whatever it was he was going to
say out in the open before she lost her poise.

His words, however, though not the warning or dismissal she'd expected, threatened to shatter her reserve
all the same.

"Have I done something to offend you, Mrs. Mowbray?" the earl asked, his usually good-natured expression clouded with concern. "Because for the life of me
I cannot remember anything which might have put us
at loggerheads. With the exception, of course, of my
engagement to your friend, the young dowager Duchess of Ormond, the breaking which, I am quite sure
you know, he was her choice."

Georgie stared at him for a moment. Of all the scenarios she'd imagined, this one had never crossed her mind.

"I'm not sure I know what you mean," she responded, pretending confusion to buy herself some time.

"Do not brush me off, madam," he said, deliberately leaning in so that she had no choice but to meet his gaze. "I know there is something I've done to make you uneasy in my company and I wish to know what it was. And barring that, I'd like to know what I might do to make amends so that my aunt will not be forced in the next week to feel the tension between us. She is obviously not in the best of health right now and I do not wish to worry her."

Georgie was taken aback by his directness. But she supposed he was right. It would bother Lady Russell to see them at cross-purposes and Georgie did not wish to worry her. She'd grown quite fond of the older lady during the past few months.

And it was hardly Lord Coniston's fault that Georgie thought him an undisciplined fribble. Lettice had been perfectly correct when she'd said it was his right to behave as he wished. He could hardly be expected to live his life according to Georgie's standards of correct behavior. And he clearly adored his aunt, which was certainly a point in his favor.

Addressing the earl, she made herself look him in the eye. "You are correct when you say that your aunt is not in the best of health, Lord Coniston," she agreed. "And if my manner toward you has given offense, I sincerely apologize. I may have been a bit stiff, but that is simply my own cow-handed manners, not anything purposely insulting at any rate." To her own surprise what she said was the truth. She hadn't intentionally been cool toward him. She simply did not know how to go on with him. She was hardly in the company of handsome earls every day.

"Then what is the problem?" Coniston demanded, his brows drawn together. He stood so close to her that Georgie could smell the sandalwood of his cologne, and see the laugh lines fanning out from the corners of his eyes.

"There is no problem with you, per se," she explained, willing her attention back to the matter at hand. "I am simply not all that comfortable around . . ." She paused, searching for a word. "Gentlemen," she forced herself to say aloud.

Coniston's pique turned to puzzlement. "You're afraid of me?" he asked in a bewildered tone. "Whyever for? If I've done something to give you a fear of me, I do sincerely apologize, Mrs. Mowbray. It was certainly never my intention." If the situation were less serious, Georgie would have been amused at the echo of her own earlier apology.

"It's nothing you've done," she assured him with a smile. "Indeed, you have been a perfect gentleman. I have simply not been accustomed to moving in such elevated circles and I fear that my own natural reticence coupled with my diffidence in the company of gentlemen has made me seem less than friendly. Which has certainly not been my intention."

It wasn't that she disliked him, personally, she suddenly realized. Just that he seemed so much like the titled officers she'd known in the army. Which was hardly his fault.

Unaware of her mental struggles, Coniston rubbed his chin thoughtfully, his eyes troubled. "I must admit, I had not considered that you might find me intimidating," he said with a frown. "I do not mean to brag, but I have a rather easy rapport with most of the people I encounter. And though, yes, I am an earl, I hardly think myself to be so fearsome that I would cause a spirited lady like yourself to cower before me." The twinkle in his eyes let her know that this last was meant to be a jest.

"I would hardly call it cowering," said Georgie with a roll of her eyes. "It's more that I do not know how to be comfortable in your company."

He was clearly nonplussed by the whole situation, Georgie could see that by the shadow that lurked behind his affable smile. Still, he did not give up or decide to wash his hands of her. "I hope that over this week, Mrs. Mowbray, you will give me the chance to prove to you that I am not the brute you think me."

Before she could protest his characterization of himself as a brute, Coniston continued, "In fact, I insist upon it."

"Oh, but surely there's no need," she began, feeling a bit sheepish at his declaration. Even if she didn't find him the most comfortable companion, he was under no obligation to ease her mind.

"I believe there is every need," he said firmly. "And I warn you I won't take no for an answer."

Georgie sighed. She supposed she had no choice.

And at least this might allow her to gain enough familiarity with him that Lady Russell would not be made uncomfortable by her own unease.

"All right," she said with a rueful smile. "But you must agree that if by the end of the week I still feel this way, then you will leave me in peace with my shyness."

He held out his gloved hand. "Agreed."

This might not be a particularly comfortable week, Georgie thought as she shook his proffered hand, but it would certainly be interesting.

Two

*D*inner that evening was a spirited affair, with Lady Russell's nieces and nephews recounting stories from their childhoods and their time on the Coniston estates in Essex. Though he'd not particularly looked forward to a week in the company of his relatives—who could be a trial if one were in the wrong sort of mood—Con enjoyed himself far more than he would have expected.

He was displeased to notice, however, that Mrs. Mowbray was ignored by virtually everyone. Her dinner companions were his uncle Bertie, who was deaf as a post, and his cousin Lydia, who was, as far as he could tell, as shallow a young lady as he'd ever met. Since Mrs. Mowbray could contribute nothing to her popularity in the *ton*, Lydia saw no reason to pay her any mind. There were far more important people to converse with, such as their cousin Roderick who drove a high-perch phaeton and had once dined with Byron.

His aunt's invitation for the week's festivities had come as something of a shock to Con on two fronts. First, that his aunt was celebrating her seventieth birthday. It was impossible to imagine that the vital woman who had cared for him when his own parents had been too self-involved to do so was at an age when it became reasonable to speak about bequests and inheritances. That in itself had been enough to ingest, but along with her announcement of the birthday celebration, his aunt had included a request that he attempt to learn just what it was that bothered her companion so much. Of course, Con hadn't known at the time that her companion was Mrs. Mowbray. But her identity did not change the fact that he would do whatever his aunt asked of him, which in this case included assisting the woman who wished he would go to the devil.

When the gentlemen rejoined the ladies in the drawing room after the obligatory port and cigars, Con noted that Mrs. Mowbray had retired to a seat in the corner with some sewing while the rest of the ladies chatted animatedly on the other side of the room.

"Con!" Lydia greeted him as he entered the room with the rest of the men. "You are just the man we need! I've been trying to convince Mama to let us take an excursion to the abbey ruins at Farley Castle tomorrow. She says we've only just arrived and should go to the Pump Room first." She gripped him by the arm and pulled him into the circle of ladies—the younger on the left and the elder on the right. "Everyone knows that the only people who come for the Bath season these days are unfashionable ladies who failed to take during their London seasons, and elderly people who come for the waters. It's so deadly dull. I cannot possibly remain here if we're to be confined every day to the Pump

Room for our entertainment. And the assembly isn't until Wednesday evening."

Unsurprised to hear his cousin's complaints, he extricated himself from her viselike grip on his arm. "What can I possibly say or do to change your mother's mind, Lydia?" he asked, with a glance at his cousin Clara, Lydia's mother, who frowned at her offspring. "She's correct to say that you've only just arrived. I doubt you've even said two words to Aunt Russell."

"I have too." Lydia pouted, drawing a series of surreptitious eye-rolls from her fellow cousins. The girls were used to her exaggerations and dramatics, and the boys were simply indifferent. Aunt Russell, Con noticed, was pretending to snooze, but taking in every word that was said. "I'm sure she'd be perfectly content with us going on a bit of an excursion tomorrow. Wouldn't you, Aunt?"

"Lydia," her mother chided, "hush. Let your auntie rest."

"I'm not asleep, Clara," the old woman said, opening her eyes. "I was simply resting my eyes for a bit." Turning to her great-niece, she said. "I do not suppose I would mind for you young people to take in the outdoors hereabouts. It was not so very long ago that I was young, you know. And I remember being incredibly impatient with my parents for trying to keep me cooped up indoors. Of course, back then Bath was the height of fashion and all my friends and I were desperate as could be to be seen in the Pump Room. How things change."

"Aunt, you are being too polite," Clara said firmly. "I won't have my daughter offering you such disrespect.

Lydia, I've a great mind to send you back to stay at home with your younger brothers."

Seeing the mulish set of his young cousin's jaw, Con interceded on her behalf. "Clara, would you be more agreeable to Lydia's scheme if Mrs. Mowbray and I agreed to go along with them? That way you and the rest of the parents could have the day to yourselves. And I do think that Aunt is sincere when she says that they should go." And the time alone with Georgina would give him a chance to make her more comfortable around him.

Seeing that Con was serious, Clara looked to her aunt who nodded her approval. Raising her hands in capitulation, she said, "I suppose if you are willing to go along, I cannot object. But only if you wish to do it, Cousin. I know what it is like to lead a dozen or so young people on an expedition. And what of poor Mrs. Mowbray? She hasn't even the excuse of being related to these wretches to save her."

But to Con's surprise and pleasure, Mrs. Mowbray had left her sewing and come to stand near the little group. "I shouldn't mind it at all, Lady Clara," she said with a smile. "I've been wishing to see Farley Castle myself, so Lydia's suggestion is quite welcome. If, that is, Lady Russell can spare me."

"Of course I can, my dear," said Lady Russell with a delighted smile. "I was just beginning to feel a bit guilty for keeping you tied to me all this time and this excursion is just the thing to relieve my conscience."

"Do not argue with her, Mrs. Mowbray," Con said before Georgina could object again. "Just agree to come with us."

"As long as Lady Russell is agreeable," Mrs. Mowbray said with a smile, "then so am I."

A huzzah from the young cousins went round the room.

"You won't regret this, Mrs. Mowbray," Lydia said brightly, as she led her cousins to the other side of the room so that they could discuss the next day's outing.

"Thank you, Con," Clara said with feeling. "I will feel much better knowing you and Mrs. Mowbray are looking after Lydia and the others. They can get up to mischief at times."

"Better you than me," said their cousin Lord Payne, from his chair near the fire. "I'd rather visit the tooth drawer than be ordered about by Lydia. That chit has the devil's own mind when it comes to scheming."

"What a horrible thing to say about my daughter," Clara said with a laugh. "Not that I don't agree, but even so, it is horrible."

"I know how to handle Lydia," Con said easily. "I'll simply let her think that everything is her idea. She may order me about as she likes, but I will only obey her as I wish to do so."

"But what of Mrs. Mowbray?" Aunt Russell demanded. "I won't have my companion being treated like a glorified housemaid. By Lydia or anyone else."

At her words, Con's eye flew to Mrs. Mowbray, who only betrayed her embarrassment with a slight flush. "Lady Russell," she said in a soft voice, "you mustn't trouble yourself. I am sure that Miss Lydia will be all that is proper. Besides, I truly do wish to visit the ruins, so her notion to go there was a very welcome surprise."

"Then it's settled," Con said, wanting to spare Mrs.

Mowbray any further upset. "We shall all go and enjoy the ruins. I for one am looking forward to bringing my sketchbook. It's been some time since I simply focused on capturing a scene in charcoal."

At that the conversation turned, and to Con's relief, no more was said about Mrs. Mowbray's position in the household.

Georgie closed her bedchamber door firmly behind her and relaxed for the first time all evening.

Located at the far end of the corridor, her room was small enough that she had at first wondered if it had begun life as a closet. No matter how small, however, she loved the tiny chamber. First as a child, then as a wife, living in the army's world of limited privacy she'd longed for nothing more than a room of her own. So, any place that had a door and didn't require her to share with someone else Georgie counted as a luxury.

Not to mention that having this tiny room was the first step toward her ultimate goal of owning a small cottage in the country, just as she'd always dreamed. Though her wages from Lady Russell were hardly more than room and board, Georgie tucked every bit into her nest egg in the hopes that one day she would be her own mistress.

Stepping further into the chamber, she lit the lamp beside her bed with the taper she'd used to come upstairs, appreciating the glow of light on the rosewood furnishings.

What a change this evening had been from the night before, she reflected, stretching a bit to relieve the ten-

sion in her neck. She'd known that the arrival of Lady
Russell's family would herald an end to the peace she
and her employer had enjoyed since she'd taken the position as her companion three months ago, but she hadn't
realized just how trying the family would be. And at
the top of her list was the enigmatic Lord Coniston, who
had kept a watchful eye on her all evening.

From the moment he entered the drawing room, she'd
felt his scrutiny like a staying hand. She could understand why he felt so protective of his aunt. Lady Russell had told Georgie about how she and her late husband
had acted as surrogate parents to the young boy while
his own parents lived out their tumultuous romance in
London and Paris and wherever the whims of their fast
set took them. He would of course wish to ensure that
his aunt's companion was someone he could trust. Despite her friendship with Perdita, he needed to vouch
for her himself before he let her remain in his aunt's
employ.

Unbuttoning her gown, which had been made with
the fastenings in front since she hadn't a maid of her
own, Georgie didn't wait to take it off before she began
to loosen the stays beneath. Sighing with relief, she set
about making herself ready for bed, washing with the
cold water in the basin, changing into a nightgown, and
brushing out her hair before the small mirror on the
makeshift dressing table.

As she followed her nightly routine, the various bits
of conversation and chatter she'd overheard that evening played through her mind. At the forefront, always,
was Lord Coniston.

She had to admit, she thought, braiding her long

blond locks so that they wouldn't get tangled in the night, that he was as handsome a man as she'd ever seen. More than once during his betrothal to Perdita she'd noticed as much, though of course she had not allowed herself to think more than that. Yet, despite the dissolution of his betrothal, he was still off limits. Not only was he her employer's nephew, he was also an earl. While she was simply an army man's daughter who'd had the good fortune to form a friendship with a pair of aristocratic sisters.

Now Georgie felt as close to Isabella and Perdita as if she were related to them by blood. But, as she was reminded when Lord Coniston looked at her, no matter how comfortable she felt with the two aristocratic ladies when they were alone together, there was still an ocean's width of difference between them when it came to how the rest of the world perceived them. And she needed to remember that when dealing with her employer's nephew, who for all that he'd set out to win her over, was still an earl and could demand to be treated as such by the likes of her.

While she prepared for bed, the wind outside had picked up a bit. The years of following the army had left her with an abiding need to breathe fresh air when she could, so Georgie had left the window open earlier that day. Now, however, the evening was growing chilly, so she stepped over to close the window and the curtains for the night.

The moonlight was bright, and as she paused to appreciate the way it illuminated the world outside, she was startled to see a figure standing in the garden below. Taken aback, she shivered as she realized the person—a man—was peering up at her. When he lifted his head a bit and the moonlight shone on his face, she let out a startled cry.

The man was her dead husband.

Despite the early hour, Con had decided against going out to the tavern with his younger male cousins and instead retired to his bedchamber to look over the papers his estate agent had given him before he left for Bath. He'd learned the hard way that ignoring his holdings could lead to trouble—a missive from his steward read too late had led to a costly repair to the roof of Coniston Grange last summer—and he was not so wealthy that he could afford another such mishap. Besides, when his cousins had tried to tempt him out with the promise of pretty wenches, for reasons he was not willing to contemplate, his mind had conjured up the image of Georgina, her blond hair gleaming in the lamplight.

He must be more fatigued from the journey to Bath than he'd thought. She was an attractive woman, he conceded, but hardly the sort to inspire flights of fancy. As his aunt's companion she was out of bounds anyway. Instead of carousing with his cousins, he'd do much better to get some rest and put the pretty, if stubborn, lady from his mind.

No sooner had he shrugged out of his coat, however, than he heard a startled cry from down the hall.

His reverie broken, Con's head snapped up as he met his valet's gaze.

"What was that?"

"Like as not someone has seen a wee mousie, my lord," Burns said with a frown. "'Tis the time of year when outside creatures long to come in."

"Even so, I'm going to see what's amiss," Con said, heading for the door. He was probably just imagining things but the cry had sounded feminine. And terrified. It would do no harm for him to investigate the source of it. He was, after all, the head of the family despite the fact that the house belonged to his aunt.

Pulling his coat back on, he strode out of his chamber and into the hallway beyond. His family members, in various stages of undress, were standing in their doorways. They all denied having made the sound, and when he reached the far end of the hall he saw his cousin Clara speaking to Georgina.

"Is aught amiss?" he asked, as he reached them. Georgina, he noted, was pale but otherwise appeared unharmed.

"I was just telling your cousin that I am quite fine, my lord," she said, tucking a stray lock of blond hair behind her ear. She'd braided it in preparation for bed, and he couldn't help but imagine what it would look like spread out upon a pillow. Oblivious to his thoughts, she continued, "I do apologize for disturbing everyone but, really, I am well. I simply thought I saw a mouse in the wardrobe. I feel so foolish for mistaking a balled-up stocking like that."

Everything she said sounded plausible, but Con was quite sure that she was lying. He'd played cards since his youth and had come to figure out that there were certain ways to tell when a fellow player was telling an untruth, and for whatever reason, Georgina was doing so now. He could see it in the way she didn't look at them as she told her story.

"We've all done it, my dear," Clara said, touching the other woman's arm. "I mistook a potted plant for a man once after I'd spent the entire evening before reading one of Mrs. Radcliffe's gothic tales. I will never fail to be amazed by the degree to which the mind can be fooled. It is really quite extraordinary."

"But you're sure it was a stocking?" Con demanded, watching as Georgina blushed under his scrutiny. She might well blush, he thought, given how she was fibbing to Clara. "There was no other reason for you to be upset?"

But before Georgina could respond, Clara placed herself between them. "Really, Con, you needn't glare at her as if she's a common criminal. The poor woman's had a fright. We should all just leave her be and get back to our own bedchambers."

The relief on Georgina's face was enough to tell him that she was indeed hiding something. Still, he could hardly press her further when Clara was here to stand as watchdog.

"I beg your pardon, Mrs. Mowbray," he said with a stiff bow. "I did not mean to alarm you. I was merely attempting to assure myself that you are recovered from your fright."

"I am quite well, my lord," Georgina responded, her features once more schooled into a mask of calm. "I do, however, wish to ensure myself that your aunt hasn't been disturbed by my foolishness."

Clara, however, forestalled her from leaving. "Never fear, my dear, I will go check on Aunt Russell. You return to your bedchamber and get some rest."

One by one, his cousins had returned to their bedchambers, leaving Con alone with Georgie in the hallway.

"Are you sure there's nothing amiss?" he asked once Clara was out of earshot. "I somehow do not think you are the sort of woman who would shriek at the sight of a mouse."

"I'm afraid you do not know me well enough to make such an assessment, my lord," the widow said with a frown. "We've not met above a dozen times at most. How can you know what might startle me or not?"

"That is true enough," he said, not fazed by her setdown in the slightest. "I will perhaps get to know you better now that we are to be in such proximity to one another for the next week."

Realizing what that must have sounded like, he added, "To ensure that you are the right person to care for my aunt, I mean."

"I believe it is up to your aunt to make that decision, is it not?" Georgina asked, not backing down an inch. He found himself impressed even as he was annoyed by her refusal to cow to him.

"It is," he agreed, "but that doesn't mean that I cannot ensure that her choice is a wise one."

She looked as if she might wish to argue, but said, "My lord, it has been a long day. And we must be awake bright and early to accompany your nieces and nephews to the ruins. Do you suppose we might argue over who knows best for your aunt tomorrow?"

He realized then that she was still pale, and upon closer inspection, he saw that there were purple shadows beneath her eyes. Dammit, when had he become the sort of man to browbeat a woman into doing his bidding? "My apologies, Mrs. Mowbray," he said sincerely. "I was merely concerned for your and, by connection, my aunt's safety. As you say, we must accompany my young relations to the ruins tomorrow. I will bid you good night."

With a bow, he turned and strode back down the hall toward his bedchamber.

Behind him he heard her shut her bedchamber door and then set the lock with a firm snap.

Safe inside her bedchamber, Georgie leaned back against the door with a sigh of relief.

It would have been easy to hide the unease that gripped her if Lord Coniston hadn't been there watching her with his gaze that seemed to see straight into her very soul. She'd never been a particularly skilled liar, but had his lordship not been there watching her, she was quite certain she'd have been able to pass the incident off without anyone suspecting anything was amiss.

Remembering the moment when she'd realized just who the man in the garden was, she began to shiver uncontrollably. Moving away from the door and changing back into her night rail, she lifted the counterpane, climbed beneath, and curled into a protective ball.

No matter how she tried to tell herself that it was impossible, she could not deny that the face looking up at her from the garden was that of her brutish, cruel, vindictive, and very much deceased husband. The husband she'd seen dead of his wounds on a battlefield in Belgium.

Throughout her horrific marriage to Colonel Robert Mowbray, the one thing she'd relied upon was the fact that no matter how out of control his behavior became, her own mind was always to be relied upon. Robert might fume and curse and strike out at her, but Georgie would remain in control of her own emotions. And that, above all things, gave her the inner strength she needed in order to survive.

Little wonder, then, that seeing Robert, or his double, in the garden behind Lady Russell's house had sent Georgie into shock. The notes referring to Ormond's death had been disturbing, certainly, but they hadn't made her question her own sanity.

"He is dead and gone," she said, wrapping her arms around herself to keep the chill at bay. Over and over she repeated the words, like a prayer.

It was a long, long time before she slept.

Three

The next morning dawned far too early as far as Georgie was concerned, but she could hardly complain when she'd been the one to cause her sleeplessness.

In the cold light of day, she was amazed at her own foolishness of the night before. How could the man in the garden have possibly been Robert? The short answer was that he couldn't. Ashamed of her own foolishness, she marveled at the way she'd allowed a trick of moonlight to frighten her. Her dead husband, indeed. Georgie was quite sure she'd never been so foolish as she had been last night. She'd tended Robert's wounds herself when he'd been brought back from the battlefield at Waterloo. His medals were tucked away in her jewelry chest. Medals awarded to him posthumously, for heaven's sake. What she'd seen last night had been the conjuring of a tired brain after a day spent preparing for Lady Russell's guests.

Nothing more, nothing less.

Dressing quickly, she put the finishing touches on

her hair and hurried from her bedchamber to visit her employer.

She found Lady Russell tucked up into her bed still, a cup of chocolate on the tray before her. "Ah, Georgina," she said with a smile. "I am glad to see that you are recovered from your fright last night. I cannot account that I heard none of the to-do last night. I suppose I was more tired than I at first thought. I hope you are none the worse for wear."

"Not at all," Georgie said, sitting down on the side of Lady Russell's bed. "It was a trick of the light. I am fit as a flea now thanks to a good night's sleep.

"Now, enough of me, what of you? Are you certain that you will have no need of me today? I can still tell Lord Coniston that I am unable to accompany them to the ruins. In fact, I'd prefer it, I think. I'll just ring for a footman to let him know."

But Lady Russell reached out a staying hand and placed it on Georgie's arm "You will do nothing of the sort. I will be quite well here with my sisters to keep me company. You have spent the past three months watching over me like a mother hen. I insist that you have a bit of amusement yourself while you may."

Georgie frowned. How could she possibly tell the older woman that her nephew was not the sort of amusement that she wished for?

Aloud she said, "But I am here to act as a companion to you. Not for my own amusement."

"Oh, piffle," the elderly lady said with a frown. "You are a fine companion. But you are a young woman yet. You need the company of young people from time to time to remind you of it."

Georgie would have protested further, but was prevented by the arrival of Lady Russell's maid who had come to dress her for the day.

"Away with you," Lady Russell said with a finality that Georgie knew would not be gainsaid. "I expect to receive a full report of your day's adventures when you return."

Knowing she was beaten, Georgie returned to her bedchamber to get her hat. She met Lord Coniston at the bottom of the stairs where he was leaning elegantly against the newel post while his six younger cousins stood about chattering.

"Good morning, Mrs. Mowbray," he said, straightening to offer her a bow, which was graceful despite the sketchbook tucked beneath his arm. "I trust you were able to sleep after your fright last evening. Mice can be so alarming."

She studied his expression to look for any sign of sarcasm, but found none. Offering him a brief curtsy, she said, "I thank you, my lord. I am quite well. And eager for our outing."

A quirk of his dark brow let her know he suspected that last to be an exaggeration at best, but he merely offered her a short nod. Accepting his hat and gloves and walking stick from the butler, he called his cousins to attention and they set out.

The ladies rode in an open carriage while the gentlemen rode alongside, Georgie remaining silent as Lord Coniston spoke up now and then to engage his cousins in conversation. They seemed to be a close family, and Georgie found herself wishing she'd been part of a larger family. With only her parents and a sister, she'd been able to count the army as a family of sorts, but that hardly replaced the comfort of actual kin.

Still, she had Perdita and Isabella to turn to. And Lady Russell treated her like a daughter, though Georgie knew better than to mistake that relationship for anything other than what it was—that of employer and employee.

By the time they reached the well-worn drive to the Farley Castle grounds, the sun had slipped from behind the clouds. Taking in a deep breath, Georgie allowed herself a moment to simply appreciate the feeling of the sun on her arms and the breeze on her skin.

"I never would have guessed it," Lord Coniston said, bringing his mount alongside the carriage. Turning, she found him watching her with a wry half smile.

"What?" she demanded, reaching up to ensure that her hat was securely fastened. "Is there something on my face?" she asked warily, bringing a gloved hand up to wipe at her cheek.

"You're a country girl," he said with a tone that might almost have been accusing. The hint of a dimple in his cheek took away any suggestion of ill will.

"I'm sure I don't know what you're talking about," she said with a self-conscious tug of her shawl around her arms. For some reason she felt as if he'd seen her in her shift or some equally revealing state.

"I don't suppose it should matter," he continued, his eyes intent upon her, "but it simply never occurred to me. I've always seen you in town."

"Why should that matter?" she asked, glad that the others were engaged in a spirited conversation of their own, so they wouldn't hear the querulous tone in her voice. It would not do for her to seem too familiar with her employer's nephew. "It is hardly a crime for me to enjoy the open air."

"No, of course not," Lord Coniston said with a maddening sense of his own certainty. "I am only remarking upon the fact that you seem far more comfortable out of doors than in. You're positively aglow with it."

Feeling self-conscious, Georgie felt a blush steal into her cheeks. "It is true, I do enjoy the outdoors. I suppose it comes of army life.

"Though it is hardly to be expected," she continued. "Any number of ladies who followed the drum were happy beyond words when their husbands returned to England and they could spend their days in drawing rooms and nights in houses with sturdy roofs."

"But not you," he said, his eyes crinkling at the corners as he smiled at her.

"I happen to enjoy the countryside," she said, trying to suppress the flip in her stomach that came of being in the gaze of such a handsome man. "And I happen to dislike the feeling of confinement one gets after several days indoors. I hardly think that makes me completely out of the ordinary."

"I suppose not," Lord Coniston said with a shrug, completely oblivious to his effect on her. "It is simply unusual in the ladies of my acquaintance."

"That is because the ladies of your acquaintance would never dream of suggesting anything is more appealing than your fascinating conversation," she said with a wry grin, as much for her own weakness as for theirs.

He laughed. "You might be right about that, I'm

afraid. There is far too much dishonesty exchanged in the drawing rooms of the *ton*. I am relieved, in fact, that we are having this discussion in the open air, so I need not fear such dissembling from you, Mrs. Mowbray."

"Or so you think," she said pertly. "Fresh air is hardly a guarantor of truthfulness."

"Why, Mrs. Mowbray, I had no idea you were capable of such taunting," he said, with a grin.

"For shame, my lord," Georgie said, looking up at him from beneath the brim of her bonnet. "You forget that I also spent my formative years surrounded by scores of young soldiers with hours between battles to spend flirting."

That seemed to give him pause, for he lost his customary poise for a moment and gaped at her. Then, almost as quickly as he'd dropped it, his charming mask returned.

"Were you a flirt?" he asked, dipping his head slightly to look her in the eyes. "I somehow doubt it."

She fought the instinct to look away, knowing somehow that she had to hold his gaze. "Not so much as my sister," she admitted with a shrug. "But I had my moments."

"I'll bet you did," he said, evidently seeing something in her gaze that satisfied him. He nodded and that elusive dimple appeared again.

They continued on in companionable silence for the rest of the ride, the ebb and flow of conversation of the group ahead of them an accompaniment.

* * *

"I don't suppose you'd like to tell me what happened last night," Con said, resuming their conversation once they'd left the horses and carriage behind and continued the rest of the way on foot. "What made you cry out."

Though he'd known the question would break the ease between them, he also knew that the question had to be asked. He felt her stiffen beside him, but when she made to remove her arm from his, he clamped down on her hand and held her there. "Do not fly up into the boughs. I merely ask as a friend."

"As a friend?" she asked skeptically. "There is no such thing as friendship between an earl and a lady's companion, my lord."

"Why not?" he asked, diverted from his original question. "You are a friend to not one but two duchesses. And they are far more elevated than a mere earl."

"Do not attempt to cloud the issue, my lord," Georgina responded firmly. "I thought I saw a mouse. That is all. Nothing to concern yourself with. Nothing that could endanger your aunt. You must know that I care enough about her not to keep something from you that might truly endanger her."

"But there is a difference, Mrs. Mowbray, between something that you think might endanger her and something that I think might endanger her. We are of two different perspectives after all."

"You are splitting hairs, my lord," Georgina said tightly, and Con could see that she was growing frustrated. "It is my concern and no one else's. And has absolutely no bearing on your aunt's safety."

At last.

"Then you admit that there was more to last night's to-do than an imagined mouse?" he demanded, stopping and grasping her arm to pull her to a halt as well.

She stopped, but wrenched her arm free. "Yes," she hissed, keeping her voice low, though his cousins were long gone down the path. "Yes, something other than a mouse upset me last night, but I assure you that was all. A simple trick of the light. Nothing more."

He could see from her expression that whatever had happened frightened her more than she was willing to admit. "It worries you," he said. It was a statement, not a question. He did not like to see a woman like this overset by anything. She was too strong for that. And it was a mark of just how dangerous whatever had disturbed her was, that it could cause her real fear. "Doesn't it?" he prompted.

Her expression softened under his gaze. "I am quite well," she assured him. Then, laughing, she said, "It was nothing. Really, it's amusing in the light of day."

Con clenched his jaw. There was something wrong here. He was sure of it. "I beg that you will tell me what it is so that I might share the joke," he said, unwilling to let her continue without revealing her secret.

Perhaps realizing that he did not intend to let the matter drop, Georgina's shoulders fell and she spoke in a voice that was low enough to not be heard by his young cousins ahead of them. "It was the oddest thing, but through the window last night, I thought I saw my dead husband standing in the garden." Her voice was strained as she said it, and when she made eye contact with him, he could see how hard she was trying to appear unflappable in the face of what must have been a highly disturbing moment. "There," she said brightly, "is that not amusing? That I should have thought to see a ghost? It's ridiculous."

He wasn't sure what he'd expected her to say, but it wasn't that.

Wordlessly, he took her hand and tucked it into his arm.

"What made you think it was your husband?" he asked after a few moments. "I mean, was it the man's face or his clothing, or what?"

He felt her exhale, as if she'd been holding her breath lest he didn't believe her. "I suppose it was just the general look of him. Though if one were to be exact, this man was wearing a coat and boots and breeches, whereas my husband was normally in uniform. But this man had his height and build. And his hair looked to be the same light brown shade as Robert's."

"So, it wasn't your husband as you remembered him?" Con asked. "Not as if he'd walked straight out of your memories?"

"Well, no," Georgina said after a moment. "That's odd, isn't it? I mean, if I were going to imagine him there it would surely have been as I'd seen him, wouldn't it? I could hardly remember him in a way I hadn't seen him."

"The mind is quite good at tricking us into all manner of things," Con said. "But, no, I don't think you'd remember him in a way you'd never seen him. Of course, it might have been some stranger down there who you then imagined to be your husband since you'd been thinking of him moments before."

"But I wasn't," she protested. "I was thinking of . . . other things."

Interesting, he thought, tucking away that tidbit for later. "Whoever it was, he had no business loitering in my aunt's back garden like that. I'll go take a look at the spot when we return from our walk."

"Oh, do not go to any trouble," Georgina said vehemently. "I do not wish to impose upon you with my foolish imaginings. It's the reason I told no one what happened. Not only do I feel like a flibbertigibbet, but I also did not wish to worry anybody."

"Mrs. Mowbray," he said firmly, "you are as far from being a flibbertigibbet as any lady I've ever met. And I really must insist upon checking out the scene for myself. If this man was indeed standing back there last night, then I need to know who he was and what he was doing back there. Not only for your sake but for my aunt's as well."

He felt her deflate a bit beside him. "Oh, I suppose," she said with a slight sigh of resignation. "Though I do hope you won't tell anyone else. Your cousins and their wives already think I am out of place in your aunt's house. Goodness knows what they will say if they hear I've been imagining my dead husband."

"You leave my cousins and their spouses to me," Con said, grateful to have an excuse to speak to the others. He'd been none too pleased with the way they treated her last evening, and now he could tell them to leave her be with good reason.

* * *

By the time the party reached Farley Castle, with its crumbling walls and towers rising into the sky, it was lunchtime, and their walk having given them all an appetite, the party made short work of the baskets of food Lady Russell's cook had made for them.

"It really is lovely, isn't it?" Lydia asked as she waited for her cousin James to finish peeling her apple. "I've never been very interested in old estates and the like, but even I can admit that the ivy growing over the gatehouse is quite picturesque."

Con, who had finished his lunch and taken up his charcoal and sketchbook, looked up from his work. "I am glad to hear you say it, Cousin, for I'd begun to fear there was nothing in that pretty head of yours but silliness."

"You needn't tease, Con," she responded with a frown. "Not all ladies can be as serious as Mrs. Mowbray."

Georgina had been packing their lunch things back into the basket they'd carried them in, but at Lydia's words she looked up. "Oh, I am not so serious as all that," she responded to the younger lady. "I simply do what I must to ensure that my behavior does not reflect poorly upon your aunt Russell."

Before Lydia could respond, Georgie saw Con exchange a look with James, who handed the peeled apple to Lydia and rose from the blanket they were seated upon. "Let's go take a look at the tower, Lyd," the younger man said, reaching a hand down to help her up. Georgie expected the girl to protest, but she allowed him to pull her up.

"My aunt isn't here now, Mrs. Mowbray," Lydia said, tucking her arm into James's and turning to walk with him in the direction of the far tower.

"I hope you will not refine upon Lydia's teasing, Mrs. Mowbray," Philip said from the same blanket that Lydia and James had just abandoned. "She is still quite young."

Looking at the way the young man sprawled back on the picnic blanket, one ankle crossed over the other, at his ease in that way only young men could manage, she would have liked to ask young Mr. Callow whether he was Methuselah's age, but bit her tongue before she could say the words. He was hardly to be blamed for his cousin's words, or his youth. Remembering herself at that age, she was grateful to be past it. Aloud she said, "I daresay you are correct, Mr. Callow. I thank you for your concern."

Georgie had supposed that she was quite adept by now at dampening the pretensions of young men in search of affection from an older lady, but apparently she was not as skillful at the task as she thought. For Philip's next words were to ask if she'd care to accompany him to view the intact tower ruins.

"I have been assured by friends that they are quite sound, Mrs. Mowbray," he told her, standing over her as she finished packing the basket. "There is no danger, I promise you."

Georgie was not unaware of her own appeal to the opposite sex. It was difficult to come of age surrounded by dozens of young men in search of dalliance without knowing that they liked the way she looked. But, since her return to England, she'd been careful to ensure that whatever allure she possessed was hidden beneath drab gowns and severe hairstyles. Such measures did not seem to work on Philip Callow, however.

Perhaps he was the rare man who could see past her disguise.

Then, noticing the way he glanced at his cousin Con, seated behind her, she saw that whatever had prompted the young man to ask for her company had more to do with Con than with her. Interesting, she thought.

"I should like that very much, Mr. Callow," she said to Philip, accepting the hand he offered to assist her to rise from the blanket. "I have always been fascinated by ruins."

Not surprising her in the least, Georgie heard Con flip his sketchbook closed behind her. Turning, she saw him rising as well. "I'll come along, Cousin," he said to Philip, who was not so ill-mannered as to show his displeasure, but if Georgie wasn't mistaken, was not best pleased by Con's decision to come along.

With a slight shrug, Philip tucked Georgie's arm into his and led her across the open field toward the tower on the opposite side of the castle from the one that Lydia and James had set off for.

"I suppose you've never seen something like this before, have you?" Philip asked her as they approached the ruin. "It is truly remarkable, isn't it?"

In fact, Georgie had seen any number of crumbling estates and towers in ruin as she crossed Europe with the army. Clearly Philip had no notion of what it meant to cross the continent on one's feet. "It is remarkable," she responded, ignoring the first part of his query. "I shall never become used to the sight of what must at one time have been a beloved family home falling into such disrepair."

"Oh, I daresay whoever lived here was well off enough to build another, better home," the young man said dismissively. "It is the way of the world. One house crumbles, and you buy another."

Before he could expound further on his theory, the voice of Lydia intruded. "Philip!" she called. "Philip! You must come and see! It's the most extraordinary tomb you've ever seen!"

Soon Lydia and James appeared over the horizon and hurried their way. "They are perfectly carved in the shape of the dead person, Phil. It's positively ghoulish! You must see it."

For a flash, Georgie caught a glimpse of what Philip as a little boy must have looked like. He appeared to debate within himself whether he should go with Lydia and James or continue whatever it was he wished to accomplish with Georgie.

Thinking to spare him the inner conflict, she placed a hand on his arm. "Go and see," she said firmly. "I will walk with Lord Coniston. And I've no wish to see any ancient burial sites. I've seen quite enough of death for one lifetime."

"If you are sure," Philip said a bit guiltily. He spared a look back at Con, who stepped forward to take Georgie's arm in his younger cousin's stead.

"So be it," he said, patting Georgie on the arm as if she were a favorite spaniel. "Show me these tombs, then, Lyd."

"How fickle the young men are these days," Georgie

said with a shake of her head as she watched the trio disappear back over the hill.

"You don't really mean to tell me that you are disappointed," Con said with a roll of his eyes. "I might not have years of war experiences behind me, but I wasn't born yesterday."

Allowing him to lead her around toward the back of the tower where the doorway and the stairs were located, Georgie gave what was suspiciously like a snort. "Hardly," she said with mock disgust. "I am not an ancient, but I believe I have the good sense to avoid entanglements with men as young as that."

"Aha," Con said, feeling more satisfaction at her pronouncement than he should, "then you admit to entanglements with men!"

"Well, I will hardly become involved with entanglements with women," she said calmly. When he laughed she stopped. "What is so funny about that?" she demanded. "It is only the truth."

But Con knew that now was not the time to explain just how entanglements between women might work, so he patted her on the hand and nodded his agreement. "You are perfectly correct. Forgive me. I simply thought of something that amused me."

By now they'd reached the doorway leading into the tower. On the ground around the base of the tower, blocks of stone lay in varying positions, as if they'd fallen from the top and simply stayed where they'd landed for the last several hundred years.

"Shall we ascend?" Con asked, gesturing for Georgie to go first. From his position he had a nice view of her backside as she climbed up the narrow staircase.

But soon enough it became too dark to see anything, no matter how much he'd wished to.

"It is so dark," she said from above him, and he could hear her hands pressing against the stone walls to ensure that she followed the right path.

"You're doing very well," Con said, resisting the urge to press against her body that was so close in front of him. Not so much for licentious reasons but because he wanted to ensure her safety. "Do not let go of the walls."

"I won't," she assured him. "Without it, I do not think I'd be able to follow the path."

Finally a small beam of light shone over their heads and Georgina heaved a sigh of relief. "Finally," she said, "I was afraid we'd never find the top of this tower."

By the time they'd walked a few steps farther they were in full sun. Stepping up and onto the parapet of the tower, Georgie gasped. The view of the surrounding countryside, including Bath and the river Avon, was extraordinary.

"Breathtaking, isn't it?" Con asked, stepping up beside her. "It's been years since I've been up here, but it is just as overwhelming as when I first made the climb."

"It is difficult to believe that it's all real," she said, raising her hand to shade her eyes from the glare of the sun. "Bath and all its buildings look like a child's miniature set."

"I think so too," Con said with a grin. "It is hard to believe that you cannot simply reach out and pick up Bath Abbey with your hand."

"I wonder if I can see Lydia and Philip and James,"

Georgie said, stepping forward a bit to look over the edge and at the ground below.

But instead of Con's cousins, she saw something that made her blood chill. It couldn't be him. It simply couldn't.

"What is it?" Con asked, stepping up beside her.

How could the man be so bloody perceptive? Georgie wondered with a sigh. "Nothing, my lord. I just thought I saw someone I knew."

Immediately he stilled. "Your husband again?" he demanded.

"I'm sure it isn't him," she said, not bothering to deny it this time. "It's likely some stranger who looks like—"

Con's voice cut across her words. "Where is he, Georgina?" he asked, his tone brooking no foolishness.

Knowing she had no choice, pointing, Georgie said, "There, over by the elm tree on the other side of the stables."

Silently, she watched as he shielded his own eyes from the sun and peered out across the open land at the stables which were some thousand yards from the tower.

"I see him," Con said, his voice sharp with anger. "I am going to go down. You stay here."

"Certainly not," Georgie protested. "If this person is indeed my husband, then I have every right to confront him. If he isn't, then I have the right to ask him why he is following me."

"I don't have the time to argue with you," Con said, giving up far more quickly than Georgie would have expected. "Just stay behind me and do not say anything to this fellow until I've spoken to him."

Georgie followed Con down the steps to the ground below. Once they reached the doorway, Con began to walk as quickly as he could, and Georgie had to run to keep up. When they reached the stables where they'd both seen the man who looked so much like Colonel Mowbray, they were both disappointed to find no one there.

"Where did he go?" Georgie asked, gasping as she finally slowed her pace and stopped beside Con. "He was right here."

His walking stick clutched tightly in his hand, Con strode over every square inch of ground in the little area between the trees and the stable wall. "He is gone," Con said on a muttered oath. "He must have realized you'd seen him."

"But how is that possible?" Georgie asked, feeling deflated and out of sorts now that their quarry had flown. "It isn't as if I shouted when I saw him."

"No, of course not," Con said, laying a comforting hand on her shoulder. "He must have noticed us coming down to the ground below and suspected that you might wish to confront him. Whatever the reason, he is gone now."

Her knees suddenly going weak, Georgie collapsed onto a stone bench on the edge of the trees. Unable to keep up her pretense of nonchalance, she covered her face in her hands. "Why is he doing this to me?" she asked, her voice trembling. "This person must wish to frighten me. But why?"

Lowering himself to sit beside her, Con took Georgie's hand in his and squeezed it. "My aunt told me before I arrived that something was bothering you. Could this person who is following you be connected with that other matter somehow?"

That must be his reason for watching her so closely last evening, Georgie thought with a sinking feeling. Her disappointment was absurd. Of course that was why. "Perhaps," she said. "Though I cannot tell you. About the other matter, I mean."

"I'm afraid you must tell me, Georgina," he said, calling her by her Christian name as if he had no concern for the proprieties. "I won't have someone frightening you like this. No matter how strong and independent you think yourself to be."

"It isn't that," she protested. Though perhaps that was part of it. What bothered her more was that if she told him about the threatening notes, then she'd have to betray Perdita and Isabella as well. And that was the last thing she wished to do. "It isn't my tale to tell."

"Do you think I am the sort of man who will go about town telling everyone I meet your secrets?"

"Of course not," she chided. "Don't be ridiculous."

"Then tell me," he said, knitting his fingers through hers. "Let me protect you."

"I will consider telling you," she said finally, unable to simply open up to him, but also unable to deny him outright.

"I suppose I shall have to be content with that for now," Con said, rising to his feet. "Let's gather up the rest of our party and leave this place. The ruins are not as magical as they were when we first arrived."

And to Georgie's disappointment, he was right. Allowing him to lead her away, she realized, however, that she felt safer than she had in a long while. So, perhaps the magic wasn't quite destroyed after all.

Four

$\mathcal{B}$y the time the group returned to Henrietta Street it was well past time for tea, and pleading a headache, Georgina went to bed early. There was no sign of the man in the back garden, and when she awoke the next morning, she was refreshed and ready to start the day.

Concerned that her time away the day before might have left Lady Russell without entertainment, Georgie hurried up the stairs after breakfast to check on the older woman.

Her employer, however, had not been bored in the least by Georgie's absence. When she reached Lady Russell's sitting room, Georgie found her engaged in a lively debate with her elderly sisters while they all three worked on needlepoint. Since Georgie had never been very good at needlework, she was thankful that it was her mistress's sisters and not herself who had been co-opted into the activity.

"So you see, I have survived quite well without you, my dear," Lady Russell said, looking much better than she had in weeks despite the fact that her gout-ridden foot was still propped on a stool. "Go off and enjoy yourself while my sisters are here. I vow, when I was your age I could think of nothing more dull than to be confined in a drawing room with three elderly ladies doing needlepoint."

"I am hardly a debutante, Lady Russell," Georgie argued, appreciating the old woman's kindness but not wishing to shirk her duties. "I am quite content to keep you company while you ladies chat and sew. Even if I am not any good at it. The sewing, I mean."

"It's not that she wishes to make you feel unwelcome, Mrs. Mowbray," said Lady Ayers-Ricker, who shared her sister's tendency to forthrightness, "but there are certain matters we wish to discuss that might be . . . unsuitable for you to hear."

Unsuitable? Georgie tried to figure out what Lady Ayers-Ricker meant. Then realization dawned. "Oh, do you mean childbirth and things like that? I assure you, I am quite familiar with such things. Life following the army quite relieved me of any squeamishness I might have had on that score a long time ago."

"Not childbirth, Georgina," Lady Russell said with a glare. "Other things."

Georgie stared at the older woman, trying to figure out what could possibly be more squeamish-making than childbirth.

Then it dawned on her in a horrible mental image that she would not wish upon her worst enemy.

All three sisters saw her expression and laughed. Georgie felt her face redden.

"I see now you understand," Lady Slade, the third and youngest of the Callow sisters said with a grin. "It never fails to amaze me how shocked young people can be to learn that they were not the ones to discover love-making. It's as if they think they all sprang forth fully grown from the cabbage patch."

"In that case," Georgie said, ignoring the chuckles of the three elderly ladies, "I will leave you all to your sewing and perhaps visit the lending library. Have you need of anything while I am there?"

"Not at all, my dear," Lady Russell said with a wave of her hand. "Be off with you. And for goodness' sake, enjoy yourself. There are any number of amusements here in Bath if you would but allow yourself to partake."

Shutting the door behind her, Georgie hurried away as if pursued by the hounds of hell. How was she supposed to guess that three elderly ladies would still be interested in discussing such things? She was not yet thirty and had no desire to discuss the matter. With anyone. Much less other ladies.

She'd never told another soul—not even Isabella and Perdita—but she didn't see what all the fuss was about when it came to sexual congress. When she'd agreed to marry Robert she'd been eager enough for his kisses. But she'd soon learned that the act itself left her feeling embarrassed and uncomfortable. There had been times when she thought there might be something more to it. But soon enough she'd realized she was mistaken. And whatever she'd been expecting was not going to happen, as if she'd started on the road to some fantastic destination, but had been forced to stop halfway there. But since Robert seemed to enjoy it, and it was one of the few times that he really seemed pleased with her, she submitted to it when the mood came over him. For the first few years, at least.

She never explained her puzzlement to her husband. He already found fault with her every decision and action. She could only imagine how he'd have reacted to hearing she found his lovemaking to be less than satisfactory. And after a while, he stopped coming to her bed at all, so it became a moot point.

Putting Robert from her mind, Georgie hurried into her bedchamber to prepare for her outing.

Her reticule was tucked away in a drawer of the desk she used for a dressing table, and Georgie sat down at the table for a moment to remove her purse as well so that she could count out the money she'd need.

She was dropping the coins into the drawstring bag on her wrist when a flash of light caught her eye from the window. Curious, she rose and looked out into the garden below where she saw Con kneeling in the spot where she'd seen the apparition of Robert the night before last. In his hand, he held some sort of shiny object that she presumed had caused the flash that caught her eye.

Throwing up the sash, she saw him look up and shield his eyes against the sun. Recognition dawned on his face and he gestured for her to come down.

Curious, Georgie locked her dressing table and headed downstairs to meet Con in the garden.

While Georgie was upstairs having her horizons expanded by the Callow sisters, Con had retrieved his spyglass and a small notebook from his bedchamber and set out to investigate the spot where Georgie had seen her late husband two evenings before.

The garden was well tended, if small. It was laid out in quadrants. The first two, closest to the house, were taken up by a kitchen garden, near the kitchen door, and a pretty little flower bed near the French doors off the drawing room. The left side was bisected from the right by a pretty stone pathway that curved through the greenery like a country path. The far border nearest the alleyway was marked by a curved row of shrubbery that shielded the view of the yard itself from the path running behind the row of houses. There was, however, a gate in the corner, and it was here that Georgie had seen her husband.

Fortunately, the ground on either side of the stone walk that led to the gate was bereft of any grasses or vegetation of any kind. And at some point, the man Georgina saw must have felt it necessary to step off the stone path, for it was here that Con found the clear, strong impression of a man's boot. Curious as to what sort of view a man might have from this vantage point, Con retrieved his spyglass from inside his coat and put it to his eye, scanning the back of his aunt's house until he saw Georgie's room, which was the second from the left. He could even see her there now, her head bent over some task. He'd best warn her to move whatever bit of furniture she was using away from the window.

His glass must have caught her attention, however, for she looked up and her eyes narrowed as she saw him. Realizing it would be easier to explain himself in person instead of from his current position three stories below her, he gestured for her to come down.

While he waited for Georgie to appear, Con reflected on the various reasons why someone might wish to make Georgie think that her husband was still alive. When she'd admitted to him what she'd seen he'd been inclined to suspect her of exaggerating. After all, Robert Mowbray was rumored to have been a bit of a brute, so it was reasonable to assume that she would fear that somehow he'd manage to come back. Or worse, that he'd faked his death in some sort of trick.

But yesterday at the ruins he'd seen the man who seemed to be following Georgie and the fellow had the same light brown hair and build that Georgie had described. Never having met the man himself, of course, Con had no idea whether the man resembled Robert Mowbray, but he believed that Georgie thought so.

As he stared moodily at the impression in the soil, he heard the sound of Georgie's slippers on the stone walk. Standing, he brushed his hands off on his breeches and looked up as she approached.

"I somehow hadn't expected you to begin investigating so soon," she said by way of greeting.

"I would have begun last night, but my aunt demanded my attention," Con said with a raised brow.

"I am sorry," Georgie said, her eyes troubled. "I did have a headache last night, but I should have been there to entertain her."

"Easy," Con said with a smile. "I was merely teasing you. Of course you are allowed an evening off. Especially when Aunt Russell's house is filled to the rafters with relatives who should spend more time with her."

"Oh." Georgina blushed. "In that case, thank you.

"Now," she said, indicating the area around them with a wave of her hands. "What are you doing here? Investigating the man I saw from my bedchamber?"

Con nodded. "Look at this," he said, gesturing for her to squat next to him on the path as he showed her the footprint.

"There is an easy view of your bedchamber window from here," he said, pointing up toward her room. "And after seeing that fellow following you at the ruins, I am convinced that someone wishes you to think your husband is alive, or haunting you at the very least."

"But why would someone do this?" she demanded with a puzzled frown. "I admit that I was rather . . ." She paused and Con could see that it was difficult for her to force out the words. He tensed as he guessed what would come next. "I was frightened of him. There at the last, I mean."

"I know it is none of my business," Con said quietly, "but could you tell me why he frightened you? I only ask because it might shed some light on why someone would wish to make you think him alive."

Georgina stood but Con remained where he was, close to the ground, instinct telling him that she needed to feel superior to him in this small way in order to tell her story. She rubbed her palms on her gown—she must have removed her gloves while she was in her bedchamber—and swallowed.

"The truth of the matter, my lord," she said, her voice strong despite her obvious nerves, "is that my husband was a brute. He had a temper and he didn't mind venting his spleen using his fists or his belt or anything that came in handy. It didn't much matter what I did to annoy him, he dispensed punishment for small infractions with as much force as for large ones. Though I was never quite sure what would set him off from day to day."

Though he'd suspected something along these lines, Con couldn't help but grind his teeth at her words. He knew that such men existed. He doubtless played cards with them at Whites or fought with them at Jackson's. But he found it difficult to believe that someone as measured as Georgina would fall prey to one.

"Why did you marry him?" he asked, unable to stop himself from voicing the question aloud. "Why put yourself in the hands of a man like that? You grew up following the drum. Surely your father or the other women following their regiment could have warned you."

Georgina's laugh was bitter. "Yes, you would think that a girl raised with the army as I was would have noticed the signs, wouldn't you? But you'd be wrong.

"Robert was a master at hiding the truth of his real nature from everyone," she went on. "Except of course the men he killed in battle. It was there that he was able to truly release whatever monster lurked beneath his mask of civility. When he was courting me, I thought he was the most wonderful man in the world. My father did warn me, but I thought I knew better. I know now that Papa must have heard some rumors among the camp followers or the other men. But when it seemed as if Papa would raise objections, Robert made sure to compromise me so that there would be no question of our not marrying."

"Not that you are not beautiful, but why was he so

determined to have you?" Con asked, puzzled. "Wouldn't he have chosen someone who was without family?"

"I received a quite sizable inheritance from my maternal grandmother," Georgie said bitterly. "He needed funds to pay his gaming debts. And I was foolish enough to believe that he wanted me because he loved me."

"But you are employed as my aunt's companion," Con returned. "I presume that he spent the inheritance?"

"Every cent," Georgina said with a twisted smile. "Before the first year of our marriage had ended. Then of course he was angry with me for not being a bigger heiress so that he could have had more money to gamble with."

Con was silent for a few moments while he thought how pleasant it would be to pummel the late Colonel Robert Mowbray in the face. Repeatedly.

"How did he die?" he finally asked, standing and brushing the soil from his hands.

"Gloriously in battle," Georgie said with a shake of her head. "It is inconceivable to me how a man who was so miserable a husband could be so wonderful a soldier. He was one of the first to fall at Waterloo and he died honorably. When I first returned to England I began to keep count of just how many people expressed their condolences to me in the same breath as they told me how proud I must be.

"I lost count at one hundred twenty-seven," she said wryly. "I said nothing, of course. It would be cruel to disabuse all these well-meaning souls of their notions of just what manner of man may be called hero."

"You are far stronger than many would be in that

situation," Con said with feeling. He'd never really considered how difficult it must be to be a woman. Forced to obey whatever male figure fate or her own blind choosing bestowed upon her as a guardian. Unable to fight back should he choose to strike her, or worse. He remembered what it had been like to be a child, but he'd had benevolent family to look after him. Georgina had no one to look after her.

"I did what I had to do," she responded with a shrug. "Just once, though, I'd like for every man to spend a day as a woman. So that he could see what it's like."

"I do not think you would like to see me as a woman," Con said with a speaking look. "Can you imagine?"

Though she'd meant her words in all seriousness, Georgie began to laugh. "You are correct. I should not like to see you as a woman," she said, grinning. "You are quite a handsome man, but as a woman? I fear you would have some difficulty procuring suitors."

Glad to see the tense expression she'd worn while recounting her story erased, Con raised a sardonic brow. "Do you mean that ladies over six feet tall with enormous feet and the need to shave twice a day aren't in demand? Mrs. Mowbray, you shock me!"

"It's true, I'm afraid. Even I am not in demand and I have nothing like your impediments to beauty," she said with a smile.

"If by that you mean to say that you are lovely despite your hideous gowns and insistence upon wearing your hair in those tight coils," he said, without thinking, "then you are correct."

At his words, Georgina's eyes widened and a blush

crept into her cheeks. Realizing his mistake, Con mentally smacked himself on the back of the head. "I apologize, Mrs. Mowbray. I didn't mean to be so ungallant. Of course your gowns are not—"

"I hope you will not say that my gowns aren't hideous and my hair is not unflattering, my lord," she said with a rueful smile, "because we both know that you would be lying."

Seeing the sincerity in her eyes, Con wished for a large hole to appear in the ground beneath his feet and swallow him whole.

"Besides," Georgina continued, "I intended them to be. So you are voicing only the opinion for which I devoutly wished."

Her words penetrated his wall of self-loathing well enough to reach his brain. "What do you mean, 'devoutly wished'?" he asked, furrowing his brow. "Do you mean to tell me that you wish for people to find your gowns and hair unattractive?"

"Precisely," she said, as if rewarding a particularly slow student. "I dress so that no one will notice me."

"Good God, why?" he asked, genuinely puzzled. "Why would someone as lovely as you are do such a thing?"

At his compliment, she blushed. "I thank you for the kind words, but you must know that it's not true. It's just that I seem lovely in contrast to my terrible clothes and hair. That's all."

Con reached out and grasped her by the chin so that he could look into her eyes. "Let us settle one fiction now, Georgina," he said firmly. "In a pretty gown, in a terrible gown, in a lovely hairstyle, in a hideous hairstyle, you are a stunning woman. And no amount of downplaying your looks will make that untrue."

He saw something flicker in her eyes at his words, some realization that there was truth in what he said. At least that's what he hoped. If she did not believe him, then he wasn't sure how else to show her the truth of what he said aside from demonstrating it with his body. And that was far more improper than he was prepared to embark upon in his aunt's back garden.

"I . . ." She blinked, and shook her head as if to clear her thoughts. Pulling away from his hand, she took a step back. Con felt bereft at the loss of contact. "I thank you, my lord," she continued. "I do not for a moment believe you, but I thank you all the same."

Realizing that he would have to continue this conversation later, Con gave a brisk nod. "Now, about this fellow last night," he said, glancing around at the ground to give her time to recover her composure. "He was definitely made of flesh and blood. Look here again at the footprints he left."

"So it really was just a trick of the light that made him seem ethereal?" Georgie said, sounding relieved. Con cursed himself for a fool for making her reveal so much about her husband. Now that he knew just how awful Mowbray had been, he didn't for a moment think that Georgie would have conjured him out of hope. Fear, perhaps, but she didn't strike him as the overly fanciful type to see ghosts and goblins in every dark shadow.

"Undoubtedly," he said. "Just as the man we saw at the ruins today."

"Not my imagination, then."

"Not unless we share an imagination, madam."

She relaxed visibly. "You don't know how much it relieves me to hear you say that. But how can this person look so much like my husband? For I am quite sure in the light of day that he is dead."

"Maybe," Con said, putting his hands on his hips as he looked up at her window again, "we are looking for someone who looks enough like your husband from a distance that he would cause you to mistake him for your husband."

"Like a relative," Georgie said with a gasp. "Of course! It must be some distant relative of Robert's. He never spoke very fondly of his family. I think his parents were both dead, and since he died before I returned to England, there was no occasion for me to meet any of his other family members."

"Do you know where his family hailed from at least?" Con asked. If one of Mowbray's distant cousins had been lured into perpetrating a hoax on Georgina, then he would need to visit Mowbray's relatives in order to find out if there was some male cousin who bore a resemblance to the man.

"I believe they hailed from Cornwall," Georgina said with a frown. "Penrith, I think he said."

Con nodded. He could make it to the west coast and back in a few days.

"But if it is true that one of his relations is behind this," Georgina said thoughtfully, "how would they know where to find me? It isn't as if I am in touch with them. And I did not make an announcement in the papers when I accepted the position with your aunt.

"And more important," she continued, "why? It isn't

as if I am wealthy, and even if I were my late husband's family wouldn't stand to inherit anything."

"Ah," Con said with a frown. "You're assuming that your death is what this person wants. What if their only intent is to frighten you?"

Georgie's hands tightened around her reticule. Something else was bothering her. Something connected to this business, he was sure of it. But rather than telling him what it was, she squared her shoulders and stood up straighter.

"I had hoped we would find something that would settle this business today, but I suppose it's not to be."

Impressed with her strength, despite his frustration at her refusal to tell him everything, Con stepped closer. Her blue eyes were wide as she looked up at him, showing none of the fear he might expect from a woman who had endured what she had at the hands of her husband.

"We'll figure it out," he said softly, taking her hands in his and squeezing them. "I'll keep you safe, Georgina. I promise."

He looked at their joined hands, then at Georgina's eyes. Clearly she was not quite comfortable with something as innocuous as holding hands. What sort of man would make a beauty like Georgina dread any kind of physical closeness? A dead man, his memory reminded him. A dead man he wished he'd made that way.

Con had never been a particularly violent man, but Georgina's tale of what her husband had done to her had left him with a taste for blood.

But now was not the time, he reminded himself, focusing instead on the light sprinkling of freckles on Georgina's nose.

"You want to kiss me, don't you?" she asked, the fear in her voice impossible to ignore.

"I do want to," he said, leaning his forehead against hers. "But this is not the time or the place. Besides, I can wait until a time when you want to as well."

A furrow appeared between her brows as she contemplated his words. "I don't quite know what to say to that," she said finally, her puzzled expression making his heart squeeze in his chest.

"You don't need to say anything at all," Con said with a smile. "Now, what did you have planned for this morning? Will you have someone to accompany you? I don't want you to go anywhere alone until this person is apprehended."

She looked as if she would like to argue, but seemed to realize it would be fruitless. "I planned to visit the lending library and then perhaps the confectioner's. They make the most wonderful marzipan and I know that Lady Russell would like a treat. I suppose I can see if one of your cousins wishes to come along."

Extending his arm so that she could precede him toward the French doors, Con schooled his features into a pleasant expression though he was feeling anything but.

No matter who the man following Georgina was, as far as Con was concerned he was a threat to her safety. The fact that he resembled her dead husband—a man who had brutalized her again and again—was not a coincidence, Con was sure of it. That someone— whether it was the man who followed her himself or another—was trying to terrify Georgie using the memory of Robert Mowbray indicated a degree of villainy that made the hair on the back of Con's neck stand on end.

Whoever or whatever threatened Georgie, one thing was certain.

She was in serious danger.

Five

To Georgie's relief, it was Clara who agreed to accompany her to the lending library and confectioner's. She'd been half afraid that no one but Lydia would agree, and Georgie was not prepared to spend the next two hours being condescended to by a seventeen-year-old with more hair than wit.

"I'm so pleased you asked me," Con's cousin said with a wide smile as they stepped out into the weak afternoon sunlight. Though the day had started out warm, the clouds had begun to gather just after breakfast and now there was a cool enough breeze to make Georgie glad she'd donned her pelisse before they set out. "My aunt Russell has nothing but good things to say about you, so I've been longing to meet her dear companion, Georgina, who can make her so happy."

"There is hardly any great secret to my success," Georgie said with a laugh as they passed a group of chattering young people. "I simply treat her as I would a good friend. And she treats me the same."

The other woman's eyes grew round with surprise.

"Is that all?" Clara asked, dumbfounded. "I confess, I thought there was something else."

"More than anything," Georgie explained, "when our relatives reach a certain age, they simply want to feel as if they are still relevant. As if their opinion matters. As if they haven't suddenly become doddering old fools. So, I treat her ladyship with special care by not showing her any special care."

"Brilliant," Clara said, shaking her head. "Utterly brilliant."

"Since we're discussing Lady Russell," Georgie said tentatively, "I wonder if you might be able to answer some questions for me."

To her surprise and pleasure, Clara slipped her arm though Georgie's so that they were walking side by side. "Of course, my dear. Fire away."

"I simply wished to know why Lady Russell's family is so reluctant to spend time with her," Georgie said, hoping Clara wouldn't take offense at the question. "I know it's none of my affair really, but Lady Russell is so lonely. Especially now that her sisters live so far away in Yorkshire. She has any number of friends here in Bath, of course. Far too many to interact with on a daily basis, if you want to know the truth, but it's her family she's been aching to see."

As Georgie spoke, she could feel Clara stiffen beside her, as if each word that came from Georgie's mouth contained a bit of ice that was freezing the other woman bit by bit. "I apologize," Georgie said when Clara didn't respond. "Please forget I said anything. It really is none of my affair and Lady Russell is perfectly capable of taking up her own case with you all."

"My dear," Clara said in a low voice. "Please stop apologizing. I am not put out with you in the least. It's just that I am trying to find the best way to say it."

Wondering what "it" could possibly entail, Georgie waited for Clara to go on.

"First of all," Clara said, "you must know that we all love Aunt Russell dearly and would never do anything we thought would hurt her outright."

"But?" Georgie couldn't help prodding.

"But," Clara went on, coloring slightly, "the Lady Russell you know now is not the same Lady Russell that most of us knew when we were younger."

"How so?" Georgie asked. She tried to imagine the stubborn, vibrant lady she knew in any other way and failed.

"For one thing she was much less vocal," Clara said with a sad smile. "In fact, when I was a girl I had a hard time remembering Aunt Russell was present at all during family occasions because she was so utterly soft-spoken."

"Lady Russell?" Georgie demanded. "The same Lady Russell who nearly shouted down the house last evening because she couldn't find her lorgnette?"

"Indeed," Clara said. "It's really quite extraordinary how much change she's undergone in recent years. And none of it would have been at all possible without Con."

"How do you mean?"

"I don't know how much you've been told about Uncle Walter," Clara said, "but he was as brutish a man as has ever lived."

Georgie might have argued with that assessment, but she held her tongue.

"My father and indeed all of the Earl of Coniston's sons were as even tempered as they come. But Lord Russell—Aunt's late husband—was not a kind man. He was a member of the Hellfire Club and ran in the same circles as the royal princes. And you know how ghastly they were."

Because she knew quite well how such marriages came about, Georgie didn't ask why her ladyship's parents had consented to the match with Lord Russell. She knew full well what forces worked to bind innocent young ladies to wild young men. It happened every day.

"When I was a child my grandparents did what they could to curb the worst of Uncle Russell's wildness. But he was their son-in-law, not their son, so there was little they could do."

"What effect did this have on your aunt?" Georgie asked, her own stomach in knots as she remembered what it was like to be under the control of a man such as Clara described.

"She managed well enough. When Con's parents were killed and Lord and Lady Russell were named guardians, it was Lady Russell who saw to it that Con was looked after. She was quiet as a mouse during any family or social gathering, but she made sure to speak her mind when it came to Con. She refused to be cowed when Uncle Russell tried to work things so that he drew more funds from the estate than was spelled out in the entail. Especially when it became known that he had spent all of the money she brought with her in her marriage portion."

"Why on earth did Con's parents name Lord Russell

as guardian?" Georgie asked, horrified for the little boy Con had been.

"My uncle, the late earl, was quite fond of Lady Russell, his younger sister, and so was Con," Clara said. "So, I don't believe he considered that Lord Russell would be a part of the bargain. He was only thinking that his sister would be a good caretaker for his son and heir."

"It sounds as if Lady Russell was much beloved by the family," Georgie said carefully. "So why then did she end up being ignored all these years later?"

"I'm not sure how familiar you are with the workings of large families," Clara said with a smile. "But in ours, we have a shocking tendency to place one another into very specific categories, and then, no matter how much the person has changed in personality since that original assessment, we continue to think of them in such a way."

Thinking of the way Isabella continued to treat Perdita as a younger sister despite the fact that they were grown ladies, Georgie nodded. "I think I know what you mean."

"Well, this is the trouble for Aunt Russell," Clara went on. "Though her sisters still treat her as one of their own, the rest of us recall the Aunt Russell of our childhood and have some difficulty remembering that she is no longer the cowering wife hiding from her terrible husband."

"So, what happens when your aunt does something that doesn't fall into that mold?" Georgie asked, stepping around a puddle. "Like inviting her nieces and nephews to visit her in Bath, for instance?"

"What happens in that case is that the nieces and

nephews accept her invitation but spend the entire visit marveling how out of character it was for their aunt to instigate a family gathering like that. And when we leave, we'll all likely continue to think of Aunt Russell as the timid creature we all know and love, but with the capacity for the occasional surprise."

"Remarkable," Georgie said. "I'm not sure I like the idea that my character at the time of introduction will determine how I am treated for the rest of my relationship with the person I've just met."

"It is trying, isn't it?" Clara asked as they stopped before the lending library. "But I do hope you know that we all hold Aunt Russell in great affection. And no matter how out of character we might find her decision to hold this house party, we are tremendously pleased to spend this time with her."

"I know that she would greatly appreciate knowing you feel that way, Lady Clara," Georgie said warmly. "And I do hope that you will begin to consider her as an active member of the family, rather than a frightened little mouse of a woman. Because she is one of the strongest ladies I've ever known."

"Which is why you are such a good companion to her."

The door to the lending library was propped open so as to let some of the cool breeze of the afternoon circulate among the shelves. Pausing for a moment to examine the display in the window, Georgie and Clara stepped inside to survey the massive shelves that were arranged in row after row far into the space of the shop. It looked much larger from within the shop than it did from without. And as was her custom, Georgie began to browse the shelf that was marked new books first. Clara, who had come in hopes of finding something to read while the rest of the family played cards, headed straight for the shelves of books from Minerva Press.

In the fortnight since she'd last visited the library, the stock of histories and romances had been replenished. Among the three-volume novel, Georgie saw the latest from Lady Madeline Essex, as well as volumes of poetry by Mary Robinson and Felicia Hemans. As usual Georgie was having a difficult time choosing among them.

She was reading the description in the front of the Hemans again when she heard a voice behind her.

"Mrs. Mowbray? Mrs. Georgina Mowbray?"

Shielding her eyes from the light, Georgie tried to gain a better look at her interlocutor. The shadows within the circle of the bonnet soon resolved themselves into the features of a pretty if not elegant face. One she'd not expected to see again.

"Mary?" she asked, astonished. "Mrs. Mary Kendrick? My goodness, look at you, here in Bath of all places. What a delightful surprise. Lettice will be so pleased."

Mrs. Kendrick had been the wife of another officer in Colonel Mowbray's regiment. The wives of men in the same regiment often formed bonds that were as close-knit as those of their husbands. Along with Lettice Stowe, Georgina and Mary had spent many an afternoon together while their husbands were busy with army business.

"You are a sight for sore eyes, Mrs. Mowbray," Mrs. Kendrick said with a laugh. "I have wondered what became of you when the colonel died. I know when my Jem fell at Waterloo it took me a great deal of time to recover from the loss."

The end of the war had proven to be a tumultuous time whether one had lost a husband at the final battle or not. And Georgie still could not think about those few months before she returned home with any sense of calm. She'd had no idea where she would go or how she would support herself. And she'd never thought to see her friends from the regiment again.

"It was a difficult time for all of us," Georgie said quietly. "I didn't realize that Captain Kendrick was lost in Belgium as well. I'm sorry for your loss, Mary."

The other woman shrugged. "No more than I am for yours." She looked around them, seeming to note the throngs of people who were browsing the other shelves or just chatting. "Are you free for the next hour or so?" she asked. "There is a confectioner's near here. And I'd love to chat with you a bit more."

"I am here with a friend," Georgie said, longing for a comfortable coze with Mary but knowing she couldn't simply abandon Clara.

"Bring her along," Mary said with a smile. "The more the merrier we always said, did we not?"

"Indeed. I'll see whether she wishes to join us. Either way I'll see you there within the next quarter hour."

The two women exchanged good-byes and Georgie went off in search of Clara. When that lady said she'd prefer to return home, Georgie was somewhat relieved. She would have been happy to introduce Clara and Mary, but she remembered that Mary was rather plain-spoken at times and she did not yet know Clara well enough to guess what her reaction would be.

"Do enjoy yourself," Clara said. "I know that you're doubtless considering how remiss in your duties to my aunt you'll be for taking a bit of time for yourself, but please do not refine upon it. I can assure you that Aunt is enjoying herself thoroughly with her sisters this afternoon."

Georgie squeezed the other woman's hand. "You are a dear, Clara," she said with a smile. "And please tell your aunt, or . . ." She paused, unsure whether she should mention Con's name or not. "Please tell your aunt I shan't be overlong."

Clara's lips twitched. "I shall tell my aunt and Con that you'll be back soon."

Georgie blushed, but didn't argue. Some people were just too observant for their own good.

Georgie found Mrs. Kendrick waiting for her near the entrance to Pilbury's Confectioner's Shop, which boasted some of the best candies in Bath. With a bow window that looked out over Milsom Street, it was one of the most popular meeting places in Bath outside of the Pump Room.

Once they'd gone inside and found a table, their orders of tea and cakes placed with the serving girl, the two women spent a moment chatting about their current situations. By the time their orders arrived, they were laughing and talking as if they'd never been separated.

"I was so pleased to see you here," Mrs. Kendrick

said with genuine feeling as she reached out to squeeze Georgie's hand. "I was so disappointed to find you'd left Belgium without leaving your direction."

Thinking back to those first awful days after the final battle, when Napoleon's troops had met Wellington's for the last time, Georgie knew that she'd had no choice in the matter. "There was no time, I'm afraid. But I am quite pleased to see you here now."

"And so am I," Mary said with a warm smile. "No matter how understanding my sister and her family try to be, they never quite know just how much of a change it is to be back in England."

Georgie couldn't help but agree. She'd encountered the same sorts of difficulties when she'd returned to England. Some evenings, despite what she told herself about needing fresh air, she still slept with the windows open. "So you've been living with them, then?"

Mary nodded. "Melisande and her husband, Tom, were kind enough to offer me a home with them here in Bath. I do not need to tell you just how much of a change it is to live in a thriving city, do I?"

Though Georgie knew that compared to its past days of glory, Bath was a shadow of its former self, for someone such as Mary whose whole life had been lived in the tight-knit community of the army, Bath must feel like a bustling metropolis.

"No, you don't," she agreed with a smile. "I hope you are pleased with your situation. I know we all used to daydream about just where we'd end up and what we'd do when the war ended. Have you gained even a modicum of that which you hoped for?"

A crease appeared between Mary's brows. "I cannot

help but feel grateful that my sister's family agreed to take me in. Jem had no pension and there was little I could do when I returned to keep a roof over my head. Nothing that would allow me to maintain my dignity, that is."

"Then I am grateful you had them," Georgie said with a smile. "And do you get on there?"

Mary shrugged. "I know that you will recall that Jem had certain . . . tendencies toward wildness," she said in a voice pregnant with meaning. Jem Kendrick had been a sunny-natured but reckless young man with a proclivity for gaming. His inability to resist an opportunity for a wager had led the couple into more than one vocal disagreement, which often ended up being overheard by the entire camp. It was a negative aspect of living in such close quarters.

"I do remember that, yes." Georgie said, careful to keep her expression neutral. The last thing she wished to do was add to her friend's shame over Jem's problem. "But you can trust me, Mary. You know that."

"I do," Mary said with a smile. "Your discretion was one of the few things I grew to rely on in those days." Perhaps sensing the subject had become a bit too dark, she changed it. "You mentioned Lettice earlier. I cannot believe that our own Lettice is here in Bath as well, is she?"

"She is, indeed," Georgie said with a smile. "And just as dour as ever. Though she is a dear thing all the same. We visited an art gallery together only days ago."

"Oh, dear," Mary said with a laugh. "I can only imagine what that was like."

"You were always hard on poor Lettice," Georgie

said without rancor. "She is a good friend for all that she can never see a teacup as half full instead of half empty."

"And you were always apt to take her side," Mary said with a rueful smile. "You never could resist an outcast."

At this description of herself, Georgie shrugged. For some it might be seen as a criticism, but for Georgie it was a compliment. She'd rather give an underdog her support than to always be backing the top dog. It suited her sense of fairness. "I wouldn't call Lettice an outcast," she argued. "She was simply not the most popular among the other wives. That's hardly the same as having no friends at all."

Mary shrugged. "I am hard on her, I suppose. But only because I am jealous that she's been able to spend time with you while I have not." She smiled across the table at Georgie. "I am so pleased for this chance meeting. Because I wanted to see you, of course, but also because I've needed to give you this."

Georgie watched as Mary opened the reticule at her wrist to remove a well-worn letter.

"Please excuse the state it's in," Mary said, her eyes dark with concern as she proffered the missive to Georgie. "I have carried this with me from the moment I returned to England. For I had no notion of where you might have gone after the war. But"—she smiled—"unlike our Lettice, I live in hope and I knew somehow that I should see you again."

Gingerly, as if she expected the sealed note to contain some sort of pyrotechnics, Georgie took the message from Mary's hand. Staring down at the writing that was as familiar to her as her own hand, she asked, "What is it?" But she already knew the answer.

"The night before Waterloo, your husband and mine were engaged in a particularly high-stakes card game. And they were, as they often were, together. When the word came that they were to report for battle, I suspect your Robert took a few moments to write you this note."

Staring at her name inscribed on the folded page before her, Georgie asked, "But why didn't I receive it then?"

"I'm not sure how it came to be on Jem's person," Mary said with a frown. "I only know that when I found his body, this note was in his pocket. I guessed about why he wrote it. But since I found a similar note from Jem to me as well, I supposed they were together when they wrote them."

It made sense, Georgie thought. It was common enough for soldiers to write such missives before battle. Leave it to Robert to be so careless as to neglect to actually ensure she received it.

"He may have given it to Jem thinking he would make sure you received it," Mary continued. "But for whatever reason, it didn't make it."

A thousand emotions gathered in Georgie's chest. She was grateful to Mary, for bringing her the letter, but at the same time, she wished that she'd never seen it. She had just managed to regain some equilibrium. How like Robert to surprise her with a message from beyond the grave.

"I thank you, Mary," she said aloud, placing the letter into her reticule so that she could read it later when she was no longer in view of Mary's avid gaze. She had forgotten just how inquisitive the woman could be. "I am astonished that you've carried it with you for all this time, but I cannot say that I am sorry for it. I always did wonder whether Robert had left me some last words, but always assumed there had been no time. Despite our differences I am pleased to know he was thinking of me."

The other woman squeezed Georgie's hand. "I am simply pleased that I was able to give it to you at last."

Promising that they would plan an afternoon together next week which included Lettice, the ladies parted, but Georgie wasn't altogether certain what was said. So aware was she of the note resting in her reticule that she barely recalled making her way back to Henrietta Street.

Con took a sip of the really quite passable ale served at the Angry Piglet tavern on the outskirts of Bath. He'd arranged a meeting here with the man he hoped would agree to conduct an investigation into the history of Colonel Robert Mowbray. He was astute enough to realize that there were some tasks that would be finished more quickly by someone who was familiar with the terrain. Besides, Con did not wish to leave Bath lest the man who was watching Georgina returned. And he most definitely was going to come back.

"You have a knack for choosing the most absurdly named establishments, my lord," Lord Archer Lisle said with a mix of exasperation and awe as he brushed off the seat of the chair opposite Con before lowering himself into it. Whispering conspiratorially, he added, "And I believe it would be wise to eschew the advertised pigeon pie, for I saw a few of those unhappy birds wandering drunkenly in the yard. The cook has probably lost his hunter and has taken to poisoning them."

"As I have no intention of consuming anything other than this surprisingly tasty ale," Con responded, raising his tankard in appreciation, "I have little need of your warning, though I thank you for it, Archer."

The two men were a study in contrasts. The blond Lord Archer was as fastidiously attired as the brunet Lord Coniston was dressed neatly but comfortably. And yet, for their differences, the men were friends.

"I take it that you've asked me to visit you in this sterling establishment for some reason other than to recommend the ale," Archer said, flicking a bit of fluff off the arm of his greatcoat before taking a sip from the tankard the barmaid had just set before him. "Not bad."

"I told you," Con said with a grin. "And of course I have a reason to call you here. I would hardly drag you away from the side of your beloved without one."

Archer sighed. "I've asked you not to call the Duke of Ormond my beloved. Really, what will his wife think?"

"You know damned well I'm talking about the duke's sister-in-law, old man," Con said with a sardonic smile. "Even if you aren't willing to speak the truth aloud, I am."

"By what right?" Archer asked grimly. "You're hardly in any position to throw stones."

"By the right of a former betrothed," Con said, just

as grim. "If you aren't going to admit that you're in love with her, the least I can do is say it for you."

It was an old argument, and both men had dug into their positions with the stubbornness that could only come from being born into the noblest houses in England.

"So long as you refrain from saying it in front of her," Archer said coolly, "then I suppose there's nothing I can do to stop you. Though I'm dashed if I know why you are so determined to speak of it. I had hoped that we would have got past this by now."

"This is what happens when you allow your best friend to become engaged to the woman you love," Con said with a shrug. "Especially when you don't tell the friend until after he's already asked her the question."

"It was none of your business," Archer groused. "In fact, I never would have told you at all if you hadn't dragged it out of me."

"If I hadn't dragged it out of you I'd be married to her by now," Con said with a shake of his head. "Do you know what a fiasco that would have been? Aside from the fact that the lady prefers you to me, anyway, there would have been the awkwardness of being the only person at my wedding who would have been happy about it. My vows would likely have been drowned out by the sound of you and Perdita weeping on either side of me."

"Only a little," Archer said wryly. "I haven't wept with any degree of enthusiasm since my old spaniel Greta died."

"I'd forgotten about that," Con said. "You blubbered about that for weeks."

"She was a very loyal dog," Archer said defensively. "And I was at Eton, for God's sake. If one doesn't cry once during his career there then he is made of stone.

"Besides," he continued, "I am not the one who wept when Bertie Fowlkes elbowed me in the face."

"He got me in the nose," Con defended. "I'd defy the devil himself to keep a dry eye after a punch in the nose. He had very pointy elbows, did Bertie."

"There is that," Archer said agreeably. "So, much as I enjoy being raked over the coals for failing to disclose the secrets written upon my heart to you, I believe you invited me here for some other reason. Yes?"

Quickly, Con told his friend about Georgina, the man who resembled Colonel Mowbray, and the as yet unknown problem that still bothered her.

"You should have said earlier that you wanted me to help Georgie," Archer said, sitting up straighter. "She's a dear. Of course I'll do whatever I can."

Con stared at his friend. Of course Georgina knew Archer. She was the dearest of friends with Isabella, the new Duchess of Ormond and Perdita, the young dowager Duchess of Ormond. He felt his jaw tighten reflexively.

"What?" Archer asked. "Why are you staring at me as if you're trying to decide which ear to tear off first?"

"Georgie?" Con asked his friend silkily, baring his teeth in the mimicry of a smile.

"Yes?" Archer leaned back in his chair and folded his arms over his chest. "She's called Georgie by her friends. She's given me permission to do so, as her friend. What's the trouble?"

At Con's protracted silence, Archer began to laugh.

"Oh, this is priceless," he crowed. "I vow I haven't been amused like this in quite a long time."

"What is so amusing about it?" Con demanded, failing to see the humor in the situation. He was hardly accustomed to wishing his oldest friend would take a long walk off a short pier. It was deuced uncomfortable.

"Don't you see?" Archer said, grinning widely. "This means that we're even. I forgive you for trying to marry Perdita, and you forgive me for trying to . . . well, I suppose be friends with Georgie?" Archer frowned. "That's not quite right."

"Whatever," Con said, feeling magnanimous now that he remembered Archer's affection for Perdita. "We are now even, and so long as you don't declare your love for Georgina I am prepared to put this behind us."

"So, does this mean that you're in l—"

"Stop right there," Con said sharply. "I am not in . . . that word you were about to say. I barely know the lady."

"That's not quite right," Archer said with the smile of a man who sees another fellow on his way down the same path as him. "You've known each other at least as long as I've known her. And you've been at various entertainments at Ormond House or Lady Isabella's."

"Even so," Con said, feeling a bit awkward at his friend's scrutiny. "And all this is beside the point unless I can find out who the man watching her is."

"It is a coil," Archer said, considering. "I wonder if Robert Mowbray is related to the Mowbrays of Cornwall."

"This is why I came to you," Con said with some relief. He was hopeless at remembering which families lived in which county and whether the Dauntrys with a *u* were kin to the Dantrys without. Archer had an encyclopedic knowledge of a variety of subjects and he was just the man to figure out if there was a member of the Mowbray family with the means and motive to stalk Georgina.

His mind occupied with the problem Con had presented to him, Archer nodded absently. "I'll see what I can come up with by the end of the week."

"Excellent," Con said, clapping his friend on the shoulder. "You're a good man.

"I don't suppose," he continued, "you've made any progress with Perdita since we last spoke?"

"I'd prefer not to talk about it," Archer said, his normally sunny disposition turning cloudy. "Let's just say that I have not yet found the right moment to press the issue."

"If it makes any difference," Con said sympathetically, "I do not doubt that she holds you in great affection."

"Aye," Archer said glumly. "It's just removing the cloud that bastard she married left hanging over her that I worry about. She won't see me as anything more than a friend until the bloody Duke of Ormond can be exorcised from her life like a demon."

"It appears, my friend," Con said, lifting his tankard, "that we are both beset by the ghosts of husbands past. I propose that we drink to their quick dispatch to whatever hell they both deserve."

"I'll drink to that," Archer said, clinking his own glass against Con's. "And also to the high-and-mighty Lord Coniston's succumbing to Cupid's arrow—"

Before Archer could finish, however, Con broke in. "Dammit, Archer, stop that."

The other man's eyes widened as he tried and failed to look innocent. "I don't know what you're talking about."

"You, sir, are an ass," Con said with feeling, frowning into his ale.

"I've been called worse," Archer said with a shrug.

Six

*O*nce she was safely ensconced in her bedchamber, Georgie took a seat at her desk cum dressing table and, inhaling deeply, broke the seal on the letter and unfolded it.

My dear Georgina,

I go into battle soon, so there is not much time. I have not been the best of husbands. Forgive me for the times I was too harsh. And for the ways I betrayed you—especially with those whom you called friend. It was a mistake—I see that now, but at the time I needed loving arms and yours were closed to me. If I had been a better man, or you a better wife, we might have made a happy match, but it was not to be.

I have loved you in my way,
Col. Robert Alan Mowbray

How utterly like Robert to couch his apologies in an accusation, Georgie fumed, despite the tears sliding down her cheeks.

"I needed loving arms and yours were closed to me." She thought of the times she had denied him her bed— usually when she was recovering from some injury he'd done her. For all of his faults, Robert had at least been a gentleman about that. He had never forced her. But learning he'd broken their vows with another woman removed all approbation she'd heaped upon him for his consideration.

"Especially with those whom you called friend." That one—or more—of her friends had betrayed her was almost as painful as knowing her husband had done so. And given that Georgie had called most of the women in their camp friend, the guilty party could be any one of some hundred women.

Pressing her fist against her mouth, Georgie bit back a sob. Just when she thought she'd finally come to terms with the hell Robert had put her through, he came back from the dead to punish her again. And this time it was no ghostly apparition, no look-alike playing at frightening her. No, this was Robert himself, and knowing he still had the power to upend her carefully ordered life like this was almost worse than the real thing. Because an expected pain was one thing, and surprised pain was another.

She'd never been fond of surprises.

Con knew there was something profoundly wrong as soon as he saw Georgina listening attentively to his cousin Ernestine recount the details of her performance at the annual hunt at Coniston Grange last year. It wasn't so much the subject that tipped him off. For all he knew Georgina was an avid hunter who couldn't get enough of chasing foxes cross-country on horseback. It was instead the intensity of her attention. From the moment he stepped into the drawing room, he sensed her desperation. As if letting her mind wander just a fraction away from Tina's story would result in some sort of calamity.

Fragile. That was the word he was looking for, he realized as he crossed over to join them.

He was waylaid, however, by Clara who gestured him over to a space before the fireplace.

"Clara," he began, not even looking at his cousin as he kept his eyes firmly fixed upon Georgina. "I don't have time just now. Can it wait?"

"You'd better make time, Cousin," she hissed, moving to put her face directly in his line of sight, "for I believe I can shed some light on a subject near to both our hearts."

That brought him up short. "What is it?" he asked, his attention fully focused on his cousin now.

Keeping her voice low, Clara said, "While Georgina and I were at the lending library this afternoon, she was approached by a woman whom she knew from her days with the army. I believe her name was Mrs. Kendrick. They repaired to the confectioner's and I declined to go along thinking that they would wish to have a tête-à-tête. There is nothing so unwelcome when long-separated friends reunite as a third party with no shared history. I returned to Henrietta Street and spent an hour darning stockings while the aunts chattered away like magpies."

Con took a moment to control his impatience, reminding himself that Clara was helping him. Still he couldn't help raising his brows in a questioning manner. "Well?"

"You are lucky you're my favorite cousin," Clara said with a raised brow.

Continuing, she said, "When I came into the drawing room, I saw her like this. Obviously overset by something."

Con muttered a curse. That much was obvious to anyone who had spent more than a few moments in Georgie's company. Though he supposed he now knew that this friend she'd met at the lending library had something to do with whatever troubled her.

"Thank you, Cousin," he said with a brisk nod. "That helps quite a lot."

Without a backward glance for Clara, he stalked over to Georgina.

While she listened to Ernestine, Georgina had grown progressively more relaxed.

She'd considered remaining in her bedchamber for the rest of the evening, pleading a no longer fictitious headache, but a few moments alone with her own thoughts had prompted her to go downstairs for tea.

Her time with the army had taught her to maintain her composure no matter what. While her mind was spinning like a toy top, her body at least was calm. It had taken some doing, of course, but a few moments of deep breathing and calm had allowed her to pretend as if nothing had changed since she'd left the house early that morning.

Now that the ringing in her ears had begun to subside and Georgie had become aware of the various conversations going on around her, she realized that Con had come in while she was busy gathering her wits about her.

As she watched, he stood with his arms folded across his chest talking with his cousin Clara. He looked angry about something, though Georgie could hardly guess what.

Perhaps sensing her eyes on him, Con looked up and for the flash of a moment their eyes held. She tried to read his expression, but all she saw was intense emotion. Then, he excused himself from his cousin and began making his way toward her. As she watched him, Georgie felt her heartbeat quicken.

"And then I told old Cosmo Glendenning if he didn't watch where his hunter stepped that I'd have him removed from the hunt for the next two years," the Honorable Miss Ernestine Callow said vehemently, continuing with the never-ending story of some hunt or other. Georgie had stopped listening ages ago, but found that so long as she nodded and smiled, Con's cousin seemed happy enough with the conversation. "I tell you, Mrs. Mowbray," the auburn-haired beauty said, "that horse is my pride and joy. If Cosmo weren't such a cold fish, he'd understand that they're more than just transportation. The nerve of the man!"

"Cosmo Glendenning has crossed you again, Tina?" Con asked his cousin as he stepped into their conversational circle, his apparent annoyance of a moment ago seemingly forgotten. "I wonder if you realize he's merely trying in his ham-fisted way to attract your attention. You've grown into a deuced pretty chit, you know."

To Georgie's amazement the other woman, who was quite tall and made Georgie feel rather incompetent, blushed rosily. "Con, you old flirt," she said with a rather horsey laugh. "Cosmo is forty if he's a day."

"Gentlemen do not stop appreciating pretty girls on their fortieth birthday, my dear," he said, kissing her on the cheek. "Just consider it the next time you're around him. I seem to remember him losing brain function the last time I saw the two of you in a room together."

"Why ever would he do that?" his cousin wondered, her brows drawn together. "Oh, well, I suppose I'll have to watch him more closely next time."

"I have appreciated our conversation, Mrs. Mowbray," she continued with a smile for Georgina. "Now, I'm afraid that I see Mama gesturing to me from the other side of the room. Which can only mean she has concocted a scheme to introduce me to some ridiculous gentleman at the theater tonight. It's ghastly but one does what one must."

When she was gone, Con raised a brow. "I believe you've made a staunch ally there. Tina might be socially awkward, but she's loyal to a fault. Well done."

"I did nothing more than listen," Georgie said, careful not to let her posture relax. "She is a sweet girl, if more interested in horses than I am."

"I didn't come over here to talk about Tina," he said, his eyes never leaving hers. "Clara tells me that you encountered an old army friend at the library today."

She knew that's what he and Clara had been discussing, of course, wishing she'd secured the other woman's assurance that she would say nothing about Mary. "Indeed, I did."

"I do not wish to be rude," Con began, "but Clara said you seemed to be overset when you returned to Henrietta Street. I hope you didn't receive unpleasant news. Perhaps about a mutual acquaintance from your army days?"

"You could say that," Georgie responded, wishing more than anything that she could simply turn on her heel and leave the room. She had no wish to discuss her letter from Robert. And certainly not with Con. "It really isn't the sort of thing one wishes to discuss in the middle of a Bath drawing room, however, so perhaps we could talk about it some other time?"

Georgie had no intention of discussing the matter with him at any time, but she was hardly going to tell him that now.

Con's eyes narrowed. Even so, he nodded. "All right. Perhaps later tonight, after the theater."

She gave a shrug that might have meant yes and might have meant no. She was simply too exhausted to commit one way or the other. Seeing her chance to escape, she said, "I thank you for the reminder. If I'm to be ready for the theater, I should go upstairs now and choose which slippers to wear." She felt a bit guilty for using the sort of excuses she had once mocked her

London friends for mercilessly. But, any port in a storm.

Without a backward glance she turned and hurried from the room, feeling as if Con's gaze were burning holes in the back of her gown.

Once Georgie reached the safety of her bedchamber, she heaved a sigh of relief. She'd thought being in company would improve her mood, but unfortunately, she'd been unable to escape the thoughts she'd wrestled with since reading Robert's letter.

It wasn't that she felt any sort of jealousy at learning of Robert's infidelity. She'd long ago lost any sense of ownership over her husband. He had destroyed her romantic notions about him almost as soon as the vows were said.

Was there to be no point, however, at which she could consider herself rid of Robert and his incredibly oppressive shadow? Add in the mysterious man who looked so much like him who had been watching her window, and Georgie thought the answer was no. Unless she never spoke to another person who had known him again she must be prepared for betrayals and abuse that had escaped her while he lived to surface from time to time.

The trick was, she told herself firmly, to control her own response to these revelations. It was a lesson she thought she'd learned while Robert was alive, but these last days' events had suggested that she needed to learn it again. In the meantime, she would rid herself of the physical reminder of him.

Crossing to the desk, she opened the top drawer and removed the letter Mary had given her and took it to the fireplace, where thanks to the chilly afternoon a fire was burning. Looking one last time at her name scrawled across the front in Robert's handwriting, Georgie tossed it into the flames and watched as it succumbed and transformed into just another pile of ash.

She might not be able to rid her memory of her late husband, but she could certainly rid herself of physical reminders of him.

The clock in the hall began to strike the hour and with a start Georgie realized she'd been wallowing in self-pity for nearly an hour. What foolishness to allow herself to be upset by things that no longer had any bearing on her life. Concentrating on the task at hand, she got out her one evening gown—a watered silk in robin's egg blue that brought out her eyes—and laid it out on the bed.

She was just about to remove the pins from her tightly coiled hair when a knock sounded at her door.

Opening it she saw Lady Russell's maid Holbrook.

"I beg your pardon, Mrs. Mowbray, but her ladyship wishes to speak to you before you leave for the theater."

"Of course," Georgie said, repinning the curl she'd just taken down.

Following the servant down the hall toward her employer's bedchamber, Georgie realized just how little time she'd been spending with her. Even if Lady Russell's sisters were there to see her, that was no excuse for her own companion neglecting her.

She said as much when she entered her ladyship's parlor. Tucked up into her favorite settee, Lady Russell raised her lorgnette to get a better look at Georgie as she entered the room. Georgie felt a self-conscious blush rising in her cheeks.

"I do apologize for not coming to see you sooner, your ladyship."

"Do not be foolish, gel," Lady Russell told her, gesturing for Georgie to come closer. "I told you that I was quite well enough to spend the week with my sisters and I meant it. You should take advantage of this time to see a bit more of the city, and perhaps to consider taking the waters yourself. If I don't mistake myself you're looking a little peaked today."

"I assure you, I'm fine," Georgie answered her. There was no way that she would confide what had happened concerning her late husband this afternoon. And she was certainly not going to tell her about the man she'd seen in the garden. She wanted Lady Russell to remain untouched by the ugliness that seemed to follow her wherever she went. "Indeed, I was simply napping before tonight's excursion to the theater. Won't you come with us, my lady? I feel sure we could hire a sedan chair to get you to the theater itself, then perhaps we could persuade the fellows to carry you up and into your box."

"Ah, my dear, you make it sound so easy." Lady Russell laughed. "But, thank you, no. I have seen the current production of *Much Ado About Nothing,* and have no need to see it again. I've never been a great lover of Shakespeare. Too many chits dressing up like men to suit me."

Georgie had long ago discovered her employer's aversion to the theater, but she did wish in some way to be of help to her. Especially at times like now, when the entire household seemed to have plans for the night.

"Then perhaps I'll stay here and chat with you," Georgie said with a smile. "We still have a game of chess to finish, I believe."

"Stop trying to be so blasted dutiful." Lady Russell shook her head. "When I said that you should go tonight, I meant it. You've done nothing but keep me company for the past few months and that is simply not good for a young unmarried lady."

"Widow," Georgie gently corrected. "I'm not this petite flower you think me to be."

"No, of course you aren't," Lady Russell groused. "You're as strong as an ox with a personality to match." Her grin took some of the sting out of being compared to a beast of burden. "And yes, you are widowed, but that doesn't mean that you should never marry again. You are a young woman yet, and what better place for you to see and be seen by eligible young men than the theater."

"You're trying to get rid of me?" Georgina demanded. "I hadn't thought you would be tired of me already."

Lady Russell banged her walking stick upon the floor. "I am not tired of you, you silly widgeon! I am trying to save you from ending up elderly and alone like I did. And if you can't see that it's as plain as a pikestaff that you are far prettier than I ever was, then you are far more foolish than I imagined you."

"Good gracious," Georgie said, exasperated. "Are you honestly telling me that you consider yourself to be elderly and alone?"

At that Lady Russell had the grace to look a bit sheepish. "Very well," she said with a shake of her silvery head. "I am perhaps not quite so alone or weak as I've made myself out to be. But I am an eccentric old woman who has more money than is good for her, who wishes to see her dear friend, who is also her companion, enjoy herself for a change. So I will have no more arguments out of you, miss. You will go to the theater tonight and you will enjoy yourself. Even if I have to get up from my sickbed to make it so."

As her employer became more and more vehement, Georgie's astonishment grew. Finally, when she had stopped talking, Georgie said, "I had no idea you felt this way, Lady Russell."

"Perhaps if you would stop worrying about things so much you might find yourself better able to observe."

Unable to stop herself, Georgie moved forward to give the older lady a hug. "You are a wonderful friend, Lady Russell, and I am honored to have you call me such."

Looking uncomfortable, Lady Russell gave a slight shrug. "I've been quite pleased with your service to me. I believe you care more for me than the nieces and nephews who have come to Bath only so that they might secure their inheritance from me. Do you think that I don't know how reluctant most of them have been to come here?"

Georgie moved to take a seat in the chair beside the settee. "Dear Lady Russell, I don't think they came only for the inheritance. Why, I've heard even Lydia say that you're a dear and she can't understand why the family hasn't gathered like this before."

"That's a shock," Lady Russell said, her eyes shining with amusement. "I thought the gel cared for nothing but dresses and gentlemen."

"If you would allow yourself to spend more time with them," Georgie said gently, "I feel sure you'd find that they are all quite amiable people. Aside from the fact that they're your only living relations. I've lost both parents and I cannot tell you how much I miss being able to do the very things with them that you are avoiding with your own family."

"Your mother always did love a good argument," Lady Russell said with a sigh. At Georgie's gasp, she nodded. "Yes, that was rather a bigger secret than you were planning to hear, wasn't it?"

Georgie found she was having trouble understanding just what Lady Russell had said. "Do you mean to tell me that you knew my mama?"

"Of course I do," the older woman said in exasperation. "It was long before you were born, of course, or you wouldn't be so shocked."

Grateful she was seated, Georgie gaped. "But, how . . . I mean . . . why . . . why did you not tell me? I've even told you how much I miss her and wondered about her life before she met Father. And you've known I was her daughter the entire time."

Lady Russell took one of Georgie's hands in hers.

"There, there, my dear. I didn't mean for it to remain a secret between us. But I was so concerned that you with your stubborn streak would refuse to come live with me unless it was under the guise of your acting as my companion. And every time I thought of telling you, I found myself frightened of what your response would be."

"But why tell me now?" Georgie asked, her head still reeling from the revelation. "What's different about now from all the times before?"

Lady Russell smiled. "If you'll hand me that jewel case sitting on the table, I will tell you."

Puzzled, Georgie went to retrieve the box and handed it to Lady Russell, who opened it and began sorting through the contents. Putting aside a diamond and ruby cuff bracelet, and another necklace made of opals and onyx, she seemed to be searching for one piece in particular. Finally, she stopped and removed a finely crafted necklace of matched sapphires from the case. The clasp was made of gold and was embedded with a large pearl that glinted in the lamplight.

"First of all, you should know that these are not part of the Russell entail. Just in case someone thinks to question why they are in your possession." Lady Russell stared down at the gems and seemed to see something there besides the necklace. Shaking off her reverie, she continued, "They were a gift to me from my husband upon the birth of my son."

At Georgie's questioning look, she nodded. "Yes, I had a son. Though he did not live beyond infancy. It was the greatest tragedy of my life. And of course it meant that the Russell viscountcy went to a distant cousin of Arthur's. But it was the loss of the boy that truly hurt. Not the title or the estate."

"I'm so sorry," Georgie said, clasping Lady Russell's hand. "Thank you for sharing this with me."

Blinking back a tear, Lady Russell said, "I am sharing it with you because it wasn't too long after that that my husband hit me for the first time."

Silence fell between them as Georgie considered what that confession meant.

"I tell you this because I wish for you to know that you are not alone. You are not the first woman to have felt the mark of a husband's fist, and though I wish it were not so, you are not the last. You're a strong woman, Georgina, but I think at times you forget that you have allies. That you are no longer trapped within that awful intimacy between brutal husband and abused wife."

When Georgina didn't answer, Lady Russell continued. "I want you to have these sapphires. I want you to wear them to the theater tonight. I want them to remind you that there are those like me, like Clara, like Con, who care about you. No matter what happened in the past."

Reluctantly, Georgie reached out a hand and touched one of the glinting gems. It was far warmer than she'd have imagined. Could she wear these jewels knowing they were a reminder of Lady Russell's most awful memory? Even if she insisted?

"Yes," the older woman said, as if reading Georgie's thoughts. "You can. Because they remind me not only of sad times, but also of those wonderful months before my boy was taken from me. Remember that there are good times as well as bad."

With a shaking hand, Georgie took the necklace from Lady Russell, and hoped that what the other woman said was true. She was in desperate need of some good times.

Seven

$\mathscr{A}$s he put the finishing touches on his cravat—the mathematical, which he'd mastered at Oxford and never seen much need to improve upon—Con was very aware of the fact that just on the other end of the hall, Georgina was dressing for tonight's excursion to the theater. For a brief moment he allowed himself to wonder just what that curvaceous figure looked like before it was hidden away beneath another hideous gown.

As an artist, he had always been aware of the way the right color or cut of gown could either enhance or detract from a lady's looks. Since Georgie's gowns he'd seen thus far had done nothing to improve upon the dazzling looks she'd been born with, he'd spent an inordinate amount of time imagining what she'd look like in a truly well-cut gown from Madame Celeste in a color that would bring out the blue of her eyes. Naturally, he'd spent just as much time mentally removing said gown to reveal the undergarments his imagination had also supplied.

These were just the foolish thoughts of his libido,

however. His mind also spent time lingering on Georgina's personality. Her kindness to Lady Russell, for instance. The sensible way she'd taken charge of the younger cousins on their trip to the ruins. Her sincere interest in his cousin Ernestine's interminable horse-and-hounds stories.

Mrs. Georgina Mowbray was a genuinely good person. The sort that Con had not often found himself lusting after. It was a novel enough experience that he found her quick wit and kind heart just as alluring as her pretty face.

Con checked the clock and realized he'd spent far too long ruminating. Allowing his valet to help him squeeze into his evening coat, Con gave one last tug on his cravat and stepped hurriedly into the hallway.

Only to run smack into the object of his not-so-pure thoughts.

"Oof." It was a sound so counter to the lady before him that Con almost wondered if he'd been the one to say it. Instinctively, he grabbed onto her arms, which were bare except for a thin wrap which did little to dampen the feeling of the flesh beneath.

"I am so very sorry, my lord," Georgina said, steadying herself in his arms by flattening her hands against his chest. Then, perhaps realizing what she'd done, she pulled her hands back as if he were made of flames. "Dear me," she said a little dizzily. "Forgive me. I can only blame—"

Before she could utter any more inanities, he gave in to the desire that seemed to have conjured her in the air before him. Stopping her words, he leaned forward and pressed his lips to hers.

Because she'd been in mid-sentence, her mouth was slightly open. Taking advantage of the fact, Con deepened the kiss, teasing her mouth with his questing tongue. Though a small noise in the back of her throat indicated Georgina's surprise, she was quick to respond, answering Con's stroke into her softness with her own tongue against his. Surprised, but pleased, he allowed his hands to slide over her back and pulled her closer against him, reveling in the press of her breasts against his chest, her stomach against his stirring arousal. Her hands slipped around his neck as they explored one another.

It was only the sound of a door slamming downstairs that reminded them they were in the hallway where anyone might come upon them.

Reluctantly, Con pulled away leaving both of them gasping for air. He watched her, unable to speak, as Georgina pressed a hand against her mouth. Her cheeks were pink with arousal and he was intrigued to note that the blush spread down over her chest. Vowing to explore that later, he said in a low voice, "I would beg your pardon for that, but I suspect you wanted it just as much as I did. Am I right, Georgina?"

Her eyes wide, pupils dilated, she nodded. "Yes," she said, moving the hand that had been at her lips to rest on her chest. "Yes, I did."

Though her response made Con long to toss her over his shoulder and disappear with her into his bedchamber for a few weeks, he merely nodded.

"We have an engagement, I believe," he said, offering her his arm. "Shall we go down? I believe Clara dislikes being late for anything. Let alone the theater."

Bemused, she took it. And as she did so, Con noticed that though she was wearing a gown he'd seen before in London at some function or other—not quite as ugly as her other frocks—the circlet of sapphires was something he'd not seen her wear before.

"You are looking quite well, tonight, Mrs. Mowbray," he said, putting his hand over hers where it rested on his arm. "The sapphires are lovely with your eyes."

Self-consciously, she lifted a hand to the necklace, as if she'd forgotten it was there. "Oh, yes. Lady Russell gave them to me to wear tonight."

He was unaware of his aunt even allowing her companions to wear her jewels before. But Lady Russell had been known to do stranger things, he reminded himself. "That was kind of her," he said. "I know she holds you in some affection. She rarely let's people see them, much less wear them. Did she tell you how she received them?"

"I believe she said that your uncle gave them to her upon the birth of their son," Georgina said, as she walked ahead of Con down the narrow staircase leading to the ground floor.

"That's right." Con was surprised that his aunt had told her about her son. But it proved just how close they'd become. "There's a portrait of the three of them in the Russell family seat. It's the only time I've ever seen her wear them. After the baby died, she told me she came to hate them. I think she would have let them pass into the Russell family after Uncle died and the title was inherited by a distant cousin, but the heir wouldn't hear of it. He said that she should have them as a reminder."

"Oh, dear." Georgina's hand lifted again to touch the stones. "So much sadness surrounding this beautiful piece of jewelry. I did not know about the portrait. I should, on the one hand, like to see what he looked like. The child, I mean. It is such a shame for little ones to be forgotten. But on the other hand, I do not know if I could bear to see her happiness knowing that it would so soon be snatched away from her by fate."

"Not fate," Con said, unable to stop himself from speaking the words aloud. "Fate didn't take her child away, my uncle did."

Georgie stopped, turning on the step to look at him. "I thought he died of some illness or a fever or the like."

Stepping down to the floor beneath them, Con turned and reached up to hand her down. "I'm afraid not," he said gently. "And now is not the right place to tell the tale," he continued as they were joined by Clara, her husband, John, Lydia and her escort, Mr. Demouy. "Suffice it to say it's not a pretty tale."

"What's not, Con?" Lydia asked, her inquisitive eyes darting from her cousin to Georgina and back.

"None of your affair, Lydia," her mother said pointedly. With an apologetic glance at Con, she turned to inspect Georgina."My dear, you are looking splendid this evening. Isn't she, John?"

But before her father could respond, Lydia spoke up again, "You are looking rather well, Mrs. Mowbray. Though I daresay it's the sapphires that are the real stunners. They do go well with your eyes." A silent communication passed between Clara and Lydia, Con saw. He did not envy his cousin the London season that

Lydia had yet to enjoy. It was difficult enough being her cousin. He couldn't imagine what parenting the chit would be like.

"Very nice, very nice," John said in his friendly way, completely unaware of the undercurrents in the conversation.

"I think the lady looks much better than the sapphires," Mr. Demouy said with a glance that lingered for far too long on Georgina's bosom.

Con might have said something if Lydia hadn't stepped in before him. "I had no idea you were so interested in jewelry, Mr. Demouy," the girl said with a speaking look. "Perhaps you wish to escort Mrs. Mowbray to the carriage so that you might get a closer look at her . . . sapphires?"

Choking on a laugh, Con watched as the younger man blushed all the way up to his eyebrows. "Not a chance, Lydia," he told his cousin. "Mrs. Mowbray has agreed to be my guest this evening. Mr. Demouy will have to stay with the lady he came in with, so to speak."

"I'm rather beginning to feel like the prize cow at a country fair," Georgina muttered, earning her a grin from Clara and a stifled laugh from Con.

"Not a cow, my dear," Con said, leading her out the door and toward the waiting carriage, "but definitely a prize."

Georgie felt rather like the cousin come up to town from the country as they entered the crowded lobby of the Theater Royale.

She'd seen a few plays in London with Isabella and

Perdita, but she never lost her enthusiasm for attending performances. There was something about the thrill of seeing live performers recite words on the stage that gave her chills. And for all that it was no longer quite so fashionable as it once was, Bath theater was still quite good.

Added to her excitement regarding the play was the sensation of walking into the theater on Con's arm. Again and again her mind returned to the kiss they'd shared earlier that evening. Her hand resting on his strong arm could not help but appreciate the heat of his body through the clothing that separated them. Each flex of the muscles beneath her hand reminded her of how strong his arms had felt as they'd clasped her against him.

For Con's sake, she was grateful for Lady Russell's decision to gift the sapphires to her this evening. She might not be dressed as fashionably as the other ladies in attendance, but she knew without doubt that the sapphires circling her throat were as fine a set of gems as could be found in England.

Perhaps taking note of her awe, Con pointed out the architectural highlights of the theater as they moved through the throng and up the stairs to Lady Russell's box. Because the lady lived in Bath year round she kept a permanent box which she allowed friends and relations to use as they needed it. And to Georgie's delight, it gave her a perfect view of the stage, as well as the surrounding boxes.

"I think Mrs. Mowbray and I will take the seats in the front of the box," Con said. "She is, after all, our guest."

"I don't see how," Lydia said with a pout. "She's Aunt Russell's companion. Not a friend come to visit." Then, as if realizing she'd been so uncharitable aloud, she added, "Though of course we are grateful to have her with us."

Clara, who had taken a seat in the second row, frowned at her daughter. "You forget, however, that we have all been to the theater in Bath before, while Mrs. Mowbray has not." Turning to Georgie, she continued, "I do hope you will excuse my daughter. She is in the habit of speaking her mind. A habit I fear will get her into trouble one of these days."

Ignoring the byplay between the mother and daughter, Con led Georgina into the front row. "Come and have a seat, Mrs. Mowbray, so that we can survey the room."

"Perhaps Lydia is correct," she said, hesitating before the chair. "I am hardly an honored guest. And I'm sure I shall be able to see quite as well from some other, less prominent seat. Really, my lord."

In an undertone, Con said, "But you can see everyone in Bath from here as well, which makes this the perfect place from which to search for your husband's look-alike."

When put that way, Georgie saw the wisdom of his suggestion, though she knew there would be a price to pay later in the form of unkind words from Lydia. Even so, that was likely to happen whether she took the seat or not. "I suppose you are correct," she said, reluctantly taking her seat.

"Of course I am," he said, settling in beside her. "He watched you from the garden, he followed you to the ruins, and who knows where else. I think he'll be unable to resist this opportunity to watch you from the relative safety of a crowd."

"I still don't understand what the man's aim is," Georgie said with a sigh. "He's frightened me. Made me believe I was seeing things. But that's hardly worth the time and effort it would take to frighten me properly." Though she supposed she'd been frightened *properly* enough on the other two occasions she'd seen him too.

"We'll find out when we catch him," Con said fiercely, and Georgie was grateful that he was on her side. She sensed that once roused, Con's protective instincts were strong, and that for whatever reason he considered her his to protect. Again she remembered the kiss. He had been focused on her then. She wondered what all that focus would feel like given more time and a bit of privacy.

She shivered at the thought.

"It is rather chilly in here, isn't it?" Con said beside her, oblivious to her train of thought, though the brief caress he stole under the pretense of tucking her shawl around her shoulders indicated he was perhaps not as oblivious as he seemed. "Once the masses shuffle in the temperature will warm up a bit."

Thanking him, Georgie scanned the sea of faces laughing and talking in the other boxes while they waited for the play to begin. Seeing the direction of her gaze, Con began to point out various of the more notorious members of the *ton*. "Just across the way we have the Duke of Winterson's box. You'll remember that a couple of years ago he married the daughter of the famous

Egyptologist Lord Hurston. They are here with Lord Hurston who is taking the waters for his health. And also in their box are the Earl of Gresham and his wife, as well as Viscount Deveril and his wife. Gresham's wife, Lady Madeline, is a novelist and Deveril's lady is a celebrated pianist and composer. The three wives are all cousins and are friendly with each other so they tend to come to events together."

"I had heard about them," Georgie said, taking the opera glasses from Con so that she could spy across the theater. "The duchess is involved in the Ladies' Charitable Society with Perdita and Isabella and me. She seems quite sensible. And I've read Lady Gresham's first novel. It was quite good."

"We could go speak to them during the interval if you like," Con said. "Lady Deveril has done quite a bit for veterans returning from the wars. I would have been surprised if you hadn't heard of her, considering what an uproar her own condition caused just after she married Deveril. It was quite the scandal."

Georgie's eyes widened. "Of course! She's the countess who suffered an amputation. I recognize her now." She gazed thoughtfully at the party in the opposite box. "I think I should like to meet them. Thank you for suggesting it. Though I have no idea what they'll make of me."

Con tilted his head in puzzlement. "What do you mean?" he asked. "You're hardly an antidote. And you enjoy friendship with two duchesses. I think that makes you rather special." His eyes darkened for a flash. "Among other things."

Feeling a blush rising, she forged ahead. "I am hardly

the sort that they must usually mix with. Though you are right, I suppose, that the friendship I have with Isabella and Perdita must count for something. Though I'll admit I'd never considered trading on it to gain introductions to other people in the beau monde. For the most part, I'm afraid I find society a bit insufferable."

"You are rather hard on my peers," Con said with a grin. "Not that I don't agree with you for the most part, but even so."

"I should probably hold my tongue," Georgie said with a grimace. "I am hardly in a position to criticize given my own position outside polite society."

Con took her gloved hand in his and covered it with his. "Do not speak about yourself that way," he said softly. "You are far more deserving of praise than these people. To me, anyway." Georgie thought back to that kiss again and her stomach flipped. But Con must have remembered that they were in a very public place, so he turned his head to focus on the other theatergoers again.

"Hmm, who else might we see and discuss," he said. Then turning to the right of the Winterson party, he paused. "Aha! There we have it . . ."

He continued amusing Georgie with anecdotes and bons mots regarding the rest of the assembled crowd in attendance until the play began. Then Georgie's attention was firmly riveted to the stage where the sharp-tongued Beatrice and the romance-resistant Benedick crossed verbal swords. She had no difficulty imagining herself in Beatrice's place, pronouncing that she had rather hear her dog bark at a crow than hear a man say he loved her.

By the time the first interval arrived, Georgie was thoroughly energized from what she'd just seen on stage. It was a strange aftereffect of entertainments like this that they always made her want to go out and take the stage herself. It was a ridiculous notion of course, but one that held a certain appeal to her even so.

"What must it be like to have such a talent for bringing someone else's words and characters to life?" she said to Con, who was waiting beside her for the rest of their party to make their decisions about whether to leave the box for refreshments or to remain there until the break ended.

"Exciting, I should think," was his response. "When I was much younger, Aunt and Uncle liked to throw parties where the guests performed various Shakespeare plays. I got to play Puck from *A Midsummer Night's Dream* once, and it was dashed fun."

Imagining what young Con must have looked like, with his dark curls and blue eyes, Georgie found herself smiling at the notion. "I'll bet you were adorable."

"Some would say I still am," he quipped.

"Now," he continued, "shall we remain in the box or go in search of refreshment? Or I can have refreshments brought here to the box."

Georgie felt the nervous energy pent up in her body and realized that she desperately needed to walk about a bit. "I should like to stretch my legs," she admitted.

By this time the other two couples were gone and Con and Georgie slipped out into the throng of people outside the door of the box. "Stay close," he said, "it can be quite easy to get caught up in this." He told her

the number of their box just in case they became separated.

"Yes, my lord," she said wryly, as she allowed him
to take her by the hand and lead her toward a disturb-
ingly long line where a server was handing out cups of
punch.

As they waited, Con greeted various friends and acquaintances as they passed by. Some stopped to chat
for a bit, and when Con made introductions she was
surprised that he introduced her not as his aunt's companion, but as a family friend. She supposed that either
would do, but she couldn't help but feel a bit dishonest.
No matter how Lady Russell had encouraged her to think
of herself as such earlier when she'd bestowed the sapphires upon her.

They were nearing the front of the line when Georgie felt someone collide with her and to her dismay she
lost sight of Con and was soon engulfed in the crowd
around them. Since she wished to visit the ladies' retiring room in any case, she decided simply to go there
then meet him back at the box.

They'd passed the door to the retiring room some time
ago, so she headed in the direction from which they'd
come and was soon rewarded by the sight of yet another
line. With a sigh she found the end and waited behind a
lady wearing a rather imposing turban adorned with a
peacock feather. For a few moments she waited there,
listening to the snatches of conversation coming from
the people around her.

One older woman was chastising her middle-aged
daughter for having chosen such a feckless husband. A

pair of gentlemen were discussing the figure of the actress playing Beatrice in some detail, the finer points of which made Georgie's eyes widen in surprise. She'd grown up around military men, who were as bold as any other males, but they'd been careful to edit their conversations around the daughter of their commanding officer. She supposed the men here thought their conversation would be lost amid the noise of the rest of the crowd.

Realizing that she was a lone female in a crowd of men, she searched for a member of her party, but in vain. Nervous, she began to walk briskly down the hallway toward Lady Russell's box. She'd only gone a few feet when she saw a familiar figure up ahead. The light brown hair was a bit longer than she remembered, but the height was right, even if she were convinced that it could not possibly be who she thought him to be.

It's my husband's look-alike again.

The man was walking with his back to her, his gait as fast as he could manage in the crowded hallway. Determined not to lose him, Georgie sped up herself, though she was hampered by her lack of height and the tendency of the other theatergoers to stop and talk to friends as they wandered the halls. Finally, she saw him turn down a corridor that must lead to some of the nonpublic rooms of the theater for there was no one else there when she turned to follow him but a group of gentlemen whose clothing and age marked them as likely to be just out of university.

"Pardon me," she said when it appeared that they would not simply move out of her way. "I should like to pass."

"My pleasure, my dear," said one of them, who did a double take as she edged past him. "On second thought, maybe I should just hang on to you," he said, grabbing her by the arm. "You're too delectable to let go."

"No fair, Rushton," one of the others said heatedly. "You always snag the pretty ones for yourself."

"That's just as well," a third said as Georgie struggled to remove herself from the first man's grip. "This one is going to fall for me," he continued, taking Georgie's other arm.

"Let me go," she said firmly. She'd learned long ago that wheedling didn't help in such situations. One had to be adamant and stand firm or men would ignore a woman.

"Oh-ho, you see there, Rush?" the third man said. "She wishes to come with me."

"I said, let me go," she repeated, beginning to panic a little.

It was clear that no one was able to hear her over the general noise of talk and laughter in the corridor, and she decided that since her words weren't making any difference, she'd try another tack. Her slippers were far too thin to make any kind of impact were she to try stomping on their feet, so she decided to use the method her father had taught her when she was first beginning to attract the notice of the young soldiers in camp.

With a deft twist, and grateful that the skirt of her gown was not more constricting, she lifted her knee and struck the first man with all of her might in that most sensitive part of the male anatomy.

Her first captor let go long enough for her to pull away. "You little bitch," he hissed in pain.

"Not so fast," the second man said as she tried to get out of his grip as well.

"Let. Her. Go."

"Who the hell are you?" the first man asked insolently.

"I'm the man who is going to make you wish you'd never been born unless you unhand this lady immediately," Con said, looking pointedly at the man who still held Georgina's arm.

Eight

*C*on arranged to have refreshments served to their box easily enough, but was waylaid by an aging earl who'd been a great friend of his father's and it was far longer than he'd originally intended before he made his way back to their seats. To his dismay, Georgina was nowhere to be found. In fact, no one had seen her since she left with him earlier.

Tracing his steps back to where he thought they'd been separated, he was soon moving against the crowd who were shuffling back to their seats now that the interval was almost over. He was headed in the direction of the rear stairs when he heard a masculine curse and some sixth sense urged him in that direction.

What he saw there made his jaw clench. Georgie was surrounded by four young bucks, two of whom had their hands on her as she struggled to get away. A curtain of red descended over his vision, and despite the odds of four against one, he demanded that they get their hands off her.

The relief in Georgina's face when she saw him was

palpable as he took advantage of the other men's surprise and pulled her away from them and thrust her behind him.

"Which of you wants to tell me why you thought it was a splendid idea to trap this lady?" he asked them, his voice calmer than he felt. "Though I suppose it's too much to assume that you've more than one brain among the four of you."

"Who the devil are you?" The man who'd been facing Georgina with his hands gripping her shoulders when Con approached was clearly the ringleader of the group. Con didn't fail to note how the other three had looked to him when Con arrived on the scene. Now, however, the dark-haired man looked more petulant than commanding. "This is a matter between the lady and ourselves."

"You must be incredibly stupid," Con said, his voice deceptively calm as he addressed the young man. "For if you knew anything at all you'd know that I'm reputed to be a crack shot. And what you've just done is grounds for a challenge at the very least, as this lady is under my protection."

Visibly, the three followers took a step back. It would have been amusing if Con weren't so furious.

"Now, look here, man," the leader said, his sudden pallor indicating that he'd realized that perhaps he'd chosen the wrong lady for his attentions. "I have no quarrel with you. The lady approached us. We were trying to encourage her to return to her party."

"You lie," Georgina cried, stepping around Con to confront her accuser. "I was merely trying to get past you and you grabbed me."

The young man's pallor turned to a flush of anger. "Now see here, miss . . ." he said before he could stop himself. One look at Con had him taking a step back rather than a step forward, however.

"Because nothing more happened," Con said, stepping in front of Georgie again, with a look that told her to stay put, "I will allow you to go if you all agree to leave Bath. I cannot promise what I'll do if I happen upon you at some other venue here in the coming weeks."

"I say," one of the other men said, his voice aggrieved. "That's not fair."

"Shut up, Bemis," the ringleader said, his voice clipped. To Con he said, "We'll go. Though I don't think you know just who it is you're threatening."

Con had to admit that the fellow had bottom. "And I could say the same to you, sir. I will assuage your curiosity and tell you that I am Coniston. And if you are at all familiar with sporting circles you will know I did not lie when I said I am quite nifty with a pistol."

A murmur passed among the three followers when they heard Con's name. The first man blinked. And he turned pale again. At this rate, Con thought, with dark amusement, he'd find himself shunned by his peers as the victim of some new fever.

Still, the fellow managed to bow with enough insolence to save face. "My lord, I wish I could say it was a pleasure, but it is not. I believe you'll know my father, Lord Allenby," he said. "He too is well known by reputation. I hope that you will not come to regret this night's doings."

Lord Allenby was known to be a powerful member of the Tory party, and had used his influence to see that many of the reforms championed by the Whigs were snuffed out long before they became viable. He was also reputed to have a nasty temper.

Con, however, wasn't worried. "I believe that I am quite safe from your father since I am neither weak nor powerless." Before the younger man could argue, he held up a staying hand. "We could stay here arguing all evening. Now I fear I am weary of the subject and would ask the four of you to leave us."

Though the ringleader looked as if he wished to argue, the other three soon convinced him that they would leave while they might.

Before a minute had passed, Con and Georgina were alone in the corridor.

He looked to ensure that there was no one else lurking about, and without ceremony, pulled her to him and kissed her.

Georgie had found herself battling between gratitude that Con had appeared on the scene and annoyance that he'd effectively pushed her to the side so that he might fight her battle for her. She knew well enough that some men would never see a woman's opinion as anything other than a triviality to be ignored. And she had little doubt that the young men who'd cornered her were of that ilk. However, she was still angered both by how quickly the young men did as Con said and by how he'd assumed that she'd be grateful for his protection.

Before she could voice these feelings, however, she found herself in his arms and, despite her well-formulated arguments against the wisdom of such a thing, responding with some enthusiasm to his kiss.

From the moment his lips touched hers, she lost all train of thought, except perhaps to reflect while she could that this was a far different kiss from the one they'd shared that afternoon. Gone was the gentleness of their earlier embrace. This kiss was hot and consuming and carnal. As he walked her back toward the wall, he pressed her back against it, and as he thrust his tongue into her mouth, he pressed his rock-hard erection against her softness. She gave as good as she got, meeting his mouth with her own, sliding her hands beneath his coat to feel the strong muscles of his back as he held her.

They went on like this for one, maybe two minutes more, before she felt him become still against her. He kissed her once more on the lips, and reached down to remove her hands from around his waist and took a step back. He closed his eyes for a moment, slowing his breathing before he opened them again and looked at her ruefully.

"We will have an actual bedchamber next time," he said firmly. "No more hallways."

Georgie couldn't help but laugh, though she too was short of breath. "And what makes you think a change of locale would make a difference?" she said, teasing.

His eyes still dark with passion, he smiled wickedly. "I have my reasons," he said with a raised brow.

"Now," he continued, looking serious, "I hope that you will tell me why you were foolish enough to engage those ruffians in conversation. I would have thought that given the danger we have both agreed you are in, you would take more care for your safety."

Whatever affection she might have been feeling for him after their kiss was dampened by his question. "I simply requested that they let me pass," she said tersely. "I hardly think that indicates a lack of concern for my own welfare. And since when has it become fair game for gentlemen to accost ladies in theaters like that?"

"Do not fly up into the boughs," Con said, raising a hand of surrender. "I didn't say they were in the right. But you know young men as well as anyone given your time with the army. They are as unpredictable as the weather in summer—especially when a group of them gets together. I simply wondered what reason you had for accosting them."

"I did not accost them," Georgie said through clenched teeth. "I was following someone who bore a striking resemblance to my late husband and they refused to let me pass."

At her words his brows snapped together. "That's even worse than accosting the young men. Why the devil didn't you come find me?"

"Because there was no time," Georgie said, annoyed at being called to task like a young corporal on his first mission. "I saw the man in the main hallway and knew immediately it was the same one who was in the garden the other night. And I didn't wish to lose the opportunity to find out who he was and why he was here in Bath."

Con looked as if he'd like to chastise her further, but he must have decided against it because he turned to look down the corridor. "And he went this way?" he asked. "You're sure of it?"

"I'm sure of it," Georgie said, reluctantly setting her annoyance aside for the moment. "And I might have caught him if those scoundrels hadn't blocked my way. By the time you arrived, the man was long gone. Though I believe he went through the exit at the end of the hallway."

Indicating she should follow him, Con hurried down the carpeted hall toward the door Georgie was talking about. Rather than an exit as she'd assumed, when they opened it they saw that it led to the landing for a darkened set of stairs, one rising up to the top floor, and another leading down.

"Up or down?" Con asked, surprising Georgie by allowing her to decide which direction they should take.

"Up, I suppose," she said, thinking that if Robert's look-alike were attempting to leave he'd be long gone, therefore the route downward would produce nothing of interest.

Con gestured for her to precede him, and grateful he was with her, she climbed the narrow stairs upward until they reached a doorway that marked the end of the flight.

"Let me go first," Con said before she could touch the doorknob. "If he's lying in wait, I don't want you at risk."

She would have liked to argue, but the truth of it was that Con would be better able to protect himself than she would. For the umpteenth time that evening she wished she'd brought her pistol.

"Stay here," Con said before he walked around her and turned the knob, pushing the door open and stepping out onto the roof.

Frustrated at being left behind, Georgie waited with impatience until she heard a muffled curse from Con, and ignoring his order, stepped through the doorway herself.

The air was chilly as the night sky shone down upon the city of Bath. Georgie quickly scanned the darkness for Con and saw him standing about three yards to her right. "Con?" she whispered. "What is it?" She crept over to where he stood staring down at a shadow on the floor of the rooftop. "Is it . . ." She stopped in mid-question as the shape on the roof resolved itself into something recognizable as the shape of a human body.

"Oh, dear," she said, pressing a hand to her chest.

Whoever the young man had been in life, in death he was as horrific a sight as Georgina had ever seen. Not only was the fellow—who might have been one of the men who had accosted her so closely did he resemble them—lying in an impossibly odd position. He was also showing signs of having been beaten quite badly about the head. His face was all but unrecognizable, and his shirt points, which earlier in the evening might have been as high and precise as any other young swain's, were soaked in a dark substance that could only be blood.

Though she'd seen death on the battlefield many times, she'd never thought to see it here in the heart of civilized society. Unable to maintain her composure, she turned from the body and stepped away from where Con knelt beside it. Raising her handkerchief to her mouth she fought to banish the smell of blood and death from her nostrils.

"He's dead," she heard Con say in a low voice behind her, though she'd known from the moment she saw him that the young man was no longer living. "And his skin is slightly warm, which leads me to believe that he hasn't been dead for very long."

"I want you away from here," he continued, his voice curt. "Whoever killed him might still be around here. And I don't want to risk your safety again."

The notion hadn't occurred to Georgie and she felt at once as if someone were watching her.

"Who is he?" she asked as Con came to her side, slipping an arm around her waist and leading her from the scene back toward the stairs. "Just someone who was in the wrong place at the wrong time?"

"Or the partner of your watcher who became unnecessary?" Con's voice was questioning. There were any number of possible scenarios for what might have led to the death of this man tonight and in this location. "There's no way of knowing just now."

It was then that she began to tremble. In the darkness of the stairway, Con pulled her against him. Warming her with his body. There was nothing of passion between them now. Only simple human comfort.

"You see now why I was so unhappy with you for chasing after the fellow from the garden on your own," Con said. "What if this had been you, Georgina?" he demanded, his voice fierce with anger. "Do you know what it would have done to me if I'd found your body here instead of his? Your face battered like that?"

This time when his lips descended upon hers, it was

a kiss of possession. With every touch he told her with his mouth that she was his. She had known that he wanted her, and even that he worried for her, but this kiss told her what the cost to him would be if something should happen to her—something more than simple danger, something like death.

Sometime over the course of the past few days, things had shifted between them. It was no longer possible for her to simply shove him away and tell him to mind his own business. For better or worse, Con had a stake in what became of her. Thinking what her own reaction would be if their positions were reversed, she knew without question that she would be inconsolable if it were Con lying dead on the roof of the theater.

But for now, she could only rejoice at the feeling of his body—very much alive—pressed against hers, as he kissed her.

Finally, perhaps still aware of the killer who might lurk in the shadows, he pulled back. "Please, Georgina. Do not put yourself in danger like this again."

Unable to speak, she reached out and touched his cheek, and nodded.

"We have to get out of here," he said, his hand on the small of her back as he led her into the hallway from the stairwell. "I'll send one of the ushers to let Clara know that you were feeling ill so I escorted you home. Then I'll send my man to alert the authorities once we get back to Henrietta Street. If they wish to speak to us about the matter, they can do so there tomorrow."

"But what about Robert's look-alike?" Georgie asked, for the first time worrying that the man might wish to do more than simply frighten her. The notion chilled her and she gave an involuntary shiver again. When Con's arm slipped around her as they descended the stairs, she was grateful. "If he is responsible for what happened to the man on the roof, then there must be something more to his game than intimidation."

"I'll consider the matter tonight and hopefully by morning will have arrived at some plan, whether it means confiding his actions to the authorities or striking out on our own. Either way," he continued, his hand absently caressing her bare arm, "I won't let you come to harm, you may be assured of it."

For the first time in a long while, Georgie felt protected and even, to her bemusement, cherished in some way that was as unfamiliar to her as an Indian monsoon.

Grateful for his reassurances, she allowed Con to escort her down the stairs and into the theater below.

Nine

$\mathcal{G}$eorgie spent a restless night in which she found herself dropping off to sleep only to be jolted awake by the memory of the dead young man on the roof of the theater. As a result, the face she saw in the dressing table mirror was wan with dark circles beneath the eyes. And though she tried to maintain a level of calm, she could not prevent the young man's death from casting a pall over her day.

Then there were the multiple kisses from Con yesterday to consider.

Hoping to avoid her worries, Georgie decided that she'd neglected her employer enough this week and made her way to Lady Russell's bedchamber only to find that, her gout having improved a great deal, she had gone down to breakfast for the first time in a week. Cheered at the news, Georgie searched her out in the breakfast room and was pleased to see her ladyship looking much more hearty than she had just days before.

"Ah, lovely, Georgina," Lady Russell said from the table, where she still had a cup of tea and a saucer of toast before her. "You will be able to accompany me to the Pump Room this morning, will you not? I vow it seems months since we were there—though I daresay it has only been a matter of days."

Belatedly, Georgie recalled her promise at the art gallery that she would meet Lettice at the Pump Room the next day. It felt like years since that afternoon, though it was only a few days. She hoped her friend would understand once she explained all that had gone on since their afternoon together on the day of Con's arrival in Bath.

"Of course, my lady," she said aloud to Lady Russell. "I will be more than happy to accompany you." She chose a rasher of bacon and some toast for her plate and took a seat beside Clara.

"I hope you are recovered from your headache, Mrs. Mowbray," Clara said when Georgie had taken her seat. "I was so disappointed for you to miss the second half of the play since you seemed to enjoy the first so much."

Since she and Con had agreed not to mention Georgie's altercation with the young men last night, she simply said, "Yes, thank you. I was disappointed too. But it couldn't be helped."

"What's this?" Lady Russell asked, her eyes sharp as she looked at Georgie from across the table. "I did not know you were ill. Perhaps you should stay here and rest while Clara accompanies me to the Pump Room."

"Not at all," Georgie said before Clara could speak. "I am much recovered, my lady. And perhaps I'll take the waters to see if they have any effect on my head."

It was not something she'd enjoy, but Georgie supposed the foul-tasting waters wouldn't harm her. And Lady Russell continued to drink them however Georgie might believe they'd done nothing to help the old woman's gout.

"An excellent notion." Lady Russell nodded. "You will feel much better after a drink of the waters. I thought they were not helping my gout, but now that it is improved I think they simply take time to take effect." Having finished her tea and toast, the old woman rose with the help of her walking stick. "I'll go fetch my hat and shawl and we'll be off as soon as you've finished your breakfast, Georgina."

When the older woman was out of earshot, Clara turned to Georgie and asked, "You are well, aren't you? I must admit that I was surprised when you left early last evening. The headache must have come on very suddenly, indeed."

Unsure whether she should confide in the other woman or not, Georgie merely nodded, hoping that Clara would drop the subject. She was saved from considering the matter further by Con's arrival in the room. "Aunt says that you'll be taking the waters this morning, Mrs. Mowbray," he said from the sideboard where he filled a plate with more food than Georgie could eat in a week. "I had hoped you'd be much recovered today."

At his tone, she looked up to find him watching her.

Wondering if she'd recovered from what she'd seen last night, she had little doubt.

"Will you accompany us to the Pump Room as well, Cousin?" Clara asked, looking from Georgie to Con and back again. "I know that Aunt Russell will be pleased to have you there."

"I don't think so," Con said regretfully. "I've a bit of business to take care of today, though I hope to be finished by early afternoon. Mrs. Mowbray, I have a feeling that you might be getting a call later this afternoon. Will you be here, do you think?"

"How mysterious you sound, Con," Clara said with a teasing note. "Who will you be bringing to call upon Mrs. Mowbray? A potential suitor? A friend? I must know!"

Georgie couldn't help but gasp at the other woman's inquisitiveness. Though she supposed it was to be expected when Con made things sound so havey-cavey.

"Nothing so mysterious as all that, Clara," he said with an indulgent smile. "Mrs. Mowbray and I stumbled upon a cutpurse last night before we left the theater. I plan to call upon the magistrate this morning and thought perhaps that one of his investigators might wish to speak to her."

"Good heavens," Clara said, a hand to her chest. "I had no idea. Why didn't you tell us, my dear?"

"I did not wish to overset you, my dear Clara, or Lady Russell for that matter," Georgie said, casting a speaking glance Con's way. "I shall endeavor to be back in Henrietta Street before luncheon, my lord. Will that be all right?"

Con inclined his head in assent. "I will see you then.

Though I wonder if you are able to go to the Pump Room given how severe your . . ."—he paused, looking at her with a penetrating gaze,—"headache was last evening. Do you not think that it might be safer for you to remain here this morning?"

Knowing that he feared for her safety given what she'd seen last night, Georgie felt warmth seep into her chest. Even so, she could not simply lock herself up in Henrietta Street until the danger was past. For one thing she would go mad. For another, she had a job to do.

"I'm afraid not," she said with real apology. "I really must do what I can to please Lady Russell today. I have neglected her a bit this week, so I should like to spend the day with her. And she wishes to go to the Pump Room, so I too shall go there."

"Understandable," Con said with a nod. "I shall arrange things, and if the investigator decides to call, I shall introduce you to him."

Georgie could see that Con disliked her answer and was unsurprised when he said, "I could speak to my aunt, if it comes to that. I'm sure if she knew how much you were affected by last night's ordeal she'd insist you remain behind."

The nerve of the man, she fumed. Trying to manipulate her into doing his bidding. "I'm sure that won't be necessary," she said through clenched teeth. "It is merely the Pump Room, after all. There is little enough harm to be had there. Unless one counts exposure to the waters."

He looked as if he'd like to argue, but Con finally

raised his hands as if in surrender. "As you see fit, Mrs. Mowbray," he said finally.

"Really, my dear," Clara said, oblivious to the undercurrents running between her cousin and her aunt's companion. "If we are to accompany my aunt we must go fetch our hats."

Some half hour later, Lady Russell, Georgie, Clara, and Lydia entered the Pump Room, which was somewhat crowded for this hour of the day. Immediately, Lydia excused herself to go chat with a group of young people on the other end of the bright chamber. Lady Russell, spotting a group of her own cronies, headed their way, leaving Georgie and Clara standing together near the entrance.

"Well, I call that very unfair," Clara said with mock dejection. "I suppose our conversation isn't entertaining enough for those two."

"I suspect in Lydia's case, it's more that we are not handsome or titled," Georgie said, eyeng the young men who made up part of the young lady's group.

A dimple appeared in Clara's cheek. "I fear you're right. And I suppose that leaves us on our own." She surveyed the room and her gaze rested on a pair of young matrons near the windows. "I see some friends there," she said. "Come along with me and I'll introduce you."

"I should like that," Georgie said. "But I fear I'll have to take the waters first. I'll be right over in a moment."

Clara looked over to where the server stood beside the pump, handing out cups of the noxious water. A line stretched all the way to the end of the chamber. "I daresay it would be best done quickly," she said, wrinkling her nose. "Better you than me."

Georgie bit back a laugh before urging the other woman to join her friends. With the enthusiasm of a prisoner walking to the gallows, she made her way to the end of the queue, where a pair of old gentlemen stood arguing politics as they waited.

Her mind left to wander, Georgie thought back again to what had happened last evening at the theater. A quick scan of the Pump Room had revealed no one resembling Robert. And given how he'd thus far kept to places where he would be able to effect a quick escape, she wasn't surprised. Since her husband hadn't had a twin, she suspected this man only looked like Robert. The Pump Room, with its many windows, was hardly the right venue for him to fool her. And she was convinced now that for whatever reason, this man wished her to believe her husband was back from the dead.

And the murder of the young man on the rooftop of the Theater Royale clearly indicated that the reason behind this man's attempt to frighten her was much more sinister than Georgie had first assumed. Wishing she could speak to Isabella and Perdita about the matter, she wondered, not for the first time, if this could be connected to the threats they'd all three received since the untimely death of the late Duke of Ormond. Though the circumstances had never been made public, Georgie knew that someone who wished to do her and her two friends ill did know them. And had decided that even though the duke had tried to kill all three of them that night, they were somehow in the wrong. Isabella had been tormented a few months ago at the behest of this unknown enemy. And now, it seemed, it was Georgina's turn.

Perhaps, as had been the case with Isabella's ordeal, this singular person who wished to punish them had delegated the task of antagonizing Georgina to someone else. The very idea made a chill race down Georgie's spine, as she tried to determine which of her current friends or acquaintances had betrayed her in such a way.

A hand on her arm, after the thoughts she'd just been entertaining, nearly sent Georgie to the ceiling of the Pump Room. "I'm so sorry, Georgina," said Lettice from beside her. "I did not mean to startle you. But only look who I've found!"

Turning, Georgie saw that Lettice was indeed accompanied by Mary Kendrick. "Lettice," she said, embracing her friend, "I am so terribly sorry I did not come as I said I would days ago. This week has been quite busy what with Lady Russell's family arriving to celebrate her birthday, and I've not had a morning to spare."

"From what I've heard," Mary said with a sly smile, "you've been spending a bit of time with her ladyship's nephew, the Earl of Coniston, Georgie."

Cursing the way that gossip spread in Bath, Georgie smiled, hoping she did not reveal her annoyance. "Oh, I fear that's an exaggeration, Mary. The earl is Lady Russell's nephew, of course, but we have spent time together only as part of group visits to the ruins at Farley Castle and then last evening to the theater. It is hardly to be remarked upon."

"The Earl of Coniston?" Lettice's eyes widened. "The same Earl of Coniston we saw at the art gallery, my dear? The artist? Why, Georgie, you do know him better than you let on, don't you?"

Knowing that if she allowed her friends to continue their interrogation they'd be there all day, Georgie changed the subject. "So, I see that you two have found one another," she said. "How have you been passing the time?"

The three women chatted for several moments about the various sights Lettice had been showing Mary that week, though Lettice—naturally—mourned that the weather wasn't nicer, the shops weren't cleaner and Bath in general wasn't so nice as London.

When there was a break in Lettice's complaints, Mary said, "Oh, Georgina, I meant to ask you about something the other day when we met in the lending library."

Thinking back to that uncomfortable day, Georgie braced herself for what might be innocuous but might also be painful. One never knew with Mary, she'd come to learn.

"Before he left that night for battle, my Jem mentioned that Robert had said something about ensuring his legacy." Georgie felt Mary's eyes on her face, as if the other woman were watching for some infinitesimal clue that would give away her thoughts. "I simply wondered if his letter mightn't have said something about it."

Lettice's eyes widened. "A letter?" She gasped. "You never said aught of a letter to me, Mary." Turning to Georgina, she prodded, "What did it say, Georgie?"

But Georgie had no intention of revealing the contents of Robert's letter to either of them. Especially given that Robert had confessed to an affair with one of her friends. Though she doubted it had been either Mary or Lettice, she still did not wish to share with them the knowledge that he'd been unfaithful. "I'm afraid it was private, Lettice," she said without rancor. "But there was nothing about a legacy in it, I can tell you that much."

Was it Georgie's imagination or did Mary look disappointed? Could she have been hoping for Georgie to come into some sort of property? Perhaps in the hopes that Georgie would share some of it with her dear friends?

Lettice's face fell as well. "Oh, dear. I had hoped that he'd left you an independence so that you would be able to live on your own and not as the companion of Lady Russell. I do so hate that you are under that woman's thumb."

Georgie felt ashamed at thinking so poorly of her friends. Of course they wanted to know if she would be able to take care of herself. "I'm afraid not, Lettice, dear," she told her friend, including Mary in her apologetic gaze. "And I do assure you that Lady Russell is not the tyrant you think she is."

"Come, Lettice," Mary said with a sympathetic smile for Georgie. "We will go have some tea while Georgie consumes these horrid waters."

Agreeing to meet her friend again later in the week, Georgie watched as they walked out of the Pump Room. What had Mary been talking about? she wondered. Could Robert have been more well off than he'd given her to believe? She had packed his few belongings into a small trunk which was currently being stored at Ormond House. And try as she might, she couldn't think a few books, some medals, and a few bits of jewelry he'd inherited from his parents, would be enough for him to call them a legacy.

Finally reaching the head of the line, she took the cup of cloudy water from the fellow at the pump. Stepping to the side, she took a sip and found that while it was not something she'd ever crave, the water wasn't so bad as all that. Deciding not to dally, she gulped it down without stopping.

The man who had been in the queue behind her took a spot beside her and sipped from his cup. He looked familiar but she couldn't quite place him. "I see that you are from the 'the faster the better' school of thought when it comes to drinking the waters," he said, raising his cup.

Amused, she said, "Yes, while I see that you are from the 'if I take small enough sips I won't ever actually taste it' school."

He was an average-looking sort, of middle years, whose pallor seemed to indicate some sort of ailment was part of his lot in life. "You are Lady Russell's companion, I think," he said with a smile. "I am your neighbor on Henrietta Street. Mr. Giles Corey."

Georgie realized then that she'd seen him on their street. "Of course," she said with a smile. "I'm Mrs. Georgina Mowbray, though I suppose you already know that."

"I do indeed," he said with a nod. "I had thought to meet you sooner, but I've been holed up in my house with the exception of the lending library this past week. This bad chest of mine strikes at the most inopportune moments."

"I'm sorry to hear it," Georgie said, thinking that his attitude was much more positive than hers would be under similar circumstances. "Do you find that the waters help?"

He shrugged. "I can't really say that they make much of a difference. I think I'm going to have to remove to Italy or Greece in the next month or so. England's climate is decidedly unhealthy for those with lungs as bad as mine are."

Georgie was about to voice her sadness to lose him to the Continent, when Mr. Corey's expression turned serious. "I am glad to have come across you here, Mrs. Mowbray, because I wonder if you might know anything about a man I've seen of late lurking in the mews behind our row of houses."

All thoughts of trivialities fled as Georgie took in her neighbor's demeanor. "You've seen someone in the garden too?" she asked, trying not to let her excitement show in her voice.

Mr. Corey nodded. "I have," he said. "I thought perhaps you might know him since he seems to be standing there at the behest of someone in your household."

"Why would you think that?" Georgie asked, surprised that he would think Robert's look-alike was there at the behest of someone in Lady Russell's household.

"Oh, I simply assumed," Mr. Corey said quickly, "that since he ended up in your back garden that he was there guarding the house or something."

At Georgie's puzzled look, he went on. "I wanted to know if you could ask the fellow to stop trampling my herbs. Or rather my cook's herbs. She's the most pleasant woman imaginable but when her garden is trampled she's nigh impossible to live with."

"I'm afraid I don't know who the man is, Mr. Corey," Georgina said. "But do you perhaps know whether he is there every evening or just some evenings? Is there a pattern to it, I mean."

"Oh, yes," Mr. Corey said with enthusiasm. "He's out there every night. Without fail. I should go out there and ask him to give off stomping on my cook's herbs myself, but I am in poor health, you see."

Georgie interpreted this to mean that he was afraid. Which she did not blame him for in the least. Of course a strange man in his garden frightened him.

Thanking Mr. Corey and promising that she'd do her best to see that the damage to Mr. Corey's garden came to an end, she hurried over to where Lady Russell chatted with her friends.

While Georgina and his aunt and cousin were at the Pump Room, Con visited the office of the magistrate for Bath and its surrounding area. Before leaving the theater last night, he'd informed the manager of the dead man's presence, and true to the adage "the show must go on," the man had waited until the performance was over and all the theatergoers were gone before contacting the authorities. Now, however, the investigator was determined to learn whatever he could from Con.

When he'd been shown into the man's office, Con had expected that he'd be speaking with someone a bit older than the man before him. In his early thirties, Michael McGilloway was as thin as a rail and his neck hardly looked strong enough to hold up the large whiskers he sported, much less the ears that protruded from either side of his head.

"Tell me again just what you were doing on the roof of the theater?" Mr. McGilloway asked, his sizable mustache quivering from the force of his question.

Trying to maintain his patience, Con repeated the answer to the same question he'd already been asked twice. "Mrs. Mowbray and I were searching for the man who has been stalking her. Since he disappeared into the corridor with the stairwell in it, we guessed that if he hadn't left the building he had to have gone onto the roof."

He had hoped to simply inform the man that he and Georgina were available for questions should they arise. As an earl, he was unaccustomed to having his word as a gentleman questioned, but the fact that this man kept asking the same questions again and again implied that that's just what he was doing.

"Who is this Mrs. Mowbray to you, my lord?" the investigator asked, leaning back in his chair. "Is she your mistress that you would disappear with her into a darkened corridor?"

While he was already annoyed, the man's disparagement of Georgie's good name sent Con's temper from a simmer to boiling. "Watch your tongue, man," he said through clenched teeth. "Mrs. Mowbray is a lady and a friend of the family and if you value your position you will speak of her with the courtesy to which she is entitled or our business is done here."

Seeing that he'd crossed a line, the investigator held up a staying hand. "I beg your pardon, my lord, but you must understand that I have to ask these questions no matter how upsetting they might be. What if, for instance, the man on the roof were the lady's husband?"

"We have already established that the lady's husband is dead," Con said, exasperation evident in his tone. "First, Mrs Mowbray saw the man who has been following her. Second, she tried to follow him but was accosted by four men. Third, when I had extricated her from the situation we went to the roof to see if her stalker had taken refuge there. Finally, we found a dead man on the roof. A dead man who appeared to be one of the four men who accosted her."

"Yes, my lord." McGilloway nodded like an approving parent. "Those are all the same points you've given me before. But if you have some other, deeper relationship with Mrs. Mowbray, then what is there to indicate that it wasn't you who killed the man who accosted her on the roof?"

"Aside from the fact that it was only one of them who was dead and not all four, each of whom I wanted to flay within inches of their lives when I saw them attacking her?" Con asked curtly. "Is that what you wished me to say?"

"Exactly what I wished you to say, my lord," McGilloway said, rising from his desk. "You said precisely what I needed to hear."

Con stared openmouthed at the man. "I don't follow."

"Well," McGilloway said, coming around his desk to sit on the edge. "If I were to see a lady I held in affection surrounded by four young men, like yourself I'd have wanted to tear each of those four limb from limb. I certainly wouldn't have been able to choose one of the four for punishment."

The man's explanation began to make some sense.

"So, because only one of the men was found dead on the roof, you believe I cannot have been the one to kill him," Con said, stroking his chin. There was some logic in the man's conclusion.

"I merely asked if she was your mistress to determine just where your affections lay," McAllister. "Your response answered my question."

Shaking his head ruefully, Con had to admit that he was impressed. "You know your business, McGilloway," he said. "I'll give you that."

Offering Con a short bow, McGilloway said, "I'll still need to ask Mrs. Mowbray some questions, but for the time being, I am satisfied with your responses and you are free to go."

At his words, Con paused. "I had hoped that you wouldn't need to question Mrs. Mowbray now."

McGilloway had the grace to look apologetic. "I had hoped that might be the case, but since she was the only one to see the stalker—and I've a notion that he might be the one who killed that young fellow on the roof—I shall need to speak with her. It can't be helped, I'm afraid."

Taking his leave of the other man, Con stepped out

into the street and headed in the direction of Angelini's studio.

Whenever Con was in Bath he made it a point to get a match in. Though the art of fencing was perhaps not so popular as it had been earlier in the century, there were still enough men who wished to learn at the hand of someone like Signor Angelini that the man was able to keep himself quite well, even in Bath.

He stepped into the main room of the studio to see a couple of matches already under way. Con retired to the dressing room to remove his coat and boots and was surprised to see Lord Archer there doing the same. "What are you still doing here?" he demanded of his friend.

"Not still," Archer replied. "What am I doing back?"

"What are you doing back?" Con said, feeling rather like a parrot. "I thought you were headed back to London."

"I was," Archer said, allowing one of the assistants to remove his boot. "I did go back, but found myself retracing my steps not long thereafter."

"What's happened?" Con asked in a low tone. "Did you learn something?"

His boots removed, the other man stood and flexed his shoulders. "Hardly," he said with an exasperated expression. "I was, rather, required to accompany the young dowager here."

Con's brows snapped together. "Oh, no. Please tell me that you didn't bring Perdita here to muddy the waters."

"Then I shan't tell you," Archer said, taking a couple of practice lunges with an imaginary foil. "Though you will regret not being aware of it when you find she's muddied your waters."

"It's not as if I don't already have enough to deal with, considering that Georgina refuses to leave matters to me," Con groused. "Now I shall be forced to deal with Perdita. You are a bastard, you know."

"Oh, I'm well aware of it," Archer said without affront. "I don't look a bit like my siblings."

"Don't be an ass," Con retorted. "What the devil am I going to do now? Do you even realize what a coil you've brought Perdita into?" He told his friend about what had happened the night before at the theater, and about how he and Georgina had found the dead man on the roof.

Archer whistled. "You weren't joking when you talked about muddy waters," he said. "Though I daresay that Perdita's arrival here will soothe Georgina's feelings a bit. Those two are thick as thieves and are always ready to run to one another's aid when they need it."

Con let his shoulders droop a bit. "I suppose that's something," he said with a sigh. "And I could do with your help in all this, so if having Perdita means having you here as well, that's good too."

"I didn't know you cared, old man," Archer said with a laugh. "Though you shouldn't make it sound as if we're a package deal. I merely agreed to accompany the young dowager here at her request. If the duke had needed me in town, I should have been forced to send her alone."

Con shuddered at the idea. "Do not frighten me with scenarios like that. Isabella as well? Perdita alone is as terrifying a prospect as ever I've imagined."

"You're the one who was betrothed to her," Archer said with a shrug. "Though I do feel the need to point out to you that you're speaking of the woman I love."

"How is that going?" Con asked innocently.

"Now who's the bastard, Coniston?" Archer asked, turning his back on the earl and stepping out into the studio.

"I believe that would be me," his friend responded, following. "Quite definitely, me."

Ten

*I*t was almost time for luncheon when Georgina, Clara, and Lady Russell returned to Henrietta Street.

Exhausted from her first venture out in days, Lady Russell decided to take her meal in her bedchamber, exhorting Georgie to leave her in peace. "I do not need to be coddled like a child," she insisted with exasperation. "Leave me to eat in peace and quiet. I vow I heard enough chatter in the Pump Room to last a lifetime. I'd forgotten how talkative Mr. Huntingdon can be."

Releasing Lady Russell into the care of her maid, Georgie and Clara untied their bonnets and gave them to the butler, who informed them that Lord Coniston was waiting for Georgie in the blue sitting room with another gentleman. Thinking that it was the investigator from the magistrate's office, Georgie told Clara to go on to luncheon without her, and smoothing her hair and wiping her hands nervously on her skirt, she stepped into the sitting room.

"Surprise," Perdita said, rushing forward from where she'd been seated on one of the two long couches before the fireplace and wrapping Georgie in a tight hug. "I know you hate them. Surprises, I mean. But this one couldn't be helped. I heard about the trouble you'd been having with the man who resembles . . . well, that man, and I had to come."

"I'm the guilty party, Mrs. Mowbray," Lord Archer Lisle said from his position just behind Perdita. "Coniston consulted me about the matter, and knowing the duchess would wish to be informed, I . . . well, informed her." To Georgie's amusement the man ran a finger between his collar and his neck. Leave it to Lord Archer to apologize in such a way that she couldn't be angry with him.

"Technically," Con said from his position before the fireplace, "the blame is mine. I am after all the one who told Lord Archer, so if you are to rake anyone over the coals it should be me."

"I've never heard such a load of rubbish in my life," Georgie said as she and Perdita took seats next to one another. "You're all so busy taking blame that you don't stop to consider that I might be glad for your inability to keep a secret."

"It's only that we love you, dearest," Perdita said, squeezing her friend's hand. "And knowing what Isabella went through in Yorkshire and later in London, I couldn't allow you to remain here in Bath suffering alone. I could never forgive myself."

"I understand," Georgie said, her heart full as she realized just how much she'd missed her friend. "Though I hope that this doesn't rise to the level of awfulness that Isabella's incident did, I must admit that I'm unnerved by the things that have happened here."

"Can you tell us what exactly has happened?" Lord Archer asked, his brows drawn as he stood next to Con before the fireplace. "We've heard about the incidents from Lord Coniston, of course, but I'd like to hear your own impressions if that would be agreeable to you."

So, in her own words, Georgie related to them everything that had taken place in Bath from the moment she'd seen the man who looked so like her husband standing in the garden, to finding the body on the roof of the theater, to now.

As she related her tale, Perdita became increasingly disturbed, gasping when Georgie told her about the dead man, and finally reaching out to hug Georgie when she told how frightened she'd been when she saw the body.

"This is awful," Perdita said with a shake of her auburn curls. "Simply awful. I cannot believe that this person would go so far as to kill a man simply to frighten you."

"I'm not sure it was simply to frighten me," Georgie responded, patting her friend's hand. "I suspect that the man on the roof was guilty of crossing the man who looks like Robert in some way. He'd have to be utterly mad to kill for any other reason."

"Don't be so sure of it," Lord Archer said quietly. "There are men who think nothing at all about taking another's life. I do not think your villain is one of those, however. But I shouldn't rule out the possibility completely."

"We'll know more once we've heard from Mr. McGilloway, the magistrate's investigator," Con said, his eyes intent. "I suspect that we'll find some sort of falling-out between our man on the roof and our man from the garden. But until then, we can't jump to conclusions."

"When I think about how close you came to falling into this man's trap," Perdita said with horror. "Well, it doesn't bear thinking on."

"I'm perfectly fine," Georgie reassured her friend. "In fact, I'm better than fine. For the first time since Robert's death, I feel in control of my own destiny. Even if it does mean that I'll need to vanquish this mystery man before I can truly embrace it."

"Any news from the Pump Room?" Con asked, stretching his long legs out before him. "You looked as if you had something on your mind when you returned."

Remembering what Mr. Corey had told her, Georgie related to her friends the tale of the man their neighbor had seen crossing his garden into theirs. "And since Mr. Corey said that the look-alike is there every night, we should be able to catch him at it tonight, shouldn't we?"

"How?" Perdita asked, her nose wrinkled.

"My dear Perdita," Georgie said with a wolfish smile, "because I intend to set a trap!"

"Good God," Con said, shaking his head. "Of course you can't set a trap. At least not on your own."

"Of course not," Georgie said with a grin. "I'll be with you," she said. Turning to Archer and Perdita she added, "and the two of you."

"Why do I get the feeling that this is not going to end well," Con muttered.

"Don't be such a cynic," Perdita chided him. "We'll do splendidly, won't we, Archer?"

To Georgie's amusement, the other man gave Con a look of apology before nodding at Perdita.

"Excellent!" she said. "Now we've only to make plans for our midnight ambush."

Before the others could comment, however, the butler stepped into the room and announced that a Mr. McGilloway had called and wished to speak to Mrs. Mowbray. Telling him to show the man in, Georgie was grateful that she wasn't alone to answer the man's questions about the death the night before. Not only was she terrified of saying the wrong thing, she was also worried that if she took a verbal misstep she might find herself facing more trouble than she was prepared to deal with.

From his position against the mantelpiece, Con observed McGilloway enter the room. To his amusement the man who was so self-assured with him earlier in the day was somewhat nervous outside of his own usual surroundings.

"My lord," he said, stepping forward to bow before Con, who then introduced the newcomer to Lord Archer. His greetings to the men completed, he turned to first Perdita and then Georgie. Pausing over Georgie's hand, he looked carefully at her face before allowing her to take her hand back.

"Mrs. Mowbray," he said cautiously, "I hope you will allow me to ask you a few questions regarding the events of last night at the Theater Royale?"

Once the ladies took their seats again, the investigator took a seat across from them on the couch opposite.

"I've already spoken with Lord Coniston," he continued, not looking toward the other man. "But I'd like to hear things from your point of view now, if you don't mind."

Con was pleased to see that rather than giving in to her fear, Georgie maintained her dignity and responded, "Of course, Mr. McGilloway. I am happy to help. That poor man on the roof deserves our help."

"I don't suppose you would consent to answering my questions without all these good people in attendance," the man said, in such a way that Con knew he thought the chances were slim.

"I'm afraid she will not," Con said, before Georgie could say anything. "It's not that we don't trust you, of course, but Mrs. Mowbray is rather nervous and she does not wish to speak to you alone. Aside from the fact that it would be highly improper."

"I thought not, my lord," McGilloway said with a nod. "But I had to ask all the same."

Settling back into his seat, the investigator turned back to Georgie. "All right then, ma'am," he said, "why don't you tell me about what transpired last night at the theater. When did you first know something was wrong?"

Once again, Georgie told her story, beginning with how she'd seen the man who resembled her husband and ending with finding the body of the young man on the roof. When she was finished, there was no sound in the room except for the ticking of the mantel clock.

"Was this the first time you'd seen the man who looked like your husband?" McGilloway asked.

"Not at all," Georgie said, staring at the painting on

the wall behind McGilloway's head. "He's also been seen hiding in the garden here in Henrietta Street. And at Farley Castle. But I'd never been as close to him as I was at the theater. I was able to see how much like my husband he really was in the theater. From the upper stories to the very back of the garden is quite a long way and it's difficult to judge size and distance."

McGilloway nodded. "Would it surprise you to know that the young man whose body you found has been working as an investigator himself?"

That must have given Georgina some pause, because she looked sharply at McGilloway. "You mean an investigator like you?" she asked.

"In a way," McGilloway conceded. "He was hired by a minor Italian nobleman to find the whereabouts of a piece of jewelry that was stolen from his wife just after the war."

Con saw Georgina frown. "So the dead man had nothing to do with my husband's look-alike? And he wasn't one of the four men who attacked me either?"

"He definitely was not one of the four young men," McGilloway said, his gaze intent upon her, as if he thought he could read her mind simply by staring at her. "I've spoken with all four of them."

McGilloway looked at Georgina closely. "As far as we know, your husband's look-alike was not involved in the man's death either. Though there is a strange coincidence at work there. We've spoken with an army friend of your husband's and he seemed to think that your husband was involved in some minor theft while he was in Europe. That might explain why the dead man was here. He was investigating your husband. Were you aware of any illegal activities he might have been involved in?"

Georgie shook her head, as if to clear it. "No," she said "So far as I knew he was merely a soldier. I did get the feeling he was hiding something, but I assumed that was just . . ." She paused, embarrassment lending color to her cheeks. "I assumed he was having an affair. I had no notion that he was stealing."

"With your husband's death," McGilloway said with a shrug, "there is no way of knowing one way or the other if he was involved." His eyes watching her keenly, McGilloway continued, "Unless, of course you found some unexplained valuables with his things after he died, of course. But you'd have told the authorities, wouldn't you?"

"Well," Georgina said with a frown, "it was rather impertinent, but I may as well tell you that I found nothing in Robert's things. No extra funds, no jewels, no valuables of any kind. If I had I should certainly not be employed as a ladies' companion to keep a roof over my head."

"Aye," McGilloway said with a nod. "I thought as much. Though I did have to ask."

"I can't say that I'm surprised to hear such an accusation," Georgina admitted with a shrug. "My husband was not the most ethical of men, and I often found that when he wanted something he had no compunction about taking it." Con noticed the way she seemed to shrink into herself at the memory and once again found himself damning the late Colonel Robert Mowbray.

"But what of the fellow on the roof, McGilloway?" Con asked, bringing them back to the subject at hand.

"If you believe Mrs. Mowbray, then where does that leave the investigation into his death?"

"It's possible the man was killed by someone over an entirely different matter than the one the fellow was looking into. After all, it's rare that a man like that works only one case at a time."

"It makes sense," Con said grudgingly. "But surely it is too much of a coincidence that he was investigating the husband of the woman who found him."

"I would add, however, that it's quite possible the man wasn't as convinced of Mrs. Mowbray's innocence as I am," McGilloway said. "And someone said they saw the dead man, a Mr. Potts, rushing down the hallway and he happened to run into you, Mrs. Mowbray. I believe he shoved you out of the way? Perhaps Lord Coniston didn't like that."

"Don't be ridiculous, man," Archer said, pushing himself away from the mantel. "Lord Coniston has no need to kill anyone. Especially not over something so trivial. It makes no sense."

"You may be right, Lord Archer," the investigator said mildly. "It could be that I'm chasing at windmills. But I do dislike coincidences."

"You told me I was in the clear this afternoon, McGilloway," Con said tersely.

"That was before I learned the identity of the dead man, Lord Coniston," the investigator explained. "Things are different now."

"But that's nonsense! We were there because the man who looks like my dead husband lured us there, for heaven's sake," Georgina said, standing up so that she could pace behind the sofa. "He wanted us to be blamed for the investigator's death so that he could escape suspicion."

"That's a likely scenario," McGilloway agreed. "And one that very neatly removes the two of you from suspicion. Even so, I'd like to ask you both to remain here in Bath for the next few weeks. Just until we figure out who it is that killed our young investigator."

Con clenched his teeth. He hated being trapped anywhere. Even somewhere as large as Bath. Still, he'd stay here if it meant keeping Georgina safe.

"I don't think that will be a problem," she said, raising a brow, and once more Con was awed by her ability to remain calm under the circumstances. "I am, after all, the companion to an elderly lady who lives in Bath. I'm hardly likely to go jaunting off to Scotland or the Continent. My home is here."

"And you, my lord?" McGilloway asked Con.

It was difficult to respond without giving away any of his interior thoughts on the matter. He did, however, manage it, shrugging with a nonchalance he did not feel, and saying, "Of course. I'll remain in the general area. For now."

As if he knew how much emphasis Con had placed on those two little words, "for now," McGilloway gave him a small smile, and nodded. "That's all I can ask," he said. "For now."

With that, the man excused himself, and Georgina, Con, Perdita, and Lord Archer were left alone.

The room was quiet for a few moments as they each reviewed the man's words on their own. Finally, Perdita gave her friend another hug and said, "My poor dear, you must be so devastated to learn of the accusations against Robert. I remember you being worried that he seemed to be getting money from somewhere other than his salary, but this is beyond awful. It only seems to confirm your suspicions."

Georgina, however, was having none of it. "Do not treat me like a poor martyred heroine, Perdita," she said firmly. "I was never that, even when Robert was at his very worst. I am simply a widow who has learned her husband—like any number of other husbands—was capable of more deceit than she'd imagined. It's hardly worthy of sympathy. If anything, I should be chastised for being so blind. Can you imagine how you might have felt if the situations were reversed?" She shook her head. "I already knew that Robert was a scoundrel. One more crime added to his roster is hardly enough news to inspire gasps of horror."

Her mouth twisting, Perdita nodded, though Con could see there were tears in her eyes. He thought perhaps Georgina should be left alone to contemplate the news she'd just learned, but he dared not speak the words aloud.

Seeing how overset her friend was, Georgina seemed to make a mental decision. "Perdita, I am sorry. I know you mean well, but it simply does not bother me as much as you might think."

Nodding, Perdita lifted her handkerchief to her nose and sniffed. "I know what you mean. I wouldn't have been surprised in the least to hear the same thing about Ormond. I sometimes forget how much stronger you are than me."

"Only on the outside," Georgie assured her with a half-armed hug. "I think none of us know what things are like inside a marriage. Even happy ones. And you are right on one score. I was worried about where he was getting the extra money. It's too bad it didn't occur to me what he was doing until just now."

"So, ladies," Lord Archer said, clapping his hands together. "What's to be our next adventure?"

"I don't know about you, but I'm even more determined than ever to catch our man in the garden tonight," Con said with some degree of relish. "Here's hoping that he is prepared to reveal the reasons behind his nocturnal visitations."

Eleven

While Con and Archer settled into Lady Russell's library to talk strategy for that night's ambush of the Robert look-alike, Georgie and Perdita walked the short distance to Perdita's house in Laura Place. Because the Duke of Ormond's family didn't keep a permanent residence in the spa town, the current duke, who also happened to be married to Perdita's sister, had instructed her to rent whatever she thought suitable.

"For all that he's a duke," Perdita said, sipping the cup of tea the housemaid had just brought them along with a plate of sandwiches and biscuits, "The new Ormond is certainly reluctant to spend like one. You can take the man out of the country, and all that nonsense."

Georgie bit back a laugh. "You are too hard on him," she told her friend. "I daresay he's not been accustomed to living on so lavish a scale as the rest of the family has done. And from what Con says he's rather lenient with you."

Perdita shrugged. "I daresay you're right. And I am excessively pleased that my sister has found someone who will care for her better than Wharton did. It's just difficult to adjust to having someone else in charge of things, now. I knew of course that it was always supposed to be Trevor's, but I grew rather accustomed to making my own decisions—with Archer's assistance of course. I'll get over it soon enough, I suppose."

"So, Isabella does still seem happy, then?" Georgina asked cautiously. She knew as well as anyone that marriage could sometimes start out blissfully only to dissolve into misery weeks later. "I quite liked the new duke when I met him in London. He seemed a sensible sort of man."

"Oh, quite," Perdita said with a laugh that didn't quite ring true. "My sister is fairly bursting with happiness. Before long she'll be increasing and her bliss will be complete."

Ah, Georgina thought, that was what was bothering her friend. It was only known to a few people, but when the former Duke of Ormond—Perdita's husband—had died, Perdita had been increasing. The stress of his passing, along with the violent way he'd treated her during their last encounter, had proved too much for Perdita to handle. And like so many women in that situation she'd blamed herself. Isabella and Georgina had tried to comfort her as best they could, but for many months the young duchess had been inconsolable.

"That's wonderful news," Georgina said despite her worry for Perdita. "I am so happy for her. Truly."

"So am I," Perdita said despite the tears in her eyes.

"Truly, I am. I know you must think me a beast for even a twinge of jealousy, but I find it so hard not to feel it."

Georgina reached out and took her friend's hand in hers. "I think nothing of the sort," she said firmly. "What you went through was horrible. And I wouldn't wish that sort of thing on anyone. I truly ache for you, Perdita, no matter how happy I am for Isabella and Trevor."

Perdita swallowed and squeezed Georgie's hand back. "You're a dear, Georgie," she said, "really you are. I don't know of anyone else of my acquaintance I could ever admit such feelings to."

"Just because you are envious of someone doesn't mean you cannot also be happy for them," Georgie said practically. "We are complex creatures, are we not?"

"Indeed," Perdita said with a sad smile. "And the thing of it is that I cannot wait until Isabella has a child. It's just that I wish I had a child as well. When I think of those last few weeks with Ormond, I cannot help but feel hurt and angry all over again. It's as if he weren't satisfied with attacking me in person, but he also tried to find a way to hurt me after he was gone."

"Dearest, I know it's difficult to contemplate," Georgie said. "Especially so soon after the dissolution of your engagement to Lord Coniston—"

Perdita held up a staying hand. "Stop right there, Georgina," she said. "First of all, you must know that the business with Coniston had nothing to do with love or power or any of that other nonsense that surrounds marriage among the *ton*. It was purely a business arrangement. An arrangement I found myself completely opposed to after I'd given the thing some thought."

"What's the second thing?" Georgie asked, her brows raised.

"The second thing is that if you are about to tell me that I should consider marrying someone else in the hopes that he will give me a child," Perdita said with a frown, "then you should save your breath. I have no reason to believe that I can have children at all. Remember that I had two pregnancies with Ormond, neither of which proved to be viable. Why don't I simply give up while I can?"

Georgie had heard the argument from her friend before. "But surely the reason those pregnancies didn't work out was because you were so miserable while you were married to Ormond. I haven't heard physicians say as much, but does it not make sense that a mother's happiness and well-being will affect the health of her child?"

"Dearest Georgie," Perdita said, patting her friend on the hand. "You are a far better friend than I deserve. Here I am nattering on about Ormond and Isabella and my own unhappy circumstances, while you are sitting there patient as ever letting me run roughshod over you."

Her contrition apparent on her face, Perdita poured her friend another cup of tea and continued. "Since you seem so interested in Lord Coniston," she said, "perhaps you will tell me about the undercurrent of electricity I'm feeling between the two of you. I haven't seen him look this intrigued since he was dangling after that awful Mrs. Pettibone. You remember her, don't you? She had enormous . . ." Perdita cupped her hands before her own modest breasts.

Georgina nearly choked on her tea. "That must have been before we met," she told her friend, curious despite herself at the information her friend was revealing about Lord Coniston. As a *ton* outsider, Georgie would only have known about Lord Coniston's past amours if they'd appeared in the gossip sheets. And even then she wasn't much for reading up on the comings and goings of the upper ten thousand.

"Well," Perdita said, spooning sugar into her tea, "I won't sully your ears with details but it was a rather amusing time given Mrs. Pettibone's inability to rub two thoughts together. Actually, come to think of it, it was a rather dull time. I always found myself seated next to her at dinner. I suppose because I've got a reputation for being kind. What a nuisance."

"You're a goose," Georgie said with a shake of her head. "An utter goose."

"You won't wriggle out of the question all that easily," Perdita said fiercely. "Now tell me how it is that you've ended up sharing a house in Bath with one of England's most eligible bachelors."

"For heaven's sake," Georgie argued. "You make it sound as if we live there alone. Lady Russell and countless of her other relatives are there too, you know."

"You're evading the question," Perdita said, wagging her finger. "Let me guess. You were here in Bath, minding your own business, caring for Lady Russell to the best of your ability, when who should turn up on Lady R's doorstep but the ever-so-handsome Lord Coniston?"

"Something like that," Georgie said with a surprised laugh. "And there's nothing going on between us. We're merely friends. And besides, I'm not even of his station. I'm a glorified servant girl, if you must know. That hardly means that we are destined for great happiness together."

"Hmmm," Perdita said thoughtfully. "I think you protest too much, but there is no way I'm going to convince you in a few moments. I do wish you'd give the fellow a chance though. It's obvious from the way he looks at you when you aren't aware of it that he adores you."

"Purdy," Georgina said, giving her friend a half hug, "I have missed you."

"I've missed you too, dearest," her friend replied. "And I cannot wait for tonight when we will capture this look-alike fellow. What right does he have to go about spying on private citizens? It's outrageous!"

Georgie bit back a laugh. She might have known Perdita would react that way—like a mother hen with an endangered chick. "I'm rather more concerned about the jewels the dead man was looking for. It must have something to do with the legacy Mary was telling me about at the Pump Room. But why would Robert have told Kendrick about it?"

"I don't know unless Kendrick was involved with the theft as well," Perdita said with a shrug. "And who knows why your follower continues to stalk you. He might be mad, or worse, simply determined to ruin you. But don't worry. All of us—Lord Coniston, Lord Archer, and myself—are determined to see to it that you are kept out of harm's way."

Their conversation turned to other things and without further discussion about their plans for the evening, Georgie and Perdita finally parted company so that Georgina might return to Lady Russell's to dress for dinner.

Later that evening, having declined Clara and her family's invitation to a musical evening, and having seen Lady Russell to her bedchamber for an early evening, Georgie and Con slipped out the French doors from the study to the back garden where they met Archer and Perdita. They all wore dark clothing so that they wouldn't be easily seen in the night.

They had considered how best to split up in order to maximize both safety for the ladies and the likelihood that they'd actually be able to catch their quarry. As a result, the idea of Georgie and Perdita lying in wait together was dismissed almost out of hand. Con had argued—and rather effectively, he thought—that if both ladies were to hide together it would make them more vulnerable. Even, he'd argued, if Georgie brought along her pistol. Similarly, having the four of them secrete themselves in four different locations had also been dismissed. There was safety in numbers, even if the number was only two. So eventually they'd decided that Perdita and Archer, Georgina and Con would hide in either corner of the garden—the former behind a small potting shed on the far left corner of the garden, and the latter in the shadows behind a trellis covered with climbing roses and wisteria.

"Don't forget that if either of us sees him alone,

we're to make a call like a dove," Archer said as the four of them huddled together near the back wall of shrubbery.

"And if we see him with someone else," Con said in a low voice, "we're to make the sound of a crow."

Perdita and Georgina exchanged an amused glance, which Con and Archer chose to ignore.

With a nod to Archer, Con took Georgina by the hand and led her toward their hiding place, trying to ignore the zing of awareness that he felt in such close proximity to her. This was not the time for his libido to awaken, he told himself firmly.

"If this weren't so treacherous, I'd actually be enjoying the experience of the garden at night," Georgina whispered as they settled into their positions. "It's rather lovely. Especially in the moonlight."

Unwilling to enter into a conversation about what sort of feelings his present position—which was pressing firmly against Georgina's backside—evoked, Con shushed her.

In order to fool the watcher into thinking that Georgie was in her bedchamber, Georgie and Perdita had raided the attics of Lady Russell's house and found a dressmaker's form which they'd dressed and placed in the window as if it were looking out into the garden. From their vantage point below, it looked enough like a person that it should fool the watcher. Though Con suspected its stillness might give the game away.

"Do you think he'll come?" Georgina whispered, her body relaxed against his.

Not wishing to give away their position, Con put his

mouth against her ear. "I think it's possible. Especially since Mr. Corey said he's been here every night this week."

Georgina's body shivered, presumably from the feeling of his breath against her ear. Con steeled himself not to react, though there was little he could do to prevent his cock from rising to attention. "Be still," he whispered.

Perhaps realizing what her response had provoked in him, Georgina stiffened against him. "Sorry," she whispered back.

Con closed his eyes in exasperation. This was far more punishment than he deserved for getting involved with his former fiancée's friend. This was the punishment he'd have deserved if he'd had an affair with her while he was still betrothed to Perdita. Which he had not done.

He hoped that somewhere the powers that be would reward him for his restraint.

He was imagining what sort of prize he might win for managing to get through the first ten minutes of this godforsaken exercise in self-control, when a noise at the back gate alerted him that they weren't alone in the garden.

He strained his eyes to make out the figure who pushed into the enclosure and made his way toward the tree where he'd been standing on the first night Georgina had seen him.

Con lightly pinched Georgina on the arm and gave a slight jerk of his head toward the man. Silently, she nodded, her eyes fixed on the man. They both watched as the man who looked just as Georgie had described him stood and surveyed the area around him—perhaps sensing that he wasn't alone in Lady Russell's yard.

"Who's there?" he hissed.

Twelve

*H*er eyes now accustomed to the dark, Georgie watched from the safety of Con's arms as the man seemed to relax when no one responded to his question.

Remaining silent, Georgie felt Con step out from behind her, and maintaining his cover among the shrubbery, he worked his way around the perimeter of the garden until he was directly behind the fellow. From the other side of the garden, she could see Lord Archer stepping quietly to stand on Con's other side.

Still unaware of his unwanted guests, the intruder nearly leaped a foot into the air when Con raised his weapon behind the other man, saying, "I shouldn't move if I were you."

"Who the hell are you?" the man demanded, his voice loud enough for Georgie to hear, turning to face not one but two men with guns trained at him. "This is private property, I'll have you know."

Shocked at the man's gall, Georgie strained to see his expression but the shade kept her from seeing anything other than his outline. Though the shape of the pistol in his hand was visible enough.

"You are correct. This is private property," Con said to the other man, his gun hand not wavering. "It belongs to my aunt. Try another tactic."

Georgie heard the other man curse. "You don't understand," he said. "I have a right to be here. That woman up there is my relation. My sister-in-law. I'm here to watch over her."

Something in Georgie snapped. The nerve of the man. How dare he claim to be here on her behalf! She didn't even know him. Despite Con's earlier admonishment that she stay where she was, she hurried along the garden path to where the men were standing facing one another with their pistols pointed at each other.

"I hope you don't mean me, sir," Georgie said, not caring that she sounded piqued. "I've never met you before in my life, so if you are here to watch over me as you called it, then it's certainly something I've had no notion of."

The man, his face so like Robert's and yet, this close, so unlike, stared at her. "Mrs. Robert Mowbray, I presume?" he said with something that looked like relief. "I cannot tell you what a pleasure it is to finally meet you. Especially after I've spent so long looking after you."

"What the dev . . . er, deuce," she amended, "are you talking about? I have no idea who you are, sir."

Looking from his own pistol to Con and Archer's, the man asked, "Do you mind if we dispense with these?"

Con exchanged a knowing look with Archer, who raised his brows as if to ask, "why not?" With a slight shrug, Con said, "We'll put ours away if you will do the same."

The man nodded and slowly all three men lowered their weapons and put them away. Turning to the shrubbery behind them, the man said, "Mary, you'd best come out now as well."

Georgie was shocked to see her erstwhile friend Mary Kendrick step out from the bushes. Far from looking sheepish or guilty, the woman held her head high as she stepped forward to stand next to the man who so resembled Georgie's husband.

What was going on?

"I don't wish to interrupt this charming reunion," Con said brusquely, "but might we retire somewhere indoors to complete our conversation?"

"Come," Georgie said with a nod. "We can talk inside."

If Con disliked having the man who'd been threatening her in his aunt's house, he didn't argue. "A good idea, Mrs. Mowbray," he said, offering her his arm, and extending his other arm to indicate that their two visitors—for want of a better word—should precede them.

"Wait for me!" Perdita called as she stepped out from concealment and took Archer's proffered arm. Despite her surprise about Mary Kendrick, Georgie couldn't help but smile at Perdita's excitement. "You didn't think I'd miss what promises to be the most interesting conversation to take place in Bath all year long."

To his credit, Lady Russell's butler didn't bat an eye at being asked to serve tea in the drawing room at such a late hour. Though Georgie imagined that the conversation belowstairs that evening would rival that in the drawing room for its unusual nature.

Once all six of them were seated in the drawing room with their own cups of tea, Georgie felt confident enough to start the conversation.

"Now, sir," she said to her husband's relative, "I think we should begin by having you tell us exactly who you are. I know you must be some relation of my husband, Robert Mowbray's, but I have no idea whom."

Not pretending to misunderstand her, the man gave a brisk nod and said, "I am, madam, your husband's half brother. We never met. It wouldn't have been right."

Georgie might have informed the man that he'd not missed much given Robert's unpleasant disposition, however, she held her tongue on the matter. Instead she said, "That makes sense, I suppose. Your mother was—I hate to put it this way—Mr. Mowbray senior's paramour?"

"Aye," the man said. "My name is Malcolm Lowther. My father kept my mother and me in a little house in Manchester, where he'd go on 'business' from time to time. I knew about Robert and his military career, but he didn't know about me."

"I dislike sounding ungrateful for this explanation," Con said conversationally, "but do you mind very much explaining what possible reason you might have for standing in Lady Russell's garden and frightening the devil out of Mrs. Mowbray night after night?"

At his words, Lowther reddened. "It's a bit complicated," he said, running a hand over his light brown hair.

"I think we've time to listen," Con said agreeably. "Especially if it concerns Mrs. Mowbray's well-being."

Annoyed at the way Con was taking over her interrogation, Georgie cleared her throat. To his credit, Con looked a bit sheepish. But evidently Lowther didn't notice this byplay, for he nodded, and went on. "A few weeks ago I received a letter from someone informing me that I'd lost a brother at Waterloo. This person claimed to have been with him at the last and that his dying wish had been for me to look after his wife, Georgina, whose mind had been unsettled by the war. I wasn't to approach her directly, because that would only disturb her more, but I should watch her from afar. If I protected her during her stay in Bath, where she'd become companion to a wealthy elderly lady, this person would see to it that I received ten thousand pounds at the end of three weeks."

For a few moments no one said anything. Then Archer gave a low whistle. "Ten thousand pounds is a vast sum of money for three weeks of work," he said, exchanging a look with Con.

Georgie shook her head, unable to believe what her husband's brother had just said. "Did this person never reveal who they were, or why they'd decided to play benefactor in this manner? Aside from my husband's dying wish, I mean? You must admit, it's a rather outlandish proposition."

Lowther colored. "I realize it's rather unconventional. But there is another thing that I failed to mention. I'd gotten into a bit of trouble at the gaming tables in the last couple of years. So I was, am, in desperate need of this ten thousand pounds. So I was perhaps more willing to believe them than I might otherwise have been."

"And he gave no clue as to his identity?" Con persisted. "None at all?"

The young man shook his head. "That was part of the agreement. I would watch over Mrs. Mowbray for three weeks, and if I kept her safe, and did not attempt to learn the letter writer's identity, then I would receive the ten thousand pounds."

It was a rather sly plan, Georgie thought. Because Lowther needed the money he would follow the anonymous benefactor's instructions. Which had placed him in a position to—without knowing it—terrorize her with the vision of her dead husband in the guise of following his dying wishes. It was rather brilliant actually.

"Were you following her at the theater last evening?" Con asked.

At the mention of the theater, Lowther looked abashed. "I was, my lord," he said. "And I was sorry to hear what happened to Mrs. Mowbray in the hallway. But as soon as I realized she'd seen me, I left the theater and came back to my post in Henrietta Street."

"What of the dead man on the roof?" Georgie asked, exchanging a look with Con. Surely if he'd been at the theater he was the one who'd killed the man looking for the stolen jewels.

Lowther blanched. "I don't know about any dead man," he said. "I promise you as soon as I got away from you in the theater hallway, I came straight here to wait for your return."

Con seemed to believe the man, so Georgie turned her attention to the other person they'd captured. Quickly she explained how she and the other woman were acquainted. "What was your role in this, Mary? Did you receive a letter too? Or were you perhaps trying to find out if I knew anything else about the legacy your husband told you about?"

Before Mary could respond, Lowther spoke up. "I won't have you speak like that to Mrs. Kendrick," he said sharply. "She has nothing to do with this. She was simply here tonight to keep me company while I fulfilled my end of the bargain."

But Mary Kendrick didn't appreciate the young man's chivalry, it would seem. "Don't be foolish, Malcolm," she chided. "There's no way Georgina is going to believe there's nothing more than simple coincidence here. I don't mind telling my part. I owe it to her."

Though Lowther looked unhappy about it, he didn't object further. Mary continued, "I also received a letter. You know that my husband died at Waterloo as well as Robert. And like you, I received only a small widow's portion upon which to live. I've been living here in Bath with my sister and her husband and this letter was like a gift from heaven. If I would only seek out Robert's brother in Lady Russell's back garden over the course of these three weeks, and . . ."—she colored, then forced the next words from between clenched teeth—"and attempt to seduce him in full view of your bedchamber window, then I would receive ten thousand pounds to do with as I pleased. But I could tell no one, and if I revealed the scheme to you in particular, Georgina, I would receive nothing."

The widow looked angry, but defiant. As if she resented having to tell the tale and thus lose her reward, but took some pride in the confession as well. "I couldn't see how it would hurt you," she said. "After all, it isn't as if I were carrying on with Robert himself. And I was sure if you knew what I stood to gain simply by lingering outside your bedchamber window, you'd be happy to help."

Georgie stared at her friend and wondered how she'd ever thought Mary was a good person. There had been times when Georgie had suspected the other woman of mean-spiritedness but this went far beyond anything she'd ever imagined. Not only had she kept the information about Robert's letter from her until that morning, but she'd also willfully conspired to terrorize Georgie in her own home. And thought Georgie would gladly help her if she only knew the reason.

"Thank you for telling us," Georgie said, though she was hard-pressed to say the words aloud, given her outrage.

Mrs. Kendrick shrugged, and slipped her hand into Lowther's. "I realized not too long after we began this strange business that whoever had written the letters was playing at something more underhanded than we'd at first imagined. I decided tonight that it had to stop."

Georgie forbore from pointing out that she'd only

decided this after she and Mr. Lowther had been caught out. It would do no good to antagonize the two of them when they still had some knowledge that might help Georgie and Con discover who the mysterious letter writer was. She also did not fail to notice the way the two seemed to be behaving toward one another. Perhaps some good would come of this.

"You don't seem surprised to hear her side of the tale," Con said to Lowther, apparently also interested in the couple's connection. "Did you discover it on your own or did she reveal the whole to you later?"

"I'd rather not say," Lowther said, his voice cool. "Suffice it to say that I discovered how things stood and encouraged Mary to tell me just how she'd gotten the idea to approach me in your aunt's garden."

"So you both began to come here together each evening?" Georgie asked.

Mary nodded. "At first we waited until we could see you in the window, then moved into the moonlight and played our part. Then we would swap up standing in the corner. It wasn't long into the first week that we began to wonder if the anonymous person had been overestimating just how unsettling you'd find the sight of Malcolm in your back garden. You seemed to look out every night but didn't notice us. Then earlier this week, you'll remember the night, of course, you saw Malcolm and screamed. We decided that it might be more effective for you to see him alone, since Robert is dead. And once you'd seen me at the lending library it became foolish to think you'd be frightened at the sight of me."

Georgie nodded. It was a sensible strategy. "What will you do now that you'll no longer be able to collect your ten thousand dollars?" she asked. "I daresay your mysterious benefactor will not look kindly upon your failure to keep his secret."

"I think you're quite right," Lowther said with a shrug. "But he can hardly blame us for your finding us. We could hardly have taken to the streets at a run. Regardless of how much time we had. "

"Besides which," Mary added, "we were beginning to find the whole business rather tedious. I cannot say that twenty thousand pounds for the two of us together wouldn't have been wonderful, but at this point, I'm not even sure that this person would even have given it to us after all. It occurred to me that he might simply be recruiting us to do his bidding in exchange for a prize he never intended to pay."

Con nodded. "I suspect you're correct. A person would need to be very wealthy indeed to pay out twenty thousand pounds, and it hasn't escaped my notice that many of these machinations and schemes seem to be remarkably slipshod. After all, if his intention was to frighten Mrs. Mowbray into thinking her husband was alive again, why wouldn't he or she contact her with the notion directly? As she saw his body after he died, surely she'd have to be incredibly susceptible to seeing and believing in ghosts if she were to be truly frightened at the sight of one. And as the benefactor didn't tell either Mr. Lowther or Mrs. Kendrick not to speak with Mrs. Mowbray in public, then what's to stop her from discussing seeing them in my aunt's back garden when next she sees them in town? Nothing, that's what."

At that they all six nodded. Mrs. Kendrick, her shoulders sagging, gave a yawn that was immediately replicated by the rest of them. "I do apologize, your grace, my lord, my lord, Mrs. Mowbray, but I should like to find my bed now that I am no longer beholden to the nameless benefactor."

Georgina nodded, and stood to see Mrs. Kendrick and Mr. Lowther out. When they reached the front door, they each turned to her and she shook their hands individually. "Thank you for being so frank with us tonight," she said, despite the lingering sense of betrayal she felt about Mary's role in the matter. "I greatly appreciate it."

"I'm sorry to have played you false, Georgina," Mary said. "I hope that you and your friends will be able to find out who it was that was trying to frighten you. I really do."

To her late husband's brother, Georgie nodded. "I know my husband would have enjoyed meeting you," she said. Though she knew well enough that it might not have occurred to him until it was closer to his death. For whatever reason, he'd only appreciated various people and groups when he was closest to losing them.

Malcolm Lowther smiled, and kissed the back of Georgie's hand. "I hope that you'll allow me to approach you as the family we are. I no longer have my parents but I should like very much to get to know my sister-in-law."

Georgie smiled. "I'd like that too. And please, if you recall anything else about this business—even something that doesn't seem important—let one of us know. I think the key to figuring out the motive behind this person's scheme will be somewhere in those letters."

"You don't happen to have kept them, do you?" Con asked from behind Georgie, making her feel as if they were a married couple seeing off their guests after a party.

"We did," Lowther said. "I'll send them round to you tomorrow. That way you'll be able to examine them yourself."

"I so appreciate it," Georgie said.

Bidding them both good night, they returned to the drawing room where Perdita and Archer were seated at opposite ends of the room. Odd, that, Georgie thought.

But before she could comment on it, she heard Con step into the room behind her.

"So, what we know now is that whoever wished to torment you with the image of your husband is even more diabolical than we first imagined. Who sends a brother-in-law to frighten a woman into believing that her dead husband is alive?"

"Someone who enjoys puzzles and tricks of the eye," Archer responded without batting an eyelash. "This person is an opportunist, using the resemblance of Malcolm to Robert as a way of killing two birds with one stone."

Georgie looked from one man to the other, then hurried toward the sideboard on the other side of the room. "I don't know about you all, but I believe the conversation of the past couple of hours calls for something a bit stronger than tea."

Wordlessly she poured out four small glasses of brandy and passed them round.

Thirteen

What the devil was that?" Con demanded after they'd each taken a drink of brandy. "Can they really have been so gullible as to believe that a mysterious benefactor was ready to hand over ten thousand pounds simply for watching over Georgina from afar?"

"It does call into question both Mr. Lowther's and Mrs. Kendrick's level of intellect," Archer agreed, absently stroking the edge of his brandy glass. "Either this mysterious benefactor was just extremely fortunate in his choice of minions, or—"

"Or Mr. Lowther and Mrs. Kendrick made up the tale between themselves," Georgina finished for him. "I must admit to a certain degree of incredulity when it comes to Mrs. Kendrick because of the way she duped me earlier, but what reason could Mr. Lowther have for lying? It's not as if Robert left behind a great fortune that he stands to inherit upon my death. Though there is the matter of the stolen jewels that haven't yet been found."

"It could be the jewels," Perdita said thoughtfully,

"but perhaps he's suffering from some mental malady that draws him to you? Perhaps he is jealous for what his brother had that he didn't. It could be anything."

They were silent for a moment as they each contemplated what such an illness might mean for their investigation. Con had assumed that they were searching for someone with a rational reason for targeting Georgina. Some plan to frighten her with a pretend ghost. If the person they searched for was simply a madman, then anything could happen.

"I don't think it's someone who is unbalanced," Georgina said firmly. "A madman wouldn't think to have others do his haunting for him. It's actually quite ingenious of him to have lured Robert's brother here to lurk in Lady Russell's garden. Of course I would see him and immediately think he was an apparition, since I had no notion of Robert's having a brother. And Mr. Lowther meanwhile thought he was doing something good in looking after me. He simply thought he was following the last wishes of his long-lost brother."

"And the way this seems to have been engineered from behind the scenes," Perdita said, "seems awfully familiar, does it not?"

"How do you mean?" Con asked, curious to see Georgina making a surreptitious shushing gesture at her friend. "What's familiar about it?"

"Nothing," Georgina said swiftly. "Nothing at all." She yawned theatrically. "I vow I am exhausted. Why don't we discuss all this in the morning after a good night's sleep."

But Con caught her wrist in his grip. "I think I'd prefer to hear why this seems so familiar to you and the duchess, if you don't mind. Perhaps you should start talking now."

"Don't tell me what to do," Georgina said, yanking at her imprisoned wrist. "I am at liberty to tell you or not tell you whatever I wish."

Perdita sighed loudly. "You may as well tell him, Georgie," she said. "He'll get it from Archer soon enough."

"I say," Archer protested. "I am not so indiscreet as that!"

"No," Con said pleasantly, "but when I find out what you've been hiding from me, you'll wish you were."

"Oh, stop it," Georgina said, finally managing to free her wrist. Resuming her seat, she stared down at the linen tablecloth, tracing the pattern of its lace overlay with her index finger. Finally, she said, "You were not made privy to Isabella's ordeal several months ago, when she was terrorized by someone very close to her, who was working at the behest of another."

Con listened with mounting anger as she told him about the way Isabella had received threatening notes, packages meant to terrify, and finally was held at gunpoint by someone who had been manipulated into tormenting her.

"While we never learned who it was behind the whole affair," Georgina said when she had finished, "we did suspect that he was not finished with us."

"Why was that?" Con asked silkily, though he had a suspicion.

"Because we both received similar threatening notes soon after Isabella's tormentor was captured," Perdita said firmly, her hand grasping Georgina's.

"Why did you not tell me?" Con demanded, his voice low and angry. "I can hardly be expected to do an adequate job of protecting you if I don't know all the facts, Georgina."

"See here, old man," Archer said affably, "the ladies don't particularly like it when you rip up at them. At least that's what I've heard so—"

"Archer?" Con didn't bother turning to look at his friend; instead his eyes were locked with Georgina's.

"Yes, Con?"

Before he could speak, Georgina said, "Lord Archer, perhaps you would be so kind as to escort the duchess back to her establishment?"

"That's a very good idea," Con said. "I'll see you tomorrow and we'll decide where to go from here."

Perdita took her leave of Georgina, whispering something in her ear before she and Archer saw themselves out.

"What did she tell you?" Con asked, curious in spite of his annoyance.

"She told me that I might try kissing you out of your ill temper," Georgina said without a blush.

Con raised his brows. "She thinks it's like that between us, does she?"

Georgina shrugged. "She's a romantic. Despite what happened with her husband. It never fails to surprise me."

He'd risen to pace before the fireplace, and at her words, he stopped. "Why does it surprise you? Surely resilience is one of the most reliable of human characteristics? We see it all the time in women who marry again despite previous bad marriages. And vice versa."

"You are misreading why most women marry," Georgina said with a sad smile. "It's not for romantic reasons. It's because an unmarried woman of no means with no family to take her in is likely to be destitute. If marriage is one's only respectable means of getting a roof over her head, then a woman will marry."

"As a man," Con said, "I must admit that I've not considered it that way. I think instead of man's reasons for marrying. To secure the succession, to gain property, to form alliances with other noble families. All the reasons I was betrothed to the young dowager."

"Yes, that's because you've never found yourself in the position of needing to rely on someone else for your independence," Georgina said. "You have your independence whether you are married or not. It's different for us. And your list of reasons for marriage is precisely why I have chosen never to marry again."

"Because you do not wish to bring anything to the man you marry?" Con asked, puzzled by her stance. "But surely a husband brings something to the marriage as well. A home, an estate, security. Is that not enough?"

"He brings those things only at his discretion. If he chooses, he might take them away from his wife on a whim. A wife is no more than another possession under English law. It is why so many wives find themselves in marriages like the one I had with Mowbray."

"I don't suppose I'm going to change your mind on this tonight," Con said at last.

"It is unlikely," Georgina agreed. "So, I believe you were preparing to rake me over the coals? Let's get this business over with."

Despite his earlier annoyance, Con found himself wanting to laugh at her attitude toward his proposed scolding.

"Why didn't you tell me?" he asked, once he'd schooled his features into seriousness. "If this is the same person who caused Isabella's ordeal in Yorkshire and London, then why on earth would you neglect to tell me? I cannot fight this bastard with one hand tied behind my back, Georgina."

She refused to look up at him, which Con attributed to a feeling of remorse. Though he was likely misreading that, he told himself.

"I honestly did not think the two phenomena were related," she said finally, looking up at him from where she'd taken a seat at the table. "The letters arrived before you even got to Bath. And the sightings in the garden, and even the dead man in the theater, were so completely different from a letter that I thought they couldn't possibly be connected."

"When did you realize that you were wrong?" Con asked, exasperated but no longer angry. He would save his true anger to place it where it belonged. On the head of the man who had orchestrated this coil.

"Only tonight when I heard Malcolm and Mary tell their tales of their own letter writer. It was too much of a coincidence that there should be two people who used missives as their means of controlling the situation, so I realized he'd orchestrated the entire thing."

"Yet you did not share this with me?"

He watched as she seemed to battle some inner demon for a moment, before finally she got hold of herself and said, "You must understand, my lord, that I have spent a great deal of my life making decisions for my-self. Though my mother and I followed the drum, my father was not often there to make day-to-day decisions for us. He was often involved in military business, leaving us on our own. Then, after I married, it was similar. Though my husband was less understanding about the way that life in the camps worked, even he allowed me a certain degree of autonomy. So, if I did not tell you about what I suspected regarding this person who seems to wish to do me harm, it was not because I do not trust you or because I have some secret wish to see you fail. It is more that I am unaccustomed to having someone else involved in the process of protecting me."

She looked up at him, and Con was struck by just how lovely she was. And just how alone she must have felt when she was making all those decisions for herself. He had little doubt that she was fully capable of making them, but he wondered who she turned to when she wished to simply let someone else take over for a little while. He suspected she had no one to turn to.

"And so, you did not tell me because you had no notion that you should," he said at last. "I do know now, however, and I hope that you will let me work together with you to figure out who it is pulling the strings of Mr. Lowther and Mrs. Kendrick."

"Of course," she said, her eyes large in the candle-light. "Of course I will. I need your help. I would never have been able to lie in wait for Mr. Lowther tonight if I'd been on my own."

Con stepped back over to the table and resumed his

seat there. "I think you underestimate your own bravery," he told her with a crooked smile.

His words seemed to amuse her, and she reached over to grasp his hand. They'd both discarded their gloves ages ago, and when they touched their bare hands together it felt like something that was as inevitable as the tides. "I will try not to shut you out again," she said softly. "Though I cannot make promises."

"Trying is enough for now," Con responded. "Now, tell me more about these anonymous notes you've been receiving."

"Well, there's not much to tell," she said with a shrug. "The first one I received before we'd even captured Isabella's tormentor. And I believe Perdita received one around that time as well."

"May I see them?" Con asked, thinking that there might be something about the paper or the writing or some other clue that could be gleaned from seeing the actual letters. "I promise to give them back, if that makes you hesitate."

Georgina gave a half smile. "I'm not worried about that," she said. "They're in my bedchamber. You may as well come up and I'll give them to you to look over."

Con felt his brows rise at the invitation. But she had already turned to leave the room and head upstairs, so he couldn't examine her expression for clues as to whether she meant what he thought she might mean.

Cursing his inability to tell innocent words from innuendo, he followed her upstairs.

* * *

Georgie was grateful that only she could hear her er-
ratic heartbeat as she led the way toward her tiny bedchamber. The rest of the house was quiet, none of the
other members of the household having returned yet
from the musicale they attended.

She realized that it had been nearly four years since
she'd had a man in her bedchamber. And then it had
been her husband, who had never set her pulses racing
like Con did. There was just something about Domi-
nic, Lord Coniston, that made her want to unwrap his
tidily knotted cravat and muss him up.

When she didn't hear him behind her, she turned
and found that he was there, just very quiet. He must
have had some practice at sneaking about in houses
after dark, she thought wryly. Reaching behind her, she
took his hand in hers and led him the rest of the way
until she reached her door and reclaimed her hand so
that she could open it with one hand and hold the can-
dlestick in the other.

She stepped forward to light the lamp beside her bed
and she heard Con shut the door behind them and wordlessly move over to kneel before the fireplace and light
the fire which had been allowed to die out earlier in the
day. It had grown chillier as the night wore on and
Georgie was grateful for the added warmth.

Not wishing to give up the pretext upon which she'd
invited him in, she stepped over to her small writing
table and opened the drawer where she'd placed the
notes she'd dubbed the "Last Season Letters." They
were there where she'd left them, tied up with a bit of
green ribbon.

She turned and was startled to find Con standing just behind her. "How do you do that?" she demanded, in a low voice. "I should have thought you were a green boy rather than a man grown from how light on your feet you are."

He laughed softly at her words. "I grew up in this house and I know how prone to squeaks the floors are," he said. "I learned to walk on the balls of my feet, though it's rather difficult in boots. I wish I'd worn dancing slippers instead."

She turned around to fully face him, and found herself standing in the circle of his arms. Carefully, as if she were made of spun glass, Con's hands slipped down to hold her waist while he lowered his mouth to hers. It was a kiss of reverence, as if she were as precious to him as a fragile treasure. And Georgie felt her eyes prick with unshed tears. How did he know that what she wished, what she'd always wanted deep down in her innermost soul, was to feel valued like that? All her life she'd been expected to fend for herself, to be the strong one, to bounce back from whatever blow life sent her way. What was it about this man that made him able to see just what she craved on a bone-deep level?

When he pulled back, she looked up at him from beneath her lashes to find him smiling down at her. "You don't know how glad I am that you didn't just slap my face for presuming too much," he said with a crooked smile.

"Why would I do that?" she asked, confused by his words. "You just kissed me beautifully."

"I thought perhaps I'd misinterpreted your reason for inviting me up here," he said with a raised brow. "I didn't, did I?"

Now was her chance to change her mind, she told herself. If she wished to step back from the precipice upon which they were currently poised, she could do it now. But she knew in her gut that she could no more change her mind now than she could unring a bell.

"No," she said softly, "you didn't."

His eyes darkened and he kissed her again. "Excellent," he said against her mouth. This time, she didn't allow him to keep her at arm's length like a precious jewel, but instead kissed him back with every bit as much passion as he kissed her. His lips were soft against hers as he stroked against the seam of her lips with his tongue. She opened her lips to allow him in, and tentatively, then with more assurance, stroked her own tongue against his. She felt his hands move restlessly over her waist, and up her back, pulling her closer against him, so that her breasts pressed against his hard chest. Her own hands clasped him to her, opening and closing against his strong back, stroking up to feel the softness of the hair at the nape of his neck.

"God, Georgina," he whispered against her chin, as he kissed a path down over her neck toward her collarbone where he licked into the hollow there. As his fingers slipped into the bodice of her gown, she pressed her breasts forward, wanting, needing to feel his hands touch them. He managed to slip her left sleeve down over her shoulder, freeing her left breast to the chill air. She gasped at the sensation and gasped again when his mouth closed over her nipple and suckled.

Con laughed softly against her chest at the sounds she made. "Shh. Sweetheart, you'll wake the house."

His warning brought her up short. "Oh," she whispered. "I'm sorry. I didn't mean to—"

But he kissed her and soothed her and was soon offering the same kind of salute to her right breast, and Georgie, more mindful of herself, bit her lip rather than cry out at the delicious sensation of his mouth on her. "Come over to the bed," Con said. "I want to undress you properly."

Her body awake in a way it hadn't ever been before, Georgie allowed him to pull her over to the iron bedstead, where he pulled the coverlet and sheets down to the end of the bed. Sitting on the edge of the bed, he turned her back to face him and began to unbutton her gown.

"I like this," he remarked, kissing her bare back. "Not a lot of infernal buttons to wrestle with."

"It's because I don't have a maid," she remarked dryly. "I can hardly have a gown I can't remove on my own, can I?"

"That's my Georgina," he said with a laugh. "Ever practical."

He allowed her to step out of the gown and remove her shoes, at which point, he switched places with her and she sat on the edge of the bed while he knelt before her. His eyes were dark again with passion. "You are the most beautiful thing I've ever seen," he said, sliding his hands down over her bare shoulders, over her brief corset and the shift beneath.

"Am I?" she asked, feeling almost shy. "I vow I cannot see it myself, but you do make me feel beautiful."

"You will simply have to acquit me of knowing more in these matters than you do. I am a connoisseur, you must agree."

"You're a Con-i-something." She winked, unable to resist the pun.

"Cheeky wench!" he said, biting her lightly on the knee. His mouth there gave her a tightness in her belly, and it increased as his hands stroked up over the outside of her thighs and beneath her shift.

"This will have to go, I think," he said almost to himself, as he untied the bow at the top of her corset and thread by thread unlaced it. She let out a sigh of relief as he removed it and couldn't help but rub the underside of her breasts where they'd been pushed up all day by the whalebone. "Poor darling," he said, replacing her hands with his, massaging her where it had pinched most, then stroked his thumbs over her nipples. "All this discomfort simply so that you will offer up your bosoms to us lascivious males on a silver platter."

Before she could respond, however, he leaned up to kiss her mouth, then went back to his knees before her. "Naughty Georgina," he chided. "Your attempt to distract me from my ultimate goal was bold, but ultimately futile."

She watched as he slid his hands over the outside of her thighs and shook her head. "Since I have no idea what your goal is, then I can hardly be guilty of deliberate distraction, can I?"

"No idea at all?" he asked playfully, as he slid his hands over the tops of her thighs and worked at the garters that were holding up her stockings. One by one he unfastened them, and rolled down first the right stocking, kissing his way down over each bit of skin he exposed. Then he moved to the other side, sending Georgie's pulse rate up, up, up as he kissed his way down. When both legs were bare, he kissed first her right knee then her left, and sliding his large hands over her thighs, he pulled them apart and kissed the very center of her.

It sent an instantaneous jolt of intense pleasure through her. So much so that Georgie had to cover her mouth with her hand to keep from crying out. As Con's tongue and fingers and mouth worked against her sensitive skin, Georgie felt wave after wave of passion surge through her, and unable to remain passive beneath his ministrations, she lifted her hips again and again, following him every time he pulled away. Until, that is, he placed one forearm across her hips and kept her from moving, which somehow made the sensations of his mouth on her sex even more intense.

He stroked his tongue over the most sensitive bundle of nerves and at the same time thrust first one finger, then another inside her, the tandem motion of his tongue and thrusting fingers nearly driving her to madness. When he replaced his fingers with his tongue, Georgie thought she would explode, and despite his strong arm across her belly, she tried desperately to move against his maddening mouth.

Finally, it was too much for her to endure and Georgie felt herself splinter into a million pieces and float up outside of herself into nothingness.

When she came back to herself, it was to find Con trying to remove his boots beside her, and cursing beneath his breath. "Damn boots, why didn't I take the bloody things off before I got started? Foolish, Coniston. Damn foolish."

Drowsy with passion's aftermath, Georgie giggled at his annoyance. She reached out to touch him on the back and was surprised at how tense his muscles were. "I wouldn't do that if I were you, Georgina," he said, finally getting his second boot off, and standing beside the bed to remove his coat and waistcoat and to pull his shirt off over his head. "I am likely to explode," he said through clenched teeth as he indicated the bulge in his breeches. "I want to be gentle, but I'm damned if I know how I'll manage it."

She giggled again, which only earned her a scowl. She scrambled back onto the bed and gave him some room to climb up onto the bed. "You think this is funny, do you?" he asked once he'd removed his breeches. Stretching out beside her, he took her in like a lion surveying his prey.

"This is as serious as serious can be," he said, though even as the words left his mouth he grinned. "I'm clearly not serious enough to maintain the degree of gravitas necessary for a true ravishment."

Georgie kissed him and worked between them to touch his erection. "No ravishment here," she said against his mouth as she stroked his bare flesh between them. "The lady is more than willing."

She felt him gasp at the touch of her hand and was pleasantly surprised to feel his arms harden around her as he flipped her onto her back, then grabbed her shift and proceeded to split it from neck to hem. "Well," she whispered, "that's one way to remove a shift."

"It is indeed," he said against her neck as he brought her left leg over his right hip and stroked against her.

Con looked up then, and his gaze met hers. Georgie felt the intensity of their connection right down to her toes. And she knew that whatever it was between them, it was far more dangerous than anything she'd shared with Robert. To her surprise she felt tears well. Before she could hide them, Con leaned forward and kissed her, the motion bringing their bodies together, and with one sure thrust, they were joined.

There were no more words then, only the desperate feel of skin against skin, and the build of sweet passion as they each worked toward crisis. Georgie had never been as overwhelmed by sheer need as she was now, with Con's strong body against her, in her. It was impossible to remember where she left off and he began. And with each beat of her heart she felt the threads of their souls knitting together in a fabric no amount of strife could unravel.

Never had she thought to once again make herself vulnerable to a man. The very idea had been impossible to contemplate a week ago, but she felt as if she knew more about Con, about his innate sense of decency, his goodness, than she'd ever gleaned from her husband's character. She was not a woman who took pleasure lightly. There had been more than one opportunity for her to take lovers. A certain type of gentleman gravitated to widows in their search for bed partners. And though she'd been tempted, she'd never allowed herself to succumb. Until now. And that said more about Con's character than anything. She was not a woman who trusted easily, but she knew in her gut that whatever his faults, Con would never deliberately set out to harm her. It wasn't in his nature.

All of this and more flashed through Georgie's mind, until she found further thought impossible and the passion Con stoked in her overtook conscious thought. And when she felt her body climbing toward that place where they'd dissolve together, she held on to him for dear life. As spasm after spasm rocked through her and she clenched around him, she felt him go over the edge too, following her into bliss, as he thrust one last time into her and she was lost.

Fourteen

They made love again before Con regretfully left the cozy warmth of Georgina's bed to return to his own bedchamber. He did not wish his aunt to be disturbed by tales of bed-hopping, and aside from that, he wanted the fact of whatever was between himself and Georgina to remain their own secret for now.

If he were to act purely based on his own wishes, he'd be riding hell for leather to Coniston Grange to retrieve his mother's wedding ring, with a brief detour to the Archbishop of Canterbury for a special license. But a good hunter knows not to rush his fences. And for all that Georgina had been willing to share her body with him, he sensed even now a reluctance to make things more permanent between them.

Oh, she was quite willing to be with him, and perhaps even to give him her heart, but he wasn't sure she was yet ready for marriage to any man, let alone himself. But he remembered what she'd said last night when they were talking of marriage and a woman's reasons for marrying. Perhaps he was being overly cautious, but he would rather err on the side of caution than risk alienating her forever. That did not mean that he would not let her know that he wanted to marry her, however. Just that he would wait to ask her.

Some hours later, he found her alone in the breakfast chamber and had the devil of a time walking past without touching her. He managed it, however, and he even greeted her without sounding like a lovesick swain before loading a plate for himself from the sideboard and taking the chair opposite hers.

"I trust you are well," he said, imbuing the words with far more meaning than they connoted on their own. "You are looking quite well this morning. I daresay it was all that sleep you got last night."

To his amusement her cheeks colored prettily. "Indeed, my lord," she said calmly despite her blush. "I tried a new sleeping aid. It seems to have worked rather well. Though it had to be repeated in the night. One does wish to ensure such methods are thoroughly tried before abandoning them."

Con nearly choked on his toast. "I should hate to think of your abandoning such an effective method. Perhaps you should give it a while to ensure that it takes."

"Oh, I shall continue the treatment so long as I am able," she said with a cheeky smile. "It depends of course on the availability of the . . . ah . . . proper tool, so to speak."

He did choke then, which turned into a coughing then laughing fit. "I had no idea you were so skilled at the art of innuendo, Mrs. Mowbray," he said as he wiped his streaming eyes. Grateful for the solitude of the breakfast parlor, he looked at her seriously now. "I do hope you are truly well and not suffering any after-effects of, um, you know . . ." He waved his hand in the air.

Now it was Georgina's turn to laugh. In a low voice she said, "I am quite well, my lord. Indeed, I am feeling quite invigorated and ready to embark upon the search for the person or persons responsible for threatening me. If you will recall, we got a bit distracted from our purpose last evening when I was supposed to show you the letters."

Con was slightly disappointed at the change of subject, but supposed that they could hardly go on exchanging lascivious puns in Aunt Russell's breakfast parlor all morning. Aloud he said, "You are correct. Perhaps we can see if the young dowager and Lord Archer would care to join us in a picnic on the grounds of the ruins?"

"An excellent notion," she said with a smile. "I'll go have a word with cook. Perhaps you can send a note along to the dowager and to Lord Archer?"

The matter settled, they went about their proposed tasks, and it was nearly two hours later that they found themselves in Lady Russell's open carriage. The weather was, for Bath, quite good, and though there was a bit of autumn chill in the air, the sun coupled with warm shawls for the ladies prevented them from becoming too cold.

"Georgie," Perdita said in a low voice as the gentlemen discussed a prizefight that was scheduled to take place later in the week. "What's amiss between you and Lord Coniston? I don't believe you've spoken two words to one another since we entered the carriage."

Fighting the urge to tell her friend everything that had happened between herself and Lord Coniston the night before, Georgie swallowed before she pulled her shawl tighter around her shoulders. "I'm sure I don't know what you mean. We are as we ever have been. I daresay he didn't sleep very well last night and is in a bit of a mood. Nothing to concern yourself over."

Perdita's eyes narrowed as she contemplated her friend. "Why do I get the feeling you're fobbing me off?" she asked with a suspicious look between Georgie and Con. "Either the two of you have been fighting about something—probably your refusal to tell him about the letters last season—or, if I didn't know you would never do so without informing me first, I would almost suspect that the two of you were engaging in some sort of clandestine affair."

Georgie felt her jaw drop, and was about to confess all when Perdita began to laugh. "What a nonsensical idea," she said, shaking her head at her own foolishness. "I know I suggested you kiss him last night, but I was only teasing. I know better than to suspect such a thing of happening. You're friendly enough with one another, but he could hardly take up with his aunt's companion. What a scandal that would be."

Feeling a gnawing pain in her belly, Georgie made herself join in her friend's laughter. Perdita's assessment of just how society would view any sort of connection between herself and Con was likely accurate. It had not occurred to her in the haze of last night's bliss, but now in the light of day, she saw their pairing as others would see it and fought the desire to howl with frustration. Not that she had intended to make the arrangement permanent, of course. That would be up to Con, at any rate, and since he hadn't come to her in a fit of conscience this morning and offered marriage, she knew that he would never do so. If he truly considered her virtue besmirched by their carnal knowledge of one another, then he would have done something about it.

Forcing herself to grin at Perdita, she told her just how silly her idea had been. "It's almost as hilarious as the notion of some kind of match between you and Lord Archer," she said with a giggle. "Can you possibly imagine?"

To her surprise, for the briefest of moments, rather than joining in the laughter, Perdita looked as if she were in genuine pain. Then, almost as if Georgie had imagined it, she was her old self again and giggling. "Yes, it's quite the joke, isn't it? After all, Lord Archer was my husband's private secretary. What would people say? Why, they'd probably conjecture that I killed Ormond so that I could finally be with my lover Lord Archer."

"People are imbeciles," Georgie said, suddenly feeling sorry for both of them and their hypothetical scandals. "They should mind their own business."

"It's the way of the world, my dear," Perdita said with a sad smile. Georgie knew in that instant that the idea of a romance between her friend and Lord Archer wasn't as far-fetched as Perdita made out. At least on Perdita's side of things.

"You aren't . . ." Georgie gestured in the air with her hand. "You know . . ."

Perdita shook her head. "No. We are just good friends. Indeed, I don't know what I'd do without Archer. Why ruin such a good friendship with something as treacherous as romance?" But her words and her expression were saying two different things and Georgie felt a pang of sadness for her friends. Not only was Perdita denying the possibility that she might share something more than friendship with Lord Archer, he was being denied the chance at such a match as well. At the direction of her thoughts, she shook her head in exasperation. Clearly last night with Con had instilled in her the desire to make matches where none had previously existed.

Schooling her features to amusement, she said, "Listen to us. The gentlemen are going to begin teasing us for being silly romantics any moment."

"Did someone say 'silly romantics'?" Con said from across the carriage. "You know I cannot bear to hear Mr. Wordsworth's reputation besmirched, my dear."

"Bah," Archer said with a shudder. "Do not tell me you find him superior to Coleridge. Now there's a poet with imagination. Give me Xanadu and 'Kubla Khan' before yet another poem of the beauties of nature any day."

And thus they were launched into a discussion of poetry until they reached the landscape surrounding Farley Castle. Clearly they were not the only people in Bath to have the idea for a picnic that afternoon, and to avoid the other visitors, they followed the path leading to a stream marking the boundary of Farley estate.

"Here's a likely spot," Con called from where he'd walked on ahead, carrying the picnic basket with him. The others agreed and within minutes they were all seated on the blanket Archer had carried from the carriage, their luncheon feast spread out before them. Fruit, bread, cheese, baked chicken, and raspberry tarts were eaten with relish along with wine from a small decanter. When they had all eaten their fill, amid pleasant chatter, Georgie packed the remains of the meal back into the basket and set it aside.

"I cannot fault Lady Russell's cook," Archer said, stretching his arms over his head. "But I must admit that what I long for more than anything is a nap."

"Here," Con said, tossing him a shiny red apple. "This will help keep you alert while we discuss things." He himself moved to sit with his back against the large elm tree they'd chosen for its shade. "Now, ladies, I believe you have something to tell me about some letters?"

Holding her hat against the wind that was trying to send it flying away, Georgie exchanged a look with Perdita, who gestured for Georgie to begin. "We have already spoken of what happened to Lady Isabella, or rather the Duchess of Ormond, last year. Well, what we did not tell you, Con—for Lord Archer knows by dint of his presence in the Ormond household when it began—is that both Perdita and I received letters shortly after Isabella's tormentor was captured. And when Isabella was being taunted, she also received letters that we later discerned had not come from the person who was conducting the campaign against her in person, as it were."

"So," Con said thoughtfully, "it was similar to what happened with Lowther and Mrs. Kendrick, in that someone else was directing their movements?"

"Yes," Georgie said firmly. "It was as if whoever was controlling the business couldn't help but add his own threats into the mix. Which to my mind is rather foolish, because if he stayed out of things, no one would know about his involvement at all. And the people he had performing his dirty work would have been blamed for it."

"It is curious," Archer said, biting into his apple. "It's almost as if the fellow cannot stand being left out. Reminds me of a land steward my father used to employ. The man couldn't delegate to save his life. He'd send one of the gardeners off to trim some hedges and before you knew it Hixton was out there trimming them himself because he couldn't trust them to get the thing done right."

"It's a thought," Con agreed, drawing one knee up before him. "May I see the letters?"

Georgie and Perdita nodded. Georgie removed the reticule from her wrist and loosened the drawstring to remove the bundle of letters. "These are mine."

"And these," Perdita said, removing her own bundle of letters from her reticule, "are mine."

"So you've received two more than the duchess at this point," Con said, comparing Georgie's large stack to Perdita's smaller one. "Is that because you're in the midst of the campaign of terror, so to speak? Whereas the duchess's has yet to begin?"

"When you put it like that it sounds so . . ." Perdita paused, looking a little pale. "Inevitable."

"I'd like to catch the damned coward," Archer said vehemently. "I despise waiting around for him to make his next move."

"I should like to think we might be able to stop things before they go any further," Con said with a frown.

Carefully, he untied the ribbon holding Georgie's letters together and opened the first one, reading it and then moving on to the next, the next, and the next.

"So the intention of these letters is to hammer home the idea that whatever you three did to cause the death of the late duke has not been forgotten."

"In a nutshell," Perdita said with a slight frown. "Though anyone who was there that night would know how preposterous it is to assume he was a helpless victim."

"Can you tell me what happened?" Con asked carefully. "It might help me understand the vehemence with which this person regards your guilt—whether it's justified or not."

Abruptly, Perdita rose from the blanket and retrieved her hat, tying it below her chin. "I beg your pardon, my lord," she said. "But I simply cannot hear the tale recounted again. Perhaps you can tell him about it, Georgie?" And with that she strode away and down toward where the stream cut through the countryside.

Archer rose and without a backward glance stalked off after her.

Con turned to Georgie with a raised brow. "I take it that the three of you were responsible for his death? Perhaps while he was in the midst of harming the duchess?"

Georgie sighed and stared down at her hands. "It's rather more complicated than that." And bit by bit, she told him how she and Isabella had found Perdita being brutalized by her husband that night and how he'd ultimately threatened to kill her outright for her disobedience. And how they were all of them, and none of them, responsible for the way his life had ended.

"Do you carry this pistol with you at all times?" Con asked, his brows knitted. "In your reticule, I mean?"

At Georgie's nod, he stared at her in amazement, and then began to laugh.

"What's so amusing about it?" she demanded. "I am just as capable a shot as any gentleman."

"It's not that, my dear," he said with wonder. "It's that I imagined myself to be some sort of Lochinvar riding to your rescue. Only to discover now that it's likely you'll be the one rescuing me should things come to a head."

Before she could stop him, he leaned forward and kissed her quite thoroughly. Then regretfully, he pulled back. "I apologize for the public display, but there was no one about. And I find the idea of being rescued quite the novelty."

"You're a very bad man," she said, though she could not help the grin she feared would tell the story of what was between them more thoroughly than a letter in the tabloids. "I will of course rescue you should the need arise, however."

"Thank heavens," he said with mock relief. Then, sobering he reached out and took her hand in his. "I tease now," he said, "but do not think for one moment that I don't regret the fact that you have felt the need to protect yourself and your friends with that pistol. In fact, it makes me quite viciously angry."

Georgie squeezed his fingers, her heart full of emotion, as she found herself unable to speak. It was a measure of how much she trusted him that she had even told him of the pistol's existence. Part of its power was in the element of surprise after all.

"I will do my best, Georgina," he said quietly, "to make sure you never have need to use that pistol again."

Before she could respond, she heard Perdita calling from where she and Archer were climbing back up from the stream toward them.

"You'll never guess, Georgie," she called. "I bested Lord Archer at skipping stones. Can you imagine? I quite think his masculine pride has been shattered forever."

At which point Archer began to argue that skipping stones properly was not even possible in a stream, which moves too swiftly for the stones to get a proper skip going.

And the moment between Georgie and Con was lost.

When Georgie and Con returned to Lady Russell's house, it was to find things at sixes and sevens.

In the drawing room, where Clara sat trying to calm Lady Russell, Con was surprised to see that his aunt's jewelry chest was sitting open on the table beside her chair.

"I know I saw them a few days ago," Lady Russell said, shaking her head tearfully. "The evening I gave Georgina the sapphires."

Spotting her companion at Con's side, the old woman reached out to her. "Georgie, dear," she said, when Georgina had reached her side. "You recall seeing my diamond and ruby cuff bracelet the other evening, don't you? I showed it to you and said that it was a piece that wasn't part of the Russell jewelry and so I'd kept it. You remember, don't you, my dear?"

Con could see from the stricken look on Georgina's face that she didn't remember the bracelet, and her words only confirmed it. "I am so sorry, my lady," she said with a shake of her head. "I don't remember seeing it that evening. But you must remember that you showed me so many pieces that night. I'm afraid I had difficulty keeping them all straight."

The disappointment in his aunt's face made Con ache for her. His aunt had always prided herself on her sharpness of mind, and if she was unable to recall where she'd put a piece of jewelry then it did not bode well for her state of mind.

"Could you perhaps have put it somewhere other than your jewelry chest, Aunt?" he asked, allowing Clara to rise and pour his aunt a cup of tea from the tray, before taking her place beside her. "I must admit that I let my valet deal with all my sticks and fobs and whatnot. It's far too much for me to keep straight."

"No," Lady Russell insisted, her eyes red from tears. "I have always ensured that I kept my things in the chest. My mama was adamant that a lady needed to keep track of her own jewels because one could never be too sure that the servants were honest. Of course, I don't suspect anyone in my house of dishonesty. I trust my maid and all the rest implicitly. But if the cuff cannot be found, I fear I will have no choice but to have their rooms searched."

"Lady Russell," Georgina said to her employer, "why don't I go up to your sitting room and search there. It's where you showed me the jewels that evening and perhaps the cuff fell between some cushions or someplace like that."

The gratitude in his aunt's face made Con vow to thank Georgina for her patience later. His aunt had a tendency to hysteria from time to time, and Georgina clearly knew how best to handle her in moods like this.

When Georgina was gone, Clara came forward and sat by Lady Russell. "I dispatched Lydia to speak to the housekeeper about conducting a discreet search of the servants' rooms. I know you dislike doing so, Aunt," Clara said with a sad smile, "but I'm afraid that sometimes one must take matters like this in hand before they get out of control. The sooner we know that none of them is responsible, the sooner we can figure out where it actually is."

"Oh, Clara," Lady Russell cried in distress, "I do wish you had spoken to me first. I cannot think that any of my people would do such a thing. After all, they've been here this whole long while without taking anything. It's simply foolish to imagine such a thing tempting them at this point."

"You don't know, Aunt," Con said, trying to reassure her, but preparing her for the possibility that someone she trusted had betrayed her. "Perhaps someone has been forced to pay a debt or developed a gambling habit or some such. It's not so impossible to imagine someone who indeed holds you in some affection feeling as if there is no other way."

"But I hope they know that they can come to me if they have problems such as that," Lady Russell said sadly. "I thought we were on friendly terms."

Georgina returned just then and Con felt his hope erode when he saw her expression. "I'm afraid I didn't find it, my lady," she said. "I even looked in your bedchamber and your dressing room and it was in neither of those places. I found only a bit of crimson ribbon and a bunch of dried flowers which appear to have come off a hat. I am sorry."

"Do not worry over it, my dear," Lady Russell said, gripping Georgina's hand. "I thank you for looking. I do hate the idea that someone took it, but at this point I fear there must be little alternative."

A fracas outside the drawing room door, which concluded with a sharp gasp, drew their attention to the doorway, where the housekeeper, her face reflecting her chagrin, stepped forward and stopped before Lady Russell.

"We've located your bracelet, my lady," she said carefully, her eyes straying to no one else in the room. "I'm afraid we found it in the room of one of the servants."

Lady Russell covered her mouth with her hand. "Oh, dear," she said with some degree of upset, "I was so hoping it wouldn't be one of them."

"It's all right, Lady Russell," Georgina said, placing a steadying hand on the old woman's shoulder. "We'll see to it that the bracelet is returned to you and whoever took it is dismissed."

"Who was it?" Lady Russell asked, looking as if she were awaiting a death sentence. "Go ahead and tell me, Mrs. Marks, for I don't know if I can bear the suspense."

Something about the stillness of the housekeeper's countenance gave Con a bad feeling. And it was with a sense of inevitability that he saw her turn to Georgina. "Begging your pardon, my lady," the woman said, her words directed to her employer but her eyes on the companion, "we found the cuff in Mrs. Mowbray's bedchamber."

Fifteen

Georgie had been surprised at certain times in her life, but nothing had ever prepared her for the shock she felt as she heard the housekeeper accuse her of stealing Lady Russell's diamond and ruby cuff.

Not only had she not stolen it, but she'd been so focused on soothing her employer's eviscerated nerves that it had literally never occurred to her that the bracelet might be found in her bedchamber. She was just as shocked as the others in the room. With the possible exception of Mrs. Marks, who had never been Georgie's greatest advocate.

"It's impossible," Georgie said before she could contemplate the wisdom of speaking at all. "I don't even recall the bracelet's existence, so why on earth would I steal it?"

"Perhaps friendship with duchesses and earls and the like has given you ideas above your station, if you don't mind my saying so," the housekeeper said with pursed lips.

Before Georgie could object, Con snapped, "That's enough, Marks. That will be all for now."

With an insolent curtsy, the housekeeper stalked out of the room, leaving the rest of the occupants in stunned silence.

Finally, Lady Russell regained her powers of speech. "Why would you take it from me, Georgina?" she said, shaking her head. "I treated you like the daughter I never had. Indeed, I loaned you a necklace worth three times as much as that cuff. Why would you betray me like that?"

"But I didn't, Lady Russell," Georgie said, cut to the quick that even for a moment Lady Russell would believe such a thing of her. "I swear to you I had no notion the cuff even existed before today. And I certainly have no need of the funds. If I wished it—and I did not, mind you—I could have sold the sapphires instead of returning them to you. It makes no sense."

She looked to Clara who, to her astonishment, would not meet her eye. "It's difficult to deny the evidence, Georgina," Con's cousin said sadly. "I had thought that you were far too fond of my aunt to ever do something like this, but who's to say what lengths people will be driven to when they are in need of funds. I daresay your husband's death left you with a great deal of debt. It's not an altogether uncommon tale."

Georgie tried not to look at Con because if he condemned her as well, she'd be unable to contain the tears gathering behind her eyes. But she couldn't help herself, and when she saw the set of his jaw she nearly cried out, the pain was so intense. Swallowing and forcing herself to remain calm, she looked at her hands rather than at any of the others. "I'll remove myself from the house at once. I'll send for my things later. My lady," she said to Lady Russell, who was weeping openly now. "I thank you for all the kindnesses you have shown me and I hope that should you choose to press charges you will give me the benefit of warning."

Holding her head high, she left the room, and still wearing the hat and shawl she'd worn on the picnic that morning, she walked out onto Henrietta Street and headed for Laura Place and Perdita's town house.

"What the hell is going on here?" Con demanded of Clara after Lady Russell had been put to bed with a ti-sane for her head. "You know as well as I do that Georgina didn't have anything to do with the disappearance of that bauble. Aside from the fact that she has no need of funds, there's the fact that she would bite off her right hand rather than betray Aunt Russell's trust like that."

"I vow, I'm as shocked as you are, Coniston," Clara said with a weary sigh. "But we cannot refute the truth of the matter. The bracelet was found in Mrs. Mow-bray's bedchamber. What further proof do you need?"

Pacing before the fireplace, Con ran through a mental list of the household's occupants, searching for one of them who disliked Georgina so much that they would cast suspicion on her like this. But no one immediately came to mind.

"Whose idea was it for Aunt to look through her jewelry chest today?" he asked. There was something rotten about this entire business. "She has never been particularly interested in her jewels," he said thought-fully. "Unless she's looking for something to wear on a particular occasion, I've never known her to be the sort to inventory them once a week."

"If you must know it was me," Lydia said from the doorway. "I wished to know if she had something for me to wear to the assembly rooms tomorrow evening," she said. "But that's not to say I intended for her to find your paramour had stolen her bracelet, Con," she said with all the arrogance of a girl just about to make her come-out. "I am entitled to ask my aunt if I might borrow her jewels, you know. It was simply bad luck that your Mrs. Mowbray was found to have sticky fingers."

"You haven't been a great fan of Mrs. Mowbray from the first, have you, Lydia?" Con asked, his eyes narrowing as he considered whether she'd disliked Georgina so much that she'd frame her for theft. "Did you perhaps slip the cuff into Mrs. Mowbray's bedchamber while we were out at luncheon?"

"Don't be ridiculous," his cousin said with a roll of her eyes. "I might not be the woman's greatest champion but I wouldn't do something that would upset Aunt like that. It's hardly likely to make her more willing to lend out her bits of jewelry, is it?"

He had to admit she had a point, though Con was still annoyed at the cavalier manner in which both his cousins referred to Mrs. Mowbray. As if she weren't worthy of their respect as any other lady would be.

"Then who is responsible for the bracelet's presence in Mrs. Mowbray's bedchamber?" he demanded, frustration making him clench his fists. Because if neither his cousins nor any of Lady Russell's other servants

were responsible for the planting of the jeweled bracelet in Georgina's room, then that meant the person who
blamed her for her role in Ormond's death had found
some way to infiltrate his aunt's household.

He turned to go after Georgina, but stopped in the
doorway of the drawing room. "I want both of you to
know that I will tolerate no more loose talk about Mrs.
Mowbray. And that goes for you and the servants in
this house. Aunt, I cannot control."

"Why on earth are you so concerned about her, Con?"
Clara asked. "I vow I'd come to like her during our stay
here, but she's hardly the sort you normally gravitate
toward."

"Don't you see, Mama?" Lydia said in a bored voice.
"He's smitten with the little companion. If it weren't so
revoltingly vulgar I'd say it was sweet."

"Con?" Clara raised her brow at her cousin. "Is she
right?"

"As a matter of fact," he said tersely, "she is. If she'll
have me, I'm going to marry her. But if either of you so
much as breathes a word of it to her or anyone else, I'll
see to it that neither of you receives anything from the
estates ever again."

"You can't do that!" Lydia hissed. "Can he do that,
Mama?"

"He's the earl, dearest," Clara said, watching the door
long after Con had left them. "He can do whatever he
wants."

Sixteen

"And then I left," Georgie said, her hands wrapped round the cup of tea Perdita had pressed into them after one look at her stricken face.

She'd spent the majority of her walk from Henrietta Street to Laura Place going over the events in Lady Russell's house in her mind and still she could not account for the way Lady Russell had turned against her. Georgie had been accused of being many things over the course of her life. But never had she ever imagined being accused of theft. Not only was it something she'd never considered—with the exception of a bit of marzipan from a cake when she was five—but she'd never really wanted something so badly she'd be willing to steal it. Material things simply weren't that important to her unless there was some sort of sentimental value to them. One look at her wardrobe would confirm that, she thought mirthlessly.

Now, however, her puzzlement had turned to a kind of sorrow for the loss of Lady Russell's good opinion. Georgie had begun to think of her as a friend rather than just an employer. And now that friendship had been shattered by someone wishing to cause her harm. Even if she were able to prove to Lady Russell that she'd not stolen the bracelet, they would never return to the easy footing upon which they'd existed for the past several months.

"I do wish we could find out who is trying to discredit us once and for all," Perdita said with a fierceness that startled Georgie. Her friend had always been loyal, but there was an underlying layer of intensity in her voice now.

"Is there something you're not telling me, your grace?" she asked, trying to discern from Perdita's face if there was anything other than simple concern there. "You've been awfully . . . fierce of late."

Perdita stared into her teacup before replying. "I am simply weary of this business. And I cannot help but feel responsible for all of it. If it hadn't been for me, neither you nor Isabella would have been there that night. Neither of you would have attracted the attention of this malevolent creature. It almost makes me wish I'd let Gervase have his way with me and left the two of you alone instead of asking for your help." She set her cup and saucer on the table and rose to poke at the fire, her back ramrod straight as she knelt before the fireplace.

"Dearest Perdita, look at me," Georgie said, putting her own cup down and going to her friend. She knelt beside her and slipped an arm around her. "You have nothing to be sorry for. You did nothing wrong. It was Gervase's crime. Not yours. And I know that Isabella would agree with me when I say that I would do the same thing again if I were given the chance to relive that night. You were in very real danger. Gervase held a knife to your throat and intended to kill you. I have little doubt of that. And if that had happened do you really think Isabella and I would have been better off? That we might have happily gone on without you in our lives? For I can tell you that I, for one, would not have preferred that outcome one bit."

All the while Georgie spoke she felt her friend shaking as silent sobs shook her slim body. It was a skill they'd all three—she, Perdita, and Isabella—perfected. Sometimes because they didn't wish their violent husbands to have the satisfaction of seeing that their blows had hit their marks. Sometimes because they didn't wish anyone else to know their shame.

When Perdita had calmed, the two women rose and ensconced themselves on the facing settees and Georgie poured them both more tea.

"I was supposed to be comforting you," Perdita said with a rueful smile. "Not the other way round."

"There is no 'supposed to be,'" Georgie said firmly. "We are both the victims of this ridiculous person. Whoever he might be."

"Or she," Perdita said with a raised brow. "I shouldn't be surprised for a moment if he turned out to be a she."

Georgie's temples began to throb. "I so wish that made me feel better. Instead it's just widened the pool of possible suspects."

"Sorry," Perdita said with a slight shrug. "I simply didn't wish you to let your guard down with ladies."

A cough from the doorway made them both turn to see the butler. "Lord Coniston and Lord Archer are here and wish to know if you are receiving visitors, your grace."

Perdita told him to send them in, and Con strode in followed by Archer. Both men looked grim.

"I've arranged for your things to be brought here by two of my aunt's footmen," Con said without preamble as he took a seat beside Georgina. "I cannot recall when I've been more angry at my family."

"I don't wish for you to quarrel with them on my behalf, Con," Georgie said, turning to take his hand. "This is the fault of whoever bears a grudge against me for Gervase's death. It has nothing to do with your aunt, and if I were in her position I'm not sure I'd have made a different decision about the matter. How she handles this will have an effect on her authority with her other servants. And if she proved too lenient with me, they might see it as an invitation to relax their own standards."

"But you aren't a servant," Con protested. "Not in the same way that they are. You are not of the nobility perhaps but you are from solid gentry stock and as such you are above them in station no matter that you were employed as my aunt's companion. And aside from all that, there is the fact that you didn't steal the bracelet. I know that as well as anyone since it wasn't in your bedchamber last night when I—"

He stopped, realizing perhaps that he'd just revealed that he'd visited an unmarried lady's bedchamber in front of two witnesses.

"Oh, don't mind us," Archer said from where he was lounging on the settee beside Perdita. He made a show of leaning forward to pick up the teapot. "More tea, Duchess?"

Her eyes bright with interest, Perdita offered her cup to Archer. "Though you do know it's highly irregular for a gentleman to serve tea, do you not, Lord Archer?"

"Somehow I think that's not the thing that's the most irregular in this room at the moment," Archer said, putting the teapot back down. He stretched an arm out along the back of the sofa and waved his hand at Con and Georgie. "Do continue," he said with an innocent smile. "I am finding this conversation quite fascinating."

"If you wish to retain possession of your liver, Lord Archer," Con growled, "you'll forget you just heard that."

"Oh, pooh," Perdita said with a dismissive wave. "As if we'd gossip about the two of you outside of this room. I'm simply pleased that my own suspicions turned out to be correct." She turned to the man beside her. "Lord Archer, you owe me a guinea."

Georgina gaped. "You wagered on whether the two of us might . . ."

"Fall in love?" Perdita asked sweetly. "Of course we did. There's little else to do for amusement in Bath. Especially given the fact that we expect to be ambushed in some way or another by the person making your life so difficult these days."

At the mention of the trouble hanging over her head, Georgie sobered. "Yes. Always back to that. I don't even see how we can think of anything else at this point.

I cannot possibly continue on as a lady's companion with a theft accusation hanging over my head."

"If it comes to that," Perdita said with a frown, "I will write you a letter of recommendation. But I shouldn't think you would wish to find another position considering . . ." She looked pointedly at Con and then Georgie.

Georgie felt her heart rise up into her throat as she squirmed under her friend's gaze. There had been no talk between herself and Con last night about any sort of permanent arrangement between them. Indeed, she'd gone into it without expectations. She'd already been married once before and it had been a disaster. She wasn't sure she wished to marry ever again. Even someone as decent as Con.

"Nothing has changed in my circumstances," she said finally. Which was the truth. She didn't allow herself to look at Con lest he decided to take offense. "If I am to keep a roof over my head, I'll need to find another position."

"Now wait just a minute," Con said, turning to Georgie. "Just because I didn't say anything last night . . ."

"We'll discuss it later," Georgie assured him. "Please, my lord. Later."

Though he looked as if he wanted to argue, Con nodded. "All right."

"Now," Perdita said, breaking into the awkward silence that had fallen. "Why don't I show you to your bedchamber, Georgina? And you can perhaps have a lie-down before dinner."

Allowing herself to be shepherded from the room by the young duchess, Georgie hoped she hadn't just made a terrible mistake.

* * *

"Damnation," Con said after the ladies had left the room. He thrust a hand into his dark curls, yanking on the ends a bit. "What did she mean she wishes to continue being a lady's companion, for God's sake?"

"I daresay she means that she wishes to continue being a lady's companion," Archer said, relaxing back against the settee.

"Don't be an ass," Con responded, stalking across the room to pace before the fire. "A woman never means exactly what she says. If that were the case then there would never be any arguments with them."

"Surely not all the time," Archer responded. "Can there really be a hidden meaning behind 'you're standing on my gown' for instance?"

"Oh," Con growled. "You know what I mean. They're always saying one thing and meaning another. In this case, it sounds to me as if Georgina is telling me that she'd rather be a damned paid servant than stoop to marriage with me."

Lord Archer sighed and stood, walked over to a sideboard on the other side of the room and poured out two glasses of brandy.

"Here," he said, pressing one of the glasses into Con's hand before taking a drink of his own. He walked back over to the settees and resumed his seat. "Now, first of all, I don't think she's professing a preference for continuing to be a companion. In the absence of an offer from you, however, she is still going to need to find some way of making a living. She has no widow's portion, does she? Or what she has is little enough that she had to seek out employment. If that is the case, then what choice does she have?"

"She has the choice to marry me."

"But," Archer continued patiently, "you've not asked her. She can hardly announce to the room at large that she's going to marry you. And it is entirely possible, though I know you don't want to consider it, that she does not wish to marry again. I am not saying whether this is the case or not, but it's a possibility that you'll need to consider."

"Damned coil," Con said, shaking his head. "Why did this bastard have to choose today as the day for framing her for theft? It's almost as if he waited until the first time we—"

"Got to know one another a little better?" Archer supplied with a raised brow.

"Yes," Con said with a roll of his eyes, "that. It's almost as if this man chose the morning after that to put the theft accusation into motion. Though I suppose if I were a better man I'd have proposed before we—"

"Held hands?" Archer supplied helpfully.

"God, you really are an ass, aren't you?" Con complained. "Yes, held hands. I should have asked her to marry me before we held hands. Then at least I would know that she wouldn't insist upon some ridiculous plan to strike out on her own again with only the pistol in her reticule for protection."

Archer nodded. "I remember that now. I'd completely forgotten about that pistol of hers."

"You shouldn't have," Con said cuttingly. "If you're as annoying to her as you are to me she might just have used it on you."

"Oh, now," Archer chided, propping his ankle on his knee. "You only find me annoying when I'm right. Which, I'll admit, is more often than not, but still."

All traces of banter gone, Con allowed his forehead to rest briefly on the mantelpiece. "What the hell am I going to do first? Ask for Georgina's hand or catch this bastard who's threatening her?"

"I know what I'd do if it were me," Archer responded, his voice sincere. "I'd settle things with Georgina. If you're going to defeat this bastard who's threatening her, then you need to be able to work together without this marriage thing hanging over your head."

Turning, Con stepped over and collapsed onto the opposite settee. Taking a long drink of brandy, he leaned back in the seat. "I suppose you're right. But I wanted to do the thing properly. With my mother's rings and at the proper time and place. Not in some ramshackle fashion while she's feeling vulnerable and disgraced."

"If I know ladies," Archer said, a bit of humor returning to his eyes, "and I can assure you that I do, I'd say that she won't care about all that folderol. A different sort might. One who stands on ceremony and is constantly concerned about rules of precedence and things like that. But that's not the Georgina you know. She's a no-nonsense, practical sort of woman. She might appreciate a bit of ceremony on your part, but she won't reject you out of hand for lack of it. If she loves you, she'll take you however she can get you. Wouldn't you say the same for yourself?"

That was true enough, Con thought. He didn't stand on ceremony and neither did Georgie.

"For once, Archer," he said to the man across from him, "you're right about something."

He rose and said to the other man, "Come with me. There are some preparations I need to make."

Without demur, the other man followed him.

Perhaps, Con reflected, he wasn't such an ass after all.

Seventeen

*I*n her bedchamber, which was finer than her room at Lady Russell's house, Georgie stood at the window looking out over the crescent while Perdita busied herself with little adjustments throughout the room. She was grateful for her friend's hospitality. Indeed, she wasn't sure what she'd have done without Perdita offering her someplace to stay. But she was somewhat uncomfortable with the opulence of her accommodations.

"You really don't need to do all of this," she said once again, turning from the window to see Perdita opening the door to a footman with Georgie's trunks. "Oh, lovely. Please just put them in the dressing room."

When the footman was gone, Perdita walked over to where Georgie stood and hugged her. "I am so glad you're here, though the circumstances are perfectly dreadful." Pulling back, she led Georgie toward the small sitting room attached to the suite and gestured for her to sit.

Georgie felt rather like she was being prepared for a

motherly scold. "What's amiss?" she asked. "Aside from the person trying to discredit me, of course."

"Why didn't you tell me about Con?" Perdita asked, her hands spread open as if she were asking the world at large. "I knew there was something different at the picnic, but I couldn't be sure. Do you know how wonderful this is?"

Her face burning, Georgie felt sheepish. "I could hardly announce it in the carriage," she protested. "And besides, he was your betrothed. I couldn't know whether you still had feelings for him or if perhaps you regretted breaking things off with him."

"Despite the fact that I've said, repeatedly, in your presence that I am ever so glad that I broke things off with him?" Perdita did not look convinced by her friend's evasion.

The expression in Perdita's face was precisely why Georgie hadn't told her about what was between her and Con. Expectations. If she told anyone about what had happened last night, then they would have expectations about what the next step should be. And for now, at least, she'd hoped to keep the intimacy they'd shared to themselves. Clearly that was not meant to be.

"Perdita," she said, trying to find the words to explain herself, "I'm not from the nobility as you are. I can't trace my ancestry back to William the Conqueror and I most certainly never expected to find myself in bed with an earl. The very notion is so foreign to anything I've ever considered might happen to me that I still wonder if there is some sort of hoax being perpetrated on me."

"Oh, please," Perdita said with a moue of distaste.

"You will not convince me that you are some sort of low-class slattern just because your father was a career army officer instead of a titled nobleman. And I do not think that has anything to do with this situation. You are simply frightened of what's passed between you and Con. I daresay because it's more passionate than whatever it was that you shared with your husband."

Georgie frowned. "Why do you say that?" she asked carefully, not wanting to reveal how close her friend had come to the truth.

"Because I know what it is to be married to a man who terrifies you. And I know that no matter how kind he might seem sometimes, there was never any question that he'd remain so forever. It's simply not how life is with a husband like that. It's a constant struggle to figure out where the next blow is coming from. What mistake will set him off this time. What misplaced word or innocent decision will cause him to hit you this time."

Perdita's eyes shone. "I know what that is like, and I know that however intense Con might be about things sometimes, he will never, ever, be the sort of man Gervase and Robert were."

Georgie realized then that Perdita was right. Her connection with Con was far stronger than what she'd had with Robert. In part because she didn't fear for herself every moment. And she knew that Con was an entirely different sort of man.

"It is more passionate," she admitted. "And more intimate. Emotionally, I mean. And that frightens me, I suppose. Because I have so much more in common with Con. There is so much more of a connection that if something were to go wrong—if he became violent or turned into a different sort of man—there would be more to lose."

She took a deep breath and clasped her hands together to keep them steady. "I don't know if I could stand it if he turned into a man like Robert."

"My dear," Perdita said, her face creased with sympathy, "I know you are frightened, but I can tell you, as someone who has known Con for most of my adult life, that he is not like them. He never has been. In part because of what he witnessed between his aunt and his uncle. From the moment he became aware of what was going on between Ormond and me, I could see how much he wished to put a stop to it. But there was little he could do. Under the law, a wife is subject to her husband. And for all that Con is an earl and powerful in his own right, Gervase was a duke. With more power."

"I hadn't realized," Georgie said, thinking of how it must have galled Con to stand by while Ormond battered Perdita.

"It was for that reason that I couldn't marry him," Perdita said sadly. "Not because he was so decent, but because I felt as if he were doing it to make up for what he hadn't been able to do while Gervase was alive. It felt like a sort of atonement. And, perhaps it's selfish of me, but I wish my next marriage to be to someone I adore and who adores me. Not someone who likes me well enough and wishes to marry me to assuage his own conscience."

It was certainly something she'd never considered, and Georgie found herself wondering if Con's attraction to her might be because, like Perdita, she'd been the victim of an abusive husband.

"Don't think for a moment that it's the same," Perdita said firmly, as if she'd read Georgie's mind. "You haven't seen the way he lights up when you enter a room. Or the way that his gaze lingers on you when you don't know he's watching. I've never seen Con like this. Not with anyone."

Georgie felt herself relax a little at her friend's words, though she still wondered whether Con would be better off with someone else. Someone who wasn't so damaged by her past.

"I'm still not sure that it's enough," she said finally. "I'm not sure if it would be right for me to tie him to me. Especially considering that there's a madman, or woman," she added, with a nod to Perdita, "who wants to do me harm."

"Georgina," Perdita said with a grin. "I don't think you've got a choice in the matter."

"What do you mean?"

"Just that," Perdita said. "I think Con is going to do whatever it takes to have you, and if that means ridding the world of whoever is trying to bring you down, then he's going to do it."

"Not if I do it first," Georgie said with conviction.

"This is going to be a very interesting few weeks," Perdita predicted.

Later that evening, Con and Archer having departed not long after the ladies had disappeared upstairs, Georgie and Perdita were just sitting down to supper when a disturbance at the front entrance interrupted their conversation.

"Curious," Perdita said with a frown. "I wasn't expecting callers at this hour."

"Perhaps it's my last trunk," Georgie said, tasting the turtle soup that had just been put down before her. "Or some friend who hasn't realized what time it is."

"We'll find out soon enough," Perdita said with a shrug.

Just then Hobson, who'd left only a moment before to retrieve the second course, returned, looking harassed. "The Duke and Duchess of Ormond," he said, just before Isabella and her husband, Trevor, the cousin who'd succeeded to the dukedom after Gervase's death, stepped into the dining room.

"Surprise," Isabella said rather sheepishly. "I am sorry for interrupting your supper, but might you have enough for a couple of weary travelers?"

"Don't be a goose," Perdita said with a wave to Hobson, instructing him to set two more places and to ask cook for two more bowls of the splendid turtle soup.

When that was finished she turned to greet her sister and brother-in-law properly. "What a delight to see you both! Whatever brings you to Bath of all places? Though we've had some excitement ourselves, Bath as a rule is duller than watching sheep graze."

"It's actually rather soothing if you're in the right mood," Trevor said, thanking the footman who'd just filled his wine glass. "Though it's no match for cows lying down."

"Darling," Isabella said to the duke, "I'm afraid Perdita and Georgina have no earthly idea whether you are joking or serious. I doubt Perdita has seen a sheep in her life."

"I have too," Perdita objected. "One of the milkmaids had one in Hyde Park."

"That was probably a cow, Perdita," Georgie said in an undertone.

Perdita frowned then shrugged. "Doubtless you are correct," she admitted. Then turning to her sister, she said, "So I ask again, why are the two of you in Bath? I thought you were leaving for the Continent this week for your wedding journey."

"Well," Isabella said, her cheeks rosy and, to Georgie's eye, particularly radiant, "we thought perhaps it would be better to postpone things until after the child is born."

Before the words had left her mouth Georgie and Perdita had both cried out with joy and were out of their chairs and hugging Isabella. By the time they'd resumed their seats, all three women were wiping away tears.

"Well done!" Perdita said again, her grin infectious. "I cannot be more pleased for the two of you."

"We're quite pleased about it ourselves," Trevor said with a grin.

"Though he does have a tendency to be a bit overprotective," Isabella said with a roll of her eyes. "The doctor has said that I'm healthy as a horse and there is no reason I shouldn't continue on with my normal activities."

"You had no business riding out in such a chill yesterday," Trevor said with mock ferocity. "Especially not without a cloak."

"I was wearing a cloak. Just not the fur-lined one, which, by the way, is unnecessary unless there is snow on the ground."

Georgie watched her friend and her new husband bickering good-naturedly and wondered if she'd ever feel that comfortable with Con. She could already tell that he had the same sort of protective streak that the duke possessed, and if given half a chance he'd wrap her up in cotton wool if their coupling the night before resulted in a child. Unbidden, an image of her holding an infant while Con held them both in the circle of his arms arose in her mind and she felt a yearning in her chest the likes of which she'd never thought to feel again.

It was at once inspiring and frightening. What if she were with child even now? She would have to marry Con then, whether she was able to overcome her fear of marrying again or not. Surprisingly, the thought wasn't as dire as she'd have thought. Perhaps she was already halfway to making a decision about him.

If he should ever ask, she reminded herself.

"So," Isabella was saying, "we decided that in lieu of a trip abroad we'd come to sedate Bath and check on how the two of you were getting on. Though you said there was some excitement. Do tell!"

One of Perdita's delicately arched brows rose. "Archer wrote to you, didn't he?"

Isabella pursed her lips. "It's Lord Archer," she corrected, "and what if he did? Am I no longer allowed to worry about how my friends are getting on now that I'm married again?"

"The man has lived in the same house with me for

five years," Perdita said, shaking her head. "I shall call him by his Christian name if I so choose. And he had no business writing to you. Especially not in your current condition."

"It's not as if he were able to sense it from afar," Isabella grumbled. "And I wanted to be here. To help."

"Isabella," Georgina said, ignoring the sisters' bickering. "I cannot tell you how much I appreciate your coming, but surely with your change of circumstances it isn't a good idea for you to be here where things are so . . . unsettled."

"But that's just it," Isabella argued. "I am here because things are so unsettled. I remember what it was like to be there in Yorkshire without the two of you to rely on." She reached out to grasp Trevor's hand and said, "I'm sorry, darling, but you know how lonely things were there for me before we became friendly."

"I do," he said, kissing the back of her hand. "And I understand both their worry for you and your need to be here. Georgina, if it's any consolation, I will do what I can to help Lord Coniston and Archer—he's my personal secretary so I can call him by his Christian name if I wish as well, Isabella—with whatever they might be planning to entrap this schemer who is trying his best to ruin your reputation."

Perdita and Georgie exchanged looks of relief. "I must admit that I do appreciate having the assistance," Georgie said with gratitude. "Though, Isabella, if you ever feel as if things are becoming too much for you to handle or if you and Trevor just want to go back to London and be alone, please don't hesitate to pack your bags and go. Indeed, you might not wish to reside in the same house with me since I doubt you've heard the latest yet."

Quickly she gave them both a summary of what had happened earlier at Lady Russell's house regarding the missing bracelet and its reappearance in Georgie's bedchamber.

When she had finished, Trevor whistled. "That's a fast and easy way to ruin a reputation," he said with a disgusted look. "Though I am most disappointed in the way that Lady Russell and her family turned on you. One would hope that they would have shown more loyalty."

"It wasn't all of her family," Perdita reminded them. "Con was quite upset about the matter and I have little doubt that he's at Lady Russell's even now trying to convince his aunt to change her mind."

"Is that right?" Isabella asked casually. A bit *too* casually for Georgie's comfort. "I wonder if it has something to do with the finer feelings that Lord Archer mentioned in his letter."

"Isabella," Trevor warned, "do not put your friend on the spot in front of me. You know that if Con and Archer sense I've overheard anything from her they won't hesitate to use the thumbscrews."

"You are all ever so amusing," Georgie said with a roll of her eyes, "but I have no intention of saying anything. Because it's none of your affair."

"Oh, an affair, is it?" Isabella crooned. "How lovely. Do tell."

"All right, Isabella," Perdita chided. "You've had your fun. Now stop haranguing my houseguest."

"Thank you, Perdita," Georgie said with gratitude.

"Haranguing her is my job," Perdita finished, to Georgie's disgust.

"Dessert had better be delicious," she groused. "It's the least I deserve if this is how you treat your houseguests."

Eighteen

The next morning, Con and Archer were leaving the White Hart where Con had removed when he left his aunt's house, and where Archer had been staying since his arrival in Bath, when they were met by Mr. McGilloway, the investigator from the magistrate's office.

"My lord," the man said, doffing his hat to them. "I wondered if I might have a few minutes of your time. Alone."

"I can assure you, Mr. McGilloway, that Lord Archer is privy to all the details of that night at the theater," Con said, curiosity gripping him. McGilloway shrugged, and suggested they repair to the tavern in the next street.

Procuring a private dining room so they wouldn't be overhead, Con waited until they'd been served small beers before he sat back in his chair and said, "Well, McGilloway, what news have you got for me?"

The investigator wiped a bit of foam from his upper lip before replying. "It's about Malcolm Lowther."

Con's brows rose. "I gave him your direction just a couple of days ago. What is this about?"

"I'm afraid, my lord," McGilloway said, "that Mr. Lowther is dead. His body was found in some rented rooms in Westgate Buildings last night. The charwoman came to clean and found him dead in 'is bed."

"How was he killed?" Con asked, wondering if the same man who'd killed the man on the roof had killed Lowther.

"Poison, it looks like," the investigator said with a moue of distaste. "Give me a shooting or even a hanging," he said. "But poison is a wretched way to go, in my humble opinion."

"One would rather not go at all," Archer said with a grimace. "So what made you come to inform Lord Coniston about the fellow's death?"

"Found one of his lordship's calling cards in his rooms," McGilloway said. "With my own name written on the back. I figured his lordship would be able to tell me what was what."

"Are the two deaths connected, do you think?" Con asked. Though he'd originally suspected Lowther of killing the man on the roof, now he wasn't so sure. As crazy as the man's tale of letters had seemed that night, knowing what he now knew about the mastermind's orchestration of any number of things using notes, Con was more inclined to believe Robert Mowbray's brother on that score.

"Well," McGilloway said, leaning back in his chair, "the fellow from the theater, John Potts, also stayed in a rooming house in Westgate Buildings, so it's like as not they knew each other. But I don't see how their deaths could be connected. One was stabbed, the other was poisoned."

"But . . . ?" Con prompted. He could see that the other man wasn't quite convinced of his own words.

"But," McGilloway admitted, "there was one thing that they had in common. Though it's probably just one of those odd things."

"There are any number of odd things about this situation," Con muttered.

"Well, even though the landlady at Lowther's rooms didn't hold with such things, she said she saw him meeting with a woman in mourning more than just a couple of times. Now, I never heard of a whore like that, but no woman with any sort of reputation is going to risk being seen in a man's rooms. And since we don't think he had a sister . . ."

"So what's the connection with Potts?" Con prompted.

"That's the thing," McGilloway said, scratching his chin. "He was seen with a woman in mourning too. His landlord wasn't so particular as Lowther's was, so she could come and go as she pleased there. And it sounded to me from what the landlord said that she was living there for nigh on two weeks."

Con pinched the bridge of his nose between his fingers. "So, we have a widow who has been seen with both of the dead men."

"And two dead men," Archer added helpfully.

"And two dead men," agreed McGilloway. "Both of whom have some kind of connection with his lordship here."

"I can tell you easily enough how I know Lowther,"

Con said. Quickly he told the other man about the way Lowther had been manipulated by some unknown person into frightening Georgina.

"So he looked enough like her dead husband to make her think he was a ghost?" McGilloway asked. "Seems to me that might make a woman pretty angry. And she is a widow, isn't she?"

"She is a widow," Con agreed, "but she has no reason to wish the man dead. And I can vouch for the fact that she's not been to Westgate Buildings. At least not in the last week or so."

"Doesn't have to travel to Westgate Buildings to poison the fellow," the investigator reminded him. "Could have poisoned a box of sweets and sent them to the man."

"Did you find a box of poisoned sweets in his rooms?" Archer asked conversationally.

"Well, no," McGilloway admitted. "But she could have removed them from his rooms after he died. Or she could have had an accomplice do it." He gave a meaningful look to Con.

"Neither Mrs. Mowbray nor myself poisoned Malcolm Lowther, McGilloway," Con snapped. "If we had you can be damned sure we'd not have left a calling card behind."

"Couldn't hurt to ask," the investigator said with a shrug. "I don't suppose you've got any idea who our murderous widow might be, have you?"

"Not offhand," Con said, though he had a very strong suspicion. He'd like to see what Georgina thought of it before telling McGilloway about it, however.

"Then I suppose I'd better be getting back to the

chase," McGilloway said, rising from the table. "If you think of anything that might help us find out who killed these coves, the magistrate's office would be grateful."

When he was gone, Con and Archer exchanged a look.

"It doesn't seem as if things are becoming any less complicated, does it?" Archer asked with a frown.

"Not particularly," Con agreed, "but I have an idea of who the widow might be. I need to confirm it with Georgina first, however."

"Then let's go tell her," Archer said, pushing back from the table.

"Poisoned?" Georgie exclaimed, pressing a hand to her chest. She'd not really known Mr. Lowther, but as it always was with death, she found it difficult to believe that the man she'd spoken with only a few days ago was now dead.

She, Perdita, Isabella, and the gentlemen were ranged about Perdita's drawing room in Laura Place, where they'd gathered when Con and Archer had arrived a few minutes ago.

"Did Mr. McGilloway have any guesses as to who might be responsible?" Georgie asked, a shiver running through her. "You don't think it might be the person who had him spying on me, do you?"

"The thought had crossed my mind," Con said, resting his booted ankle over his knee. "He was no longer of use to the mastermind and therefore Lowther was expendable."

"We've got to warn Mary Kendrick," Georgie said, suddenly realizing that if Lowther was expendable so too was the widow.

But before she could stand to go get her reticule, Con raised a staying hand. "You might wish to wait before you go to her, Georgina," he said regretfully. He told them about the sightings of the widow in mourning dress who'd been seen at the lodgings of both Lowther and John Potts.

"That could be anyone," Georgina protested. "Any woman might don mourning dress and cover her face with a veil and no one would be able to tell the difference. Just because Mary is a widow does not mean she's suspect."

"But she's the widow we found with Lowther that evening in Aunt Russell's back garden," Con reminded her. "And I didn't wish to mention it, but McGilloway asked if you might be the widow he's looking for. So be pleased that Mary Kendrick is also a possibility."

"I thought you weren't overly fond of this Mary Kendrick anyway, Georgie," Isabella said, tilting her head quizzically. "She sounds like a perfectly awful person. Especially considering that she was trying to frighten you in order to obtain ten thousand pounds. That doesn't strike me as the act of a friend."

"But she apologized for that," Georgie said firmly. "And I cannot help but sympathize with her situation. She has no widow's portion and is forced to live with her sister and her family in Westgate Buildings. I can't help thinking that I might have found myself in a similar situation if I'd been unable to find a position with Lady Russell. At least I have my independence."

"Yes, dearest," Perdita said, patting Georgie on the hand. "But you've worked hard for what you have achieved. Despite what that wretched person who planted the bracelet in your chambers did to ruin your reputation. It sounds to me as if Mrs. Kendrick is a woman who simply lets things happen to her."

"That's not fair," Georgie protested. She knew that it would be difficult for Perdita or Isabella to understand what it was like to return to England after war. To have lost the only community you'd ever known and on top of that dealing with the loss of a husband—who no matter how abusive he was still provided one with a roof over one's head—was enough to drive one to despair. And for all that Mary had seemed to be blown by every wind, she was also doing the best she could in a difficult situation. She'd stayed with her sister's family despite knowing that she was resented as another mouth to feed, and despite her brother-in-law's violence, and she'd survived. Her apology to Georgie might have been too little too late, but at least she'd given it, which was more than Georgie could say for any number of people in her life who had transgressed against her. Aloud she said, "Mary has had a difficult time of it. And yes, she did accept a bribe in order to frighten me. But that doesn't mean she's capable of poisoning someone."

"If you believe it," Isabella said, "then I am convinced."

"Perhaps we should go call upon her in Westgate Buildings," Perdita said with a smile.

Georgie could tell that she was not convinced about Mary's goodness, but she appreciated her support, nonetheless.

"I should like that," she said. "Shall we go this afternoon?"

"Wait one moment," Con said, sitting up in his chair. "I don't like the idea of you three going to Westgate Buildings on your own. It is not the best of neighborhoods. And it's where a man was just murdered."

"Not all people are able to afford the best of neighborhoods," Georgie said, something like anger tight in her chest. "It's where I might choose to live if I do not find another position soon. Though I doubt even a milliner's assistant, which is all I'm qualified for, could afford it there."

Feeling the sting of tears behind her eyes, she turned and hurried from the room.

Staring after her, Con cursed. "How the hell did that happen?" he demanded. "I wasn't being snobbish. I was worried for her safety."

"She's been through quite a bit in the past few days, Con," Perdita said soothingly. "Think of it. She's gone from thinking her dead husband was stalking her, to nearly being assaulted at the theater, to seeing a dead body, to being accused of theft. Now a woman she's known for years is under suspicion of having murdered not one but two men. I think Georgie is entitled to a bit of hysterics."

"And truthfully," Isabella pointed out, "that wasn't even true hysterics. Though for Georgie it was. She's so self-contained even her fits are controlled."

Con sank miserably into his chair. "How can I make it right? I want to protect her. And I thought she knew that there was no question of her getting another position as a companion. She won't need to."

"Easy there, old man," Archer said, clasping Con on the shoulder. "It's not the end of the world. Maybe you should go up and apologize. We'll wait down here, and when you come down we'll all set out for Westgate Buildings."

"Or better yet," Isabella said, "we'll pay a visit to Lady Russell's. I've a mind to play the duchess. Did you bring your coronet, your grace, or did we leave it at home?"

Leaving them to discuss the matter among themselves, Con headed upstairs to find Georgie.

Nineteen

$\mathcal{G}$eorgie had indulged herself in a good cry and felt much the better for it. She wasn't sure just what about the situation regarding Mary had set her off, but she suspected it had more to do with self-pity than concern for her former friend.

It was just that she'd tried so hard to maintain a positive outlook while the world seemed to be crumbling around her, and the idea that her friends might find Westgate Buildings beneath them had reinforced her fear that she was out of place among them. Neither fish nor fowl, she didn't belong in the world of Mary Kendrick but she also felt out of place in the world of Isabella, Perdita, and most painful of all, Con. That had been made abundantly clear by how quickly Lady Russell, Clara, and Con's other cousins had turned on her. It had only taken a few moments for all of Georgie's hard-won reputation to wither away.

Rinsing her handkerchief in the basin and pressing it against her tear-reddened eyes, she was surveying the results in the glass of her dressing table when she heard a tentative knock on the door. Thinking it was Perdita or Isabella she called for them to come in.

But a masculine cough made her turn to see Con standing in the doorway. He stepped in and closed the door behind him. "Perdita said I might come up and check on you," he said, looking more uncomfortable than Georgie could ever remember seeing him.

He walked a bit farther into the room, taking what Georgie thought was an unusual interest in the décor. "It's a pretty bedchamber," he said, finally looking from the walls to face her. "It suits you."

Georgie looked at his face, which had become so unutterably dear to her in the past week, and wondered how she would possibly give him up when the time came. "I thank you," she said finally, "but I suspect that you aren't here to comment upon the décor."

Con gave a short laugh. "No, I am not. But I'm damned if I know exactly what I'm meant to say." He began to pace round the room, picking up a shepherdess figurine from where it was displayed on the mantel and turning it to face the wall. Georgie rose from her seat at the vanity and walked toward the sitting room attached to her chamber. She didn't need to tell him to follow. He did.

When she was seated comfortably in a chintz chair, and Con was, if not comfortably seated, at least seated, she said, "I think I should go first."

Before he could either agree or object, she said, "You see, I think I overreacted about Westgate Buildings. In fact, I know I did. And I apologize. I realize that you wouldn't object to our going there out of any sense of superiority. And I should have known that. I've perhaps been more affected by what happened at Lady Russell's than I've realized. And I know Perdita and Isabella do not refine upon it, but the truth of the matter is, by birth I am more suited to Westgate Buildings than either Henrietta Street or Laura Place."

"But that's foolishness," Con said, his mouth twisted with anger. "You are every bit as entitled to live in Henrietta Street or Laura Place as your friends are."

Georgie smiled sadly. "Con, you cannot seriously believe that. You are an earl and you belong in the Beau Monde. And the truth of the matter is that I am not. For all that the rest of you seem to ignore it, it is the honest truth. I was born to a military officer and a vicar's daughter. And they were both of the gentry. Which means that I was never expected to mix with duchesses and earls and the like."

He opened his mouth to object again, but Georgie held up a staying hand. "That's neither here nor there. I simply wanted to let you know that my response was not about what you said, but something that I'd been thinking about myself. That's all."

She smiled, hoping that he would let the matter rest. "Now, was there something you wished to say? I hope we aren't making the others wait to go to Westgate Buildings. We are still going, are we not?"

To her surprise he thrust both hands into his hair and pulled. "Oh, dear, you are feeling put out with me, aren't you?" she asked with trepidation. She had hoped that he'd be understanding about her position on her social standing or lack thereof.

"Georgina," he said on a sigh, "I don't know that put out is the way to describe what I feel for you."

Before she could respond, he shook his head. "Do you think I lightly make love to whichever lady just so happens to be available in my aunt's house?"

"Well, of course not," she said, her brow furrowed. "That would be odd, wouldn't it?"

"Yes," he agreed. "It would be odd. It would also be odd if I did whatever I could to help aforementioned random lady find out who was trying to frighten her, kissed her witless in the theater, defended her against an accusation of theft, and in general mooned after her in a fashion that is very nearly overtaking Archer's mooning over Perdita as the most pathetic display of unrequited affection in the south of England."

Her eyes widened. "Well, if you're so unhappy about it, you can leave off with your foolish pursuit of me with my blessings."

"That's not what I want, or what I meant," Con said hotly, standing up and approaching her chair. "I only meant to say that I am bloody over the moon for you and I want you to marry me and that's why I've been such a deuced idiot about things and that's also why I'm trying like the devil to keep you safe from whoever it is who wants you to suffer." As he spoke, he very handily scooped Georgie up from her chair and, reversing their positions, deposited her upon his lap.

"Well, I don't . . ." she began, but he took advantage of her open mouth to kiss her. Soundly.

"You've been driving me mad," he said against her mouth, his hand roving down her back to cup her bottom.

"Not," she said, pulling back a little to unwrap his cravat, "as mad as you've been driving me."

"Then," he said against her chin, and making his way down over her throat, "we should do something about it."

"We are," she said, giving up on the cravat because it was taking too much concentration.

"Something else," he said breathlessly as he found a particularly sensitive spot on her collarbone. "Marriage."

She stiffened against him. Pushing against him to regain some control, she said, "We can't marry. Didn't you hear anything I just said?"

Clearly he was still muzzy from lust. "Yes, you said we should . . ." He frowned. "I don't remember exactly."

Pulling away, she tried to get off his lap, but Con's arms were wrapped around her. "I said that we come from different worlds and that you are from a higher station than mine."

Blinking, Con looked more than a little confused. But his eyes narrowed and Georgie knew he understood. "Yes," he said decisively, "you said that, but I didn't get to say what I thought about it."

"Which is?" Georgie asked, though she had a clue what he'd say.

"That it doesn't matter a damned bit."

She felt as if she were back in the army camp. "It does matter to me," she said firmly. "Do you think I wish to spend the rest of my life being condescended to by ladies who are angry with me for having married an eligible earl they were hoping would marry one of their daughters?"

"That's not even an actual thing that's happened to you," he said with a harassed look. "It's just something you've conjured from your imagination."

"It's something I've seen more than once at the charity meetings Perdita and Isabella and I attend. Gentlemen might be more forgiving, but I have my doubts about that as well."

"Perhaps that's true," he said. "But it won't all be dealing with those women. They might be upset at first, but ultimately they'll be forced to realize that if they want your approval—you will be a countess after all—they'll have to be the ones toadying to you."

"Oh, that's so much better," Georgie said with a reluctant laugh. She wasn't purposely trying to find reasons not to marry him. She'd come to the conclusion sometime that night in her bedchamber at Lady Russell's that she could quite easily spend her life with him. But she was so frightened that he'd marry her in haste and then repent at leisure. It would break her heart to know she'd trapped him into a marriage that would force his peers to shun him.

"It is better than the scenario you proposed," he said with a grin.

He kissed the end of her nose, and then her cheeks and her eyelids. Then, gently, so gently, he kissed her lips.

"I know this thing between us has happened quickly," he said, leaning his forehead against hers. "Believe me. I know. But I've been drawn to you from the first day I met you."

"When you were betrothed to Perdita?" she asked, surprised.

He nodded, looking sheepish. "It's one of the reasons I wasn't very upset when she broke things off with me. I had committed myself because as a man of honor it was my duty, but I would always have wondered about what might have been."

She stared at him, tilting her head to look more closely at him. "I would never have guessed it for a minute," she said with a gasp. "You truly are a romantic, aren't you?"

"I like to think I'm a man who knows what he wants," he said with a look of challenge. "And what I want, is you."

She stared into his eyes, which had become so familiar to her in the past days, and she wondered what she had done to deserve the affection of such a good man. She thought about the worst days of her marriage to Robert. And how she'd longed more than anything in the world to escape him somehow and to find a kind and honorable man who would cherish her in a way she suspected Robert was incapable of. Someone she could cherish in return without fear of having her every kindness thrown back in her face as proof of some imagined infraction on her part. And yet, something made her pause.

Looking down at his shirtfront, unable to meet those oh-so-trusting eyes of his, she said, "I don't know how I can possibly admit it to you, when you are being so terribly sweet. But I find I cannot go forward in this without telling you the truth." She swallowed, knowing it might make him change his mind about her. But also realizing she had to say it. "The truth of the matter is," she said quietly, "that I am afraid."

She felt the sure stroke of his hand over her back.

"Of what, sweeting?" he asked, his voice just as gentle as she'd known it would be. Making her feel all the more like a coward.

"I am afraid to risk it," she said. "I've been in this position before. I fell in love with a man, and within a year I was in misery." She leaned back to look him in the eye. She had thought to see him look offended, but all she saw was patience. And understanding. "I don't think you are even capable of the sort of violence that Robert used against me," she said finally. "But when I first married him, I had no notion that he was capable of such a thing either. The naked truth of it is that I don't trust my own judgment. I mean, look at the way Mary Kendrick fooled me. I want to believe that she's a good woman who was manipulated into a bad situation, but at the heart of things, part of me believes she's as guilty as you all think she is."

"Georgina," Con said, his voice calm and sure, "if you weren't a bit afraid to trust again after what happened with Mowbray, I'd think you were a simpleton as well as a glutton for punishment. No one who has endured what you went through could emerge without some sense of skepticism about the people around them. It would be impossible not to.

"But," he continued, "there is a great deal of difference between skepticism and blind trust. And I do not require your blind trust."

"How can we have a marriage that will possibly work without trust?" she asked, wanting to believe him but still afraid.

"That's the thing," he said. "I said nothing about a lack of trust. Just a lack of blind trust. Neither of us is going to trust the other blindly until we've got a few years of acquaintance built up. Until I've proven to you that I'm not the kind of man who would turn on you as Mowbray did."

"And that doesn't frighten you?" she demanded. "It doesn't make you question whether we can make it work?"

"Not a bit," Con said, kissing her on the forehead. "Because I do trust you. And I will spend every moment of the rest of my life proving to you that I deserve your trust."

Her eyes welled and Georgie buried her face in his neck, breathing in sandalwood and his own special scent. "I don't think it will take that long," she said finally. She pulled back a little and kissed him. "It won't take that long at all."

"But that won't stop me from trying," he said. "Now, I hate to end what might become a most enjoyable interlude. But I suppose we should go back downstairs before the afternoon is gone."

Georgie sighed and leaned her head on his shoulder. "I don't suppose you'd be interested in coming back up here tonight," she said coaxingly. "I sincerely doubt that Perdita is as scrupulous as Mr. Lowther's landlady."

Con kissed her on the mouth with a resounding smack. "I was afraid you'd never ask," he said, allowing her to stand and reaching up to straighten his cravat.

"Well, we should probably wait until we are wed—" she began, then stopped herself, realizing he hadn't actually asked.

"Say no more," Con said. "I will most assuredly be asking you properly. But now we have a mission we must undertake and I refuse to embark upon a proposal of marriage when there is not a solid block of time set aside for um . . ." He paused. "Celebration," he said finally, making Georgie laugh.

"Then I will wait until you deem the time is right," she said saucily. "Now, you'd better go look in the pier glass for I fear your poor cravat will never be the same."

Somehow neither of them seemed to mind.

"Now remember," Perdita reminded the others as they rode the short distance from Laura Place to Henrietta Street. "We are meant to be on our best aristocratic behavior." In deference to their mission, she'd chosen one of her most elegant afternoon ensembles, which included an ermine-trimmed cape to guard against the chill in the autumn air. "Do not be swayed by their attempts at toadying. We are here to ensure that they change their minds about Georgina and that means that we can take no quarter. It is do or die! Or something . . ."

"These are Con's relations you're talking about, Perdita," Georgina reminded her. "And I happen to hold Lady Russell in some affection."

"Don't mind me," Con called to Perdita from his seat beside Georgie. "Though I don't put it past scme of my relations to toady. Cousin Philip especially. But I agree with Georgina. Do not be rough on Lady Russell. She is old and infirm."

"She is quite mad, isn't she, your sister, I mean?"

Trevor said to Isabella in an undertone. Though he was a duke, he had until recently been a country farmer, so he wasn't quite used to grand displays of ducal power, the likes of which they now embarked upon.

"Oh, heavens, yes," Isabella responded, "but she is ours." She smoothed the edge of his cravat a bit and turned his stickpin to face outward. "I must admit you look rather delicious in all your ducal finery."

"No flirtation," Perdita ordered, the ostrich plume in her hat wagging at them like a finger. "We need to keep our wits about us."

"I dislike calling attention to it," Archer said with a frown, "but you do realize that we are calling upon the gout-ridden widow of a baron, do you not? I hardly think she will meet us with a volley of cannon fire or whatnot."

"An excellent point," Con agreed, offering his friend a tip of the hat. "I can assure you that there is no cannon in Lady Russell's house at present."

Perdita scowled. "Are you attempting to dissuade me from doing our level best to protect Georgina's reputation, Archer? Con? Is that what you're doing?"

When both men shrugged, Perdita's brows snapped together. Georgie was reminded of Lady Russell's spaniel, Percy, when he was deprived of a treat.

"Never mind," Perdita continued. "I do not wish to hear your argument, Archer. You've far too much experience philosophizing for Parliament. If there were a way to get around you, it would have already been done. And so far as I can tell it hasn't."

"My dear duchess," he said with a grin. "I hadn't

realized you'd noticed." He pressed a hand to his chest in mock humility. "I have been told by some that my philosophizing could convince a robin to hand over the eggs from his nest. Though of course I would never ask such a thing. Poor dear little creatures, birds."

"I'm feeling bilious," Isabella said suddenly.

Perdita gasped, her mask of haughtiness slipping. "Oh, no, darling, is it the child?"

Isabella rolled her eyes. "No, it's this ridiculous conversation. I vow you and Archer are so full of hot air you could make the carriage rise from the earth like a balloon."

"Oh!" Perdita made a sound of mocked affront. "See if I show you sympathy for your weak stomach again, Sister."

"You must admit we are a bit bombastic at times," Archer said with a shrug. "I don't blame her for complaining."

"That's mightily gallant of you, my lord," Con said, doffing his hat to the other man, who doffed his own hat in return.

"This has to be the most absurdly long carriage ride in the history of man," Isabella muttered. "Why is it taking so long to go two streets over?"

"I believe I heard the coachman complaining about an overturned cart ahead," Trevor said helpfully. "I can get out and check if you'd like," he said to Perdita.

"No." She waved his offer away. "I suppose we can wait a bit. But it does steal one's thunder when instead of a swift ride across country you arrive instead at a snail's pace across macadamized roads."

It took some minutes more but finally they arrived before the entrance to Lady Russell's house in Henrietta Street. And they took advantage of all the pomp and circumstance their positions could entail. They descended from the carriage, allowing the footmen to hand the ladies out with the gentlemen following behind.

"I'm nervous," Georgie said to Con as he handed her up the stairs. "What if your aunt or cousins refuse to see me?"

"They wouldn't dare with two duchesses, a duke, a duke's son, and the head of their family escorting you," he said, squeezing her hand. "I could have overridden my aunt's orders earlier, of course, but it is technically her house."

"I know that," Georgie said, grateful that he'd agreed to come with them at all. He might just as easily cut up rough at Perdita's plan.

When they handed the butler their cards, he gave a low bow and invited them into the hallway, and had them wait while he sent the cards to his mistress with a footman. In barely enough time for her to have glanced at the cards, the footman returned and the butler requested them to follow him upstairs to the drawing room.

"The Duke and Duchess of Ormond, the young dowager Duchess of Ormond, the Earl of Coniston, Lord Archer Lisle, and Mrs. Mowbray," the man said in stentorian tones before stepping back to stand as still as a marble statue next to the doorway.

To Georgina's amusement, the room's occupants

seemed flummoxed to be receiving a visit from such august personages. Even one of whom who was their own cousin.

"Your graces, my lord," Lady Russell, said, her gout having improved to such a degree that she was able to stand upon her bothersome foot and offer a low curtsy. "Nephew," she said, turning to Con. When she reached Georgina, she paused and her hands began to tremble. "Georg . . . ah, that is, Mrs. Mowbray, what a surprise."

"Aunt," Con said firmly, "I hope that you will see fit to welcome Mrs. Mowbray as a guest in this house."

"It has come to my attention, your ladyship," Perdita said with a slight inclination of her head, "that my dear friend Georgina was dismissed from this house yesterday for a crime she did not commit."

Looking from Con to Perdita and at the other august guests in her drawing room, Lady Russell seemed perplexed. Finally she said, "I . . . I suppose you mean Mrs. Mowbray?" she asked, her voice timid. "For if it is I feel sure there's been some sort of miscommunication. Mrs. Mowbray was guilty of stealing from me. Indeed, I didn't believe it at first either. Not until I saw the evidence with my own eyes."

"I believe I am capable of knowing whether I am or am not being fed a false tale, Lady Russell," Perdita returned, her voice cool. "And in this case, I am being fed lies, but it is not from Mrs. Mowbray's protectors. It is instead from the people who wish to do her harm. Perhaps in the name of protecting you."

Georgie could see that the older woman was taken aback by the accusation, and it took all of her might to keep from going to her former employer at once.

"Might you tell us," Isabella asked kindly, "how it came to be that Mrs. Mowbray was accused of so heinous a crime? After all, it isn't every day that a lady is accused of outright theft. Was the item something that you held in great value perhaps?"

"It was a diamond and ruby bracelet that I had only worn a few times," Lady Russell admitted. "I hadn't even realized it was gone and I wouldn't have known if my niece Lydia hadn't pressed me to let her look through my jewel chest. At first I thought she was joking when she told me it wasn't there. My next step, of course, was to figure out how the piece had been removed from my locked jewel chest and how this person was able to get into the chest without the key."

"And did you discover how it was lifted from your jewelry case?" Perdita asked. "Did someone steal the keys perhaps?"

"I never did learn the answer to that question," the elderly lady said with a shrug. "Before I could ask, my niece Clara came to me and informed me that the diamond and ruby cuff had been found. At first I was elated because I was so worried about losing such a precious item from my jewel collection that I didn't realize just what the implications of where it was found would be."

"Curious," Perdita said, her lips pursed. "Are you saying that you might not have even held Mrs. Mowbray accountable for the appearance of the bracelet in her bedchamber, if you hadn't been instructed to do so by someone else?"

"I don't care for your tone, Duchess," Clara said,

patting her aunt on the shoulder. "My aunt just told you that she didn't think of the implications at first. She said nothing about anyone else persuading her of anything."

"Remember whom you're speaking to, Clara," Con warned. Turning to Georgie, he asked, "Was that the way you remember it happening?"

"Yes," Georgie said calmly, feeling Clara's glare on her as if it were a hot brand. "I had just returned from looking for the bracelet in Lady Russell's dressing room and bedchamber when Mrs. Marks said that it had been found in my bedchamber."

"I beg your pardon, Lady Clara," Archer said, his expression one of heartfelt sincerity. "Could you possibly tell us where you were during all of this? It's just that Mrs. Mowbray has said you were such a friend to her. I wonder if you didn't perhaps go to visit her rooms while all of this was going on?"

Georgie could see that Clara was torn. On the one hand she was annoyed at being put on the spot, but on the other hand she could not help but preen under the solicitous gaze of Lord Archer. Lady Russell, Georgie noticed, was watching her niece breathlessly.

"I might have done," Clara said with a slight shrug. "Mrs. Mowbray was searching my aunt's rooms for the bracelet, and I wanted to ensure that dear Mrs. Mowbray hadn't unknowingly brought the bracelet into her bedchamber the night my aunt gave her the sapphire and diamond choker."

"Ah, what's this?" Isabella asked, leaning forward, her gaze on Lady Clara's every move. "This is the first I've heard of a sapphire and diamond choker. Why would Lady Russell lend such a valuable gift to her companion? Surely that's better suited to keeping safe within the family?"

"Which is what I thought as well," Clara said, her appreciation for Isabella's justification making her puff up with the rightness of it. "Obviously Mrs. Mowbray has been very helpful to my aunt on any number of issues, but surely nothing that warrants her receiving a family heirloom as a gift. I mean, she's barely known my aunt for six months. She doesn't deserve to have the sapphires."

Clara's dismissal of her made Georgie's blood boil. She behaved as if Georgie had wheedled the sapphires from Lady Russell. And they weren't a gift. They were loaned to her for the evening. Though it would seem that Clara hadn't known that.

"But, Clara," her aunt said, her gaze troubled, her eyes darting from here to there, unsure of where to look. "I already told you that the sapphires were not entailed. Do you believe I should hold on to the necklace for posterity's sake? Or perhaps did you wish me to bestow it upon your daughter so that she might have it instead of my dear friend Georgina who has been with me these many months when you and your family haven't seen fit to visit me once? Is that what you wish?"

"That isn't what I was saying, Aunt," Lady Clara said, turning a bit red. "I was merely suggesting that you may have been a bit premature about the sapphires."

"They are my sapphires to dispose of as I wish," Lady Russell said, stamping her walking stick upon the floor in a manner that resounded through the room like a bullet. "Really, Clara, I had no idea you were harboring such resentments against Georgina. Next you'll say that it was you who planted the ruby cuff in her bed-chamber."

"It was not!" Clara said, looking stricken. "I was not pleased that you gave her the sapphires, but that doesn't mean I would stoop to plant the bracelet in her bed-chamber. What I was going to say is that I didn't see it there."

Everyone in the room stared at Lady Clara.

"Oh, Clara," Lady Russell said with a sigh. "How could you?"

"Are you suggesting, Clara," Con demanded, his voice deceptively calm, "that while Mrs. Mowbray was in Lady Russell's bedchamber, you searched Mrs. Mow-bray's bedchamber and found nothing—only to be in-formed some minutes later that the bracelet had been found in Mrs. Mowbray's bedchamber? And did not see fit to inform the rest of us!"

"Yes," Clara cried, throwing her hands up in the air. "Yes, that's precisely what I did, so there is no pos-sible way that Mrs. Mowbray could have stolen the bracelet."

"I have never been more ashamed of a member of my own family than I am today," Lady Russell said with tears in her eyes. "And that includes all the terri-ble times with your uncle, Clara. All that included."

She held her handkerchief up to her mouth, as if to stop a cry of distress from erupting from her. Unable to let Lady Russell suffer alone, Georgie went to her side and slipped a comforting arm around her. Leading her to a settee, she helped her sit and patted her on the hand as they sat side by side.

"Who was it that first said the bracelet was found in Mrs. Mowbray's bedchamber?" Isabella asked calmly. "Because it seems to me that it's that person who is most at fault." She looked at Lady Clara. "Though there is plenty of blame to attribute to you, my lady, given that you allowed an innocent woman to sustain an accusation that might very well have ended any sort of means for her to earn her own living."

Lady Russell shook her head miserably. "I simply cannot believe it," she said again. "When I think of how I treated you when you left, Georgina. When I consider how cold I was to you. You, whom I've loved like my own daughter. What a wretched fool I've been."

"Do not think of it for another moment, my lady," Georgie said to the older woman. "You were deceived. Most horribly."

"I should hate to be the person who did this," Con said conversationally to the room at large, "if she should fail to admit as much right now."

"It was I," Lydia said, standing up from her chair where she'd been watching the rest of the room's conversation like a cat at a tennis match. "I found the bracelet in Mrs. Mowbray's bedchamber. Or rather, I put it there."

"But why?" Clara demanded of her daughter. "I thought you liked Georgina. As much as you can like anyone, that is. Was it because I complained about the sapphires?"

But Lydia shook her head in denial. "No, Mama, it was not your fault. It was mine. I allowed someone to influence me. A friend, when I should have known better than to be such a fool."

"A friend?" Clara asked, shocked. "Which friend?"

"Well, not a friend exactly," Lydia said, looking ashamed. "I received a letter."

"Of course," Con said with a groan. Turning to Lydia, he asked, "What did it offer you in exchange for framing Georgina for stealing the bracelet?"

"F-five hundred pounds," Lydia said, her eyes wide. "How did you know?"

"Let's just say this person has been practicing his penmanship on some other people in Bath this week," Con said with disgust.

"Does that mean I won't be getting the five hundred pounds?" Lydia asked, looking disappointed. "He said nothing about telling the truth later, so I thought I'd still be able to collect it."

"I simply cannot believe the two of you," Lady Russell said, looking from Clara to Lydia. "When I think about how I might have been deceived into believing the worst of poor Georgina forever. It's enough to give one a disgust of one's own family."

"Aunt," Clara said, her expression stricken, "I truly am sorry. I don't know what came over me. Other than that I was growing a bit jealous of how close you and Mrs. Mowbray had become."

"I am sorry too, Aunt," Lydia said, coming to stand close to her mother. "I was going to use some of the five hundred pounds to buy you a truly wonderful birthday present."

"You are both too much for me to endure at the moment," Lady Russell said finally, rising from her chair with the assistance of Con and Georgie, looking much older and more tired than she'd appeared at the beginning of the interview. "I thank you for your time, your graces, my lord."

Assuring Con that she was able to return to her bed-chamber on her own, Lady Russell left the room.

When she had gone, Con turned to Clara and Lydia. "I think it will be for the best if you removed your-selves from the house and from Bath altogether."

Lydia's brow furrowed. "But what about Aunt Rus-sell's birthday party?"

With a snort of disgust at her daughter, Clara led her by the arm toward the stairs so that they could retrieve their bags. "What did I say?" she could be heard asking her mother as they hurried away.

Twenty

$\mathcal{R}$emember," Con said later that afternoon as he and Georgie arrived at the house in Westgate Buildings where Lowther had been staying. "Look for anything that might tell us who sent him after you."

"I know," Georgie said, impatience creeping into her voice. "I hope that you won't be this nervous once we're inside. One look at the worry in your face will alert the landlady that there's something havey-cavey about us."

Knowing she was right, Con squeezed her hand. It wasn't so much that he expected one of Lowther's compatriots to arrive and assault them, but that he didn't wish her to be involved in any of this business at all. She wasn't meant to be digging around in rented rooms in Westgate Buildings, no matter how much she might think she was. "You are right, my dear," he said. "I will school my features to look less worried."

"Con," she said with a warning note in her voice, "we agreed that I should come with you because I might be able to recognize handwriting or other clues that would not seem important to you. And vice versa."

"There was never the possibility of vice versa," he insisted firmly. "I would never have let you come here alone."

"I might take objection to that," she said with asperity, "but I know how uneasy you are. Kindly do not make a habit of thinking yourself capable of 'letting' me do anything."

Grateful his ploy to divert her attention had worked, he nodded. "Of course. I must have misspoken." Before she could retort, he tucked her hand into his arm and knocked firmly on the door of number 13. "Remember, you're his sister-in-law."

"I remember," Georgie hissed.

Before they could speak further, the door was answered by a large woman in a gray serge gown. She looked them both up and down before saying, "I don't expect you two will be after a room, then. I 'ope you're not from them charity folk, for I've 'ad my fill 'o them."

"No, we are not, Mrs. . . . ?" Con allowed his voice to trail off, waiting for her to supply the name.

Finally, she must have decided they were worthy of speaking to, for she gave a slight nod before saying, "Barrowby. Mrs. Harold Barrowby. Now, what is it you're after, then?"

"Good afternoon, Mrs. Barrowby," Georgie said, smiling sadly. "I am Mrs. Georgina Mowbray and this is my friend Lord Coniston. I was wondering if we might have a look around the rooms of my dear brother-in-law,

Mr. Malcolm Lowther. I believe he was a boarder here?"

Mrs. Barrowby's eyes narrowed with suspicion. "He didn't say nothing about no family," she said. "Though he didn't say much of anything, come to think of it."

"Yes," Georgina agreed, her face somber. "Dear Malcolm wasn't much for conversation. I was hoping to gather his things together and bring them back to my mama-in-law. He was the youngest of her children, you see, and she'll be despondent when she receives the news of his death."

The landlady grunted. She eyed Georgina and Con with narrowed eyes, her gaze lingering on the jeweled pin at Con's throat and the lace edging on Georgina's gown. Con gave the woman three seconds before she asked for a little something in exchange for allowing them to see the room.

Three. Two. One.

"Well, I hates as much as the next to see a mother grieve for one of her own," she said slyly, "but my own children needs to keep a roof above their heads as well, don't they?"

Con wished for once that people weren't so dashed predictable. Aloud he said, "Of course, Mrs. Barrowby, we wouldn't dream of asking you to let us into your home without offering a generous token of our appreciation. Will three guineas help things along?"

If she was surprised by the generosity of the offer, Mrs. Barrowby didn't let on. "Five guineas and you can take the lot," she said firmly. "And that's generous because I know he's got some fine bits and pieces in there."

He put the coins into the woman's outstretched hand while Georgina looked on with impatience. She was ready to get past the woman and into Lowther's rooms.

Finally, Mrs. Barrowby stepped back from the doorway and ushered them into a dank and dusty front entrance hall, shut the door, and then stepped around them to ascend the stairs. She made no indication that she wished for them to follow her, but Con interpreted her acceptance of the money as consent, and taking Georgina by the arm, began following the landlady.

When they reached the second landing, she stepped into a dark hallway and paused before the second door on the right. Pulling out an enormous ring of keys, she fitted one into the door, turned the handle, and extended her arms to indicate they could go in. "Take what you want, but know that if you don't get it out of here today it's all going to the pawnshop tomorrow morning. Like I said, 'e had some nice bits and pieces and I ain't one to let things go to waste."

They told her that she could go, and with a brisk nod, she left, shutting the door behind her.

Stepping farther into the dark room, Con waited for his eyes to adjust before finding a lamp and lighting it. Immediately, a golden glow flared up and then settled out, the light casting their shadows onto the walls around them so that it looked as if visitors from the circus had come to call.

He scanned the room, noting that it had been disordered, either by the dead man himself, or someone who wished to find something within the contents.

"I'll take the bureau," Georgina said, her tone brisk, as she made her way across the room. "You might look around and see if there is a case or portfolio that might have stored letters or perhaps some sort of notes he might have received."

Con nodded, letting his eyes rove from one end of the chamber to the other, looking for anything that might be out of place, or might have been used to store important papers or valuables. On a shelf near the window, he saw a likely grouping and that one of the items there was a portable writing desk which had been turned on its side and stored like a book. Sliding it out from the shelf, he searched the sides, and finding the locking mechanism, he touched his thumbs to the clasps on either side and the lid popped open.

When the lamplight hit the items inside he gave a low whistle.

"What is it?" Georgie asked, not looking up from her task. "Did you find something?"

"Come and see for yourself," Con said, removing the papers in the box and shuffling them to get a look at all of them. "It's the letters from whoever was attempting to persecute you." He moved to the small table by the window and spread the letters out flat on the surface.

"It's just as he told us," Georgie said, sliding one note aside so that she could see the next one. "Each of them emphasize that I am in danger and the need for him to keep watch over me."

"But without being seen," Con said, examining the writing box more closely. Often, portable writing desks like this had secret compartments in them where the writer might store ink and sealing wax. He felt along the outer edges of the box with no luck, then ran his fingers along the border about the velvet-lined interior. At the back, where there seemed to be an extra large bit of cherrywood, he found it. He touched a piece just a fraction of an inch from the corner and a long, narrow drawer slid out. "Look," he told Georgie.

She peered around him at the drawer, where a coil of paper was neatly tucked into the compartment. Con nodded for her to take it, and Georgie reached down to remove it. The paper was a frequently used type of foolscap that could be had from most stationers. He saw her fingers tremble a little as she unrolled it.

They both read the first page as Georgie smoothed it out on top of the other papers on the table.

"My dear Malcolm," Georgina read. "You cannot know how much I need to tell you. About me, about the letters, about all of it. There is so much to explain and so little time in which to do it. Let me assure you that I had very good reasons for doing what I did. And they had nothing to do with wishing to harm you. There was a matter from my past which needed to be set aright. And I'm afraid I found it necessary to use your good nature to make that happen. My apologies, my love. I never meant this to seem like the betrayal you feel it is. Please find it in your heart to forgive me. Please. Ever your love."

"What the devil is this?" Con demanded. "Is this from whoever it was who sent the letters telling him to watch you?"

"That's what it appears to be," Georgina said, frowning. "And they are in the same hand, for what it's worth. Which is proof enough, I think."

"But we still don't know whose hand it is." Con

stacked the pages laid out on the table and placed them back inside the case. Finished with her perusal of the apology note, Georgie tucked it back into the secret drawer and slid it closed.

"No. We don't," Georgie said, closing the lid of the writing case and watching as Con picked it up. "I need to get back to Laura Place and see all of the writing samples side by side."

"Let's go back then," he said, gesturing for her to precede him from the room. "I don't think there's anything else in here for us to find."

They left the house and walked along Westgate Street east toward Great Pulteney Street. They'd only gone a little ways when they were met by Alfred, one of the footmen from Lady Russell's house, who was accompanied by the woman Con had seen with Georgie at the gallery.

"Thank heavens we found you," she said, her voice sharp with alarm. "Georgie, I just came from Lady Russell's house where I was hoping to find you when her ladyship suffered some sort of attack. She's in quite a bad way and the housekeeper asked me to accompany Alfred to find you, my lord. We first went to Laura Place, but were directed to find you here."

"Lettice," she said, pressing a hand to her chest. "How awful. We must go at once." She turned to Con. "We'll take the curricle and Alfred can follow us with Lettice."

"I'm afraid, Georgina," Lettice said, her face twisted with embarrassment, "I was told expressly that you were not to attend her."

That brought both Con and Georgie up short. "What

does that mean?" Con demanded. "Surely my cousins are not still holding on to their foolish ideas about Georgina."

"I'm afraid it was your aunt who insisted upon it," Lettice said apologetically. "Perhaps she isn't in her right mind?"

"That is absurd," Con said. "You will just come with me, Georgina. She will not know you're in the house at any rate. Even if she has forgotten what happened earlier."

In response, Georgie shook her head. "Why don't you go on ahead to see what must be done. I'll follow along later with Lettice."

"I don't like leaving you alone in this area of town," Con said. "Especially given what's been going on this week."

"Now is not the time for pigheadedness, my lord," Georgie told him with a gentle shove. "Now go and I'll be along before you know it."

"You are a goddess among women," Con said, kissing her hand.

Turning to Alfred, he said, "Let's be off then." He climbed up into the curricle, and Alfred took the tiger's seat. "I'll send word if there is any news."

"You can have no notion of how grateful I am that you found us, Lettice," Georgina said to her friend as they walked up a ways so that they might catch a hackney that would take them to Henrietta Street. "Whatever made you search me out today of all days?"

"I was wondering if you'd seen Mary lately," the

other woman said, her expression worried. "I haven't seen her since that day at the Pump Room and I wondered if you had perhaps received a note from her."

"No," Georgie said with a frown. "I haven't seen her. Though I don't think we'll be seeing much of her. I'm not sure if you knew this but she'd been seeing someone and I'm afraid he's been killed."

"Killed?" Lettice gasped, grasping Georgie by the arm. "How dreadful."

Georgie rubbed her arm where Lettice had grabbed it. It felt as if her friend had a sewing pin in her hand. Aloud she said, "Yes, I'm afraid it's true. He was poisoned, and I'm sorry to say it but I think Mary might be a suspect in the whole affair."

"Goodness me," Lettice said, clasping a hand to her bosom. "I don't know what this world is coming to. But surely you don't think Mary is guilty, do you?"

They had reached the juncture of Great Pulteney Street, and as Georgie watched the traffic she began to feel a bit woozy. "I'm . . . not. Lettice, I'm not feelin' well."

"There, there, dear," Lettice said, slipping a hand under Georgie's arm. "Lettice has you. There now, you're all right, aren't you?"

"N . . . n . . ." Georgie tried to make the words leave her mouth but no matter how she concentrated the words refused to leave her lips. To her horror, her head became too heavy for her to hold up and she felt her legs buckle beneath her.

Stronger than Georgie had thought her, Lettice managed to drag her into a nearby alley where Georgie felt herself being lifted into a cart of some sort. *Noooo!* she screamed, but it never left the inside of her head.

"There now," she heard Lettice say as she climbed onto the seat of the cart and began to drive her along the backstreets of Bath. "You just let Lettice carry you along to the Abbey, Georgie. Them that sins needs to repent and you've got any number of sins to repent for, don't you now? Things will be all over before you know it. When you hit the ground you won't feel a thing."

Twenty-one

$\mathcal{L}$ettice's words sent a shiver through Georgie. Having been to Bath Abbey on several occasions, Georgie was well acquainted with it. Especially with the parapets hear the bell tower. She had little doubt that Lettice meant to make her jump from one of them. Perhaps under the guise of penitence for whatever sins Lettice had laid at her feet.

Frustrated tears ran down Georgie's cheeks. If she could but move her limbs she would leap down from the cart. But she couldn't do that. Not only would she risk falling into the street, and beneath the wheels of the other vehicles, she'd also not be able to tell Con the truth about how she felt about him.

At the thought of him, her heart squeezed with fear. She had been too afraid to admit as much to him earlier that morning, but now when her life was in danger, and she risked never seeing his face again, she wished more than anything that she had found the courage within herself to admit her newly discovered love for him. She'd suspected it earlier, but unable to risk her heart again so soon after Robert, she had hidden the suspicion deep within her, where it had little chance of emerging when she saw him. Now she wished she'd told him when she'd had the chance.

"You wouldn't have expected it of your dear old Lettice, would you, Georgie?" her friend asked conversationally from the driver's seat. "But it was me who befriended young Mr. Lowther first. Not that hussy Mary. She always did think she was better than me, that one. Well, it was me, Lettice, who approached him first. And it was me who told him stories about his brother Robert's life in the army. And about his pretty little wife. And when our dear friend—you know who I mean, don't you, gel?—when our friend approached with the suggestion that I ask both Malcolm and Mary to watch after you, well, I made sure they got their offers right and tight."

So it had been Lettice who passed the letters on to Malcolm and Mary? Georgie was sick to realize what a fool she'd been about Lettice. Robert had mentioned playing her false with her own friends but it had never occurred to her that he might mean Lettice. She was a dear, if a little bit on the morose side. Never in a million years would Georgie have suspected Lettice of being the one who set all of this death and destruction into motion.

"How was I to know," Lettice continued, "that they would demand just when they could expect their money? First it was young Malcolm who asked, and I ask you, what was I supposed to do? I couldn't have him going to you about all of this, Georgie. You know I couldn't. You're like peas in a pod with an earl! How would that have looked? No, I made sure that Malcolm would keep his mouth shut. It was easy enough to put a bit of poison in his tea. And I did the same with Mary. Though she, bless her, she's not been found yet."

Georgie thought of Mary, who for all her faults, had not deserved to be murdered for them. And Malcolm Lowther, whose only crime had been being her husband's brother. And if she didn't get out of this cart, Georgie would find herself just as dead as they were.

"I've always wondered, you see," Lettice called back to her conversationally as they rode along, "if there was some reason you always seemed to land on your feet, like a cat. By the time it dawned on me, it was too late to keep you from becoming a success as a companion or as a friend to your noble set. But I could certainly do something after the fact. And in truth, it was far more rewarding to see you fall from a great height than to simply kick you while you were down."

So Lettice had been jealous of her? Georgie thought, aghast. That's what set all of this in motion?

"You must admit that you have to rise a bit in order to fall properly," Lettice continued. "First I killed the man in the theater—Mr. Potts. That was killing two birds with one stone really since he was looking for Robert's partner in crime, wasn't he? I followed you and Lowther and Potts to the theater, thinking maybe Potts would find you and think the worst. Though I suspect he was only following you to ask a few questions. But when he took too long, I decided to use him in another way. I killed him and I thought once the connection to Robert was found you'd be blamed for it. But of course nobody suspects the sweet, innocent little Georgina. Though killing him did get him off my own back—he'd figured out that Robert and I were working together to steal the jewels—so that wasn't a complete waste of effort. No one ever suspected that insignificant little Lettice would be involved in something as shocking as jewel theft!"

Georgie was horrified to hear how proud Lettice sounded about taking a man's life. She spoke of it as if she were explaining how she'd made her prizewinning pie. The gleeful way her friend spoke sent a terrified chill down her spine. Her attitude did not bode well for her plans for Georgie.

"I still needed to find a way to dispatch with you, though," Lettice told Georgie in a tone of confidentiality. "So I saw to it that Lady Russell's bracelet went missing then turned up in your bedchamber. And it worked to get you tossed out on your ear, didn't it? Though I should have known your friends from the nobility would ride to the rescue. What is it about you that makes people lose all common sense?" She made a sound of disgust. "If I hadn't thought of telling Lord Coniston that his aunt had lost her wits, I don't know how I would have gotten him to leave us alone. I might have had to harm him. You wouldn't have cared for that, would you, dear Georgina?"

The vehicle was slowing at last and Georgie, who was beginning to feel whatever Lettice had used on her wear off, braced herself to climb out as soon as it stopped. Unfortunately, Lettice must have thought of this possibility for escape as well, because pulling the horse to an abrupt stop, she leaped into the back of the cart and wrestled with Georgie until she had her hands clasped together.

Holding her in a grip that was surprisingly strong, Lettice tied Georgie's hands together with a bit of rope. "I apologize for this, my dear Georgina," her captor said, "but I'm afraid that I don't trust you to stay by my side when we get out of the cart." Leading Georgie by her hands, she pulled her to the edge of the cart and helped her jump down. Removing her own cloak she swung it around to place it over Georgie's shoulders. Pulling up the hood to cover Georgie's face, she allowed the cloak to drape before her, hiding her bound hands. "There now. No one will ever suspect things aren't as they should be. Thank goodness for this bit of cool weather so that it won't look out of place for you to be wearing a cloak like that. Though I daresay it isn't as fine as what you'd be able to get as the wife of Lord Coniston. I could almost shed a tear for the loss of that match," she said with mock sadness. "But only almost. In fact, I'll do what I can to comfort your poor distraught love. Never fear."

The thought of Con grieving for her loss made Georgie want to cry out. Still, the thought of what Con might suffer if she should die left her feeling the resolve she'd need to fight back against Lettice. She tried to channel the determination to keep the other woman from winning and pushed all of the fear and worry that had been clouding her mind away. In its place, she allowed her survival instinct and her soul-deep love for Con to focus her resolve on one thing and one thing only: getting out of this situation alive.

She could not, however, let Lettice see the change in

her demeanor. She had to make the other woman think she'd lost all hope. That she was unable to move beyond her anguish to fight back. When Georgie stumbled, Lettice grabbed her by the back of the cloak and pulled her up short. Out of the alley, they stepped past the visitors queuing up to go into Bath Abbey, and with Lettice leading Georgie by the arm, they slipped in a door just inside the entrance.

The dark hallway was short and led to a flight of stairs leading to the bell tower at the top of the ancient church. But Georgie noticed none of it. The stone walls were cool and the stairwell was much colder than the air outside had been and Georgie was glad of the cloak, though climbing the stairs was difficult given her tied hands and the inability to steady herself on the at times narrow steps.

They didn't speak as they climbed, and Georgie was grateful for the chance to plan her escape. She knew that Lettice was intending to push her from the top once they reached the tower, but she hoped that there would be a moment or two for some last words. Because it was then that she would take her captor by surprise and get away.

Finally, after a few minutes more of silent climbing, they reached the small landing with windows cut into the stones so that they could look out at the city of Bath and past it into the countryside beyond. The bell, whose chains were located in the little room where they stood, was far above them in the top of the cupola. Georgie looked up and then made the mistake of looking down and nearly lost her balance. She'd never really been fond of heights but this went beyond simple fear of heights. She'd been able to climb the ruins without any great discomfort, but this was far higher than she'd ever been and she did not like it. Not one bit.

Lettice, on the other hand, was energized. It was evident from her every movement, every word.

"It is incredible, is it not?" she asked Georgie, her eyes avid with a kind of mad excitement. "From here you can see all the way to the coast. It's a God's-eye view, and I feel at home at last. No man, or woman either, would dare cross me from this great height. It fills me with invincibility. Do you understand, Georgina? Do you feel it?"

Georgie wasn't sure what her response should be to Lettice's questions. If she agreed, Lettice might accuse her of trying to usurp her power. But if she showed fear that would give the other woman the satisfaction of knowing that Georgie was feeling exactly what she wanted her to feel. As it happened, however, it wasn't necessary for her to speak at all because a shout from the ground below them caught their attention.

Peering down, Georgie saw Con staring up at the bell tower from the street, where he was joined by Mr. McGilloway, the investigator for the magistrate's office, Perdita, Archer, Isabella, and Trevor. He said something to his companions then shouted upward toward them. "I'm coming, Georgina. Don't move."

"Oh, lovely," Lettice said with a beatific smile. "We'll have an audience. I suppose this will be easy enough to explain. I shall simply tell them you've been livid with me ever since you learned of my affair with your late husband. Which, of course, you didn't speak of to anyone because you were so ashamed of being played false. It will be no great trouble to convince them that you led me up here then tried to push me off. I had no choice but to fight for my life. You're quite strong for such a tiny thing, after all. And what a terrible tragedy it will be, when, in a fit of sorrow at seeing you fall to your death, your dear Lord Coniston follows you down. Really, it's a beautiful tale of love. It might be marred a bit by the news of all those murders you committed before you died, but then there is always a bit of bad news to leaven the good."

Georgie stared dumbfounded. Lettice sincerely believed that she'd be able to convince the authorities that the crimes she, Lettice, had committed had instead been perpetrated by Georgina. All evidence to the contrary conveniently forgotten in the haze of her madness.

Still, Georgie had an idea that she hoped would enable her to escape. If only she could get Lettice to cooperate.

Aloud she said, "Lettice, how on earth are they going to believe I threatened you when my hands have been tied up this whole while? I think you'd better remove the rope before I go down, don't you?"

Lettice watched her for a moment, her eyes narrowed with suspicion. "Why would you point that out to me? You aren't going to convince me that you really wish to fall to your death. You're too fond of your own hide to want that."

Even so, she walked closer to where Georgie stood next to one of the stone pillars holding up the cupola. "Give me your wrists," she said with impatience. "I'm getting tired of your foolishness and we might as well make sure you fall before Lord Coniston gets up here. He'll be more easy to control when you're gone."

Obeying, Georgie offered the other woman her bound wrists, and rather than trying to untie the knot she'd tied there, Lettice pulled a knife from her reticule and sliced through the bindings. "There," she said, while Georgie rubbed the raw flesh on her wrists. "Now, it's time for you to pay for your myriad sins, my dear friend."

As Georgie had hoped, Lettice couldn't resist the urge to point the knife at Georgie's chest while they were standing so close to one another. She pressed the point into Georgie's breastbone. Georgie remained still while Lettice spoke.

"You really don't like this knife, do you?" she asked, her eyes narrowed with delight. "I must admit, it would be so satisfying to sink it right into your flesh." She smiled, her eyes focused on the place where the knife bit into Georgie's skin. "You saw the bayonet wounds after battle, did you not?" she asked, looking at Georgie. "Where the blade had sliced through skin and sinew and sometimes bones or organs. It was terrible, but at the same time, there was a sort of beauty to it all. The way the blood turned from red to crimson then to black. The way the flesh parted, like a melon split open in the sun."

Georgie's stomach turned at the other woman's descriptions, but she steeled herself against the image her words conjured. Instead she focused on the knife, and on the lilt of Lettice's words. She'd just chosen her moment when several things happened at once.

First, she brought her right hand up from where it

rested at her side and grabbed the hand in which Lettice gripped the knife.

Next, they heard pounding steps coming up the stairs.

Georgie took advantage of the other woman's surprise, and using the pillar behind her for balance, she pressed down on Lettice's knife and tried to wrest it away from her. They struggled for a few moments until Lettice, who was wearing boots and not slippers like Georgie, brought her booted foot down on Georgie's foot. Hard. Surprised, Georgie lessened her grip for a split second, and before she knew it Lettice, pulling at the knife, propelled them both away from the pillar and up against the balustrade, where she pushed Georgie's head and shoulders over the edge.

She'd just brought the knife against Georgie's throat, when Con burst through the doorway pointing a pistol at Lettice.

"Drop the knife, Mrs. Stowe," he said fiercely. "And let Georgina go."

Twenty-two

Oh," Lettice said, not frightened in the least, "you'd like that, wouldn't you? Then you and your little mouse could live happily ever after. Isn't that right? Well, why should I care one way or another what you want, Lord Coniston? Your sort has never given a hang for me."

"But perhaps that's why, Lettice," he said, softening his tone. Georgie could hear the fear underlying his façade of calm, however. "Perhaps Georgina and I can see to it that you get the respect you deserve. I am an earl after all. I'm quite powerful and could see to it that you get everything you deserve. But only if you let Georgina go. If you don't then I'm afraid I'll do everything in my power to destroy you."

"Oh, la, my lord," Lettice said with a giggle. "Listen to you making such a threat. And me with my knife right here on your little love's neck. Let's just see what happens if I bring the knife closer." She increased the pressure on the blade and Georgie felt the sharp sting of it against her neck, where her pulse hammered with fear. She clenched her teeth against the pain rather than give Lettice the satisfaction of hearing her cry out.

"No!" Con cried. "No. Stop. Do not hurt her. I apologize for threatening you, Lettice. Only please don't hurt her. I . . ." Georgie could see the fear in his eyes, and she felt the burn of tears behind her eyes as she watched him. "I love her," he said, his voice breaking. "I'll do whatever you wish. Just please don't harm her."

"Will you put your gun down?" Lettice asked, her voice lilting as if she were singing a nursery rhyme. "Will you put your gun down and promise not to interfere again? Your little love and I have some unfinished business to attend to."

"Yes, of course," Con said, his voice strong, but still with a thread of fear behind it. "I'll leave you alone. And I'll put the pistol down. Here?" He gestured to the sill nearest him.

"That's better," Lettice said, nodding her approval. "Now, you may stay here. But keep quiet. And remember not to interfere. I so hate interfering gentlemen."

Con nodded, but his eyes found Georgie's and held them for only a moment. But it was long enough for her to feel the power of his love for her. And silently she vowed to get out of this situation so that she and Con could have and enjoy the happily ever after that Lettice had just scoffed about.

"Now," Lettice said to Georgie, "where were we?" She kept Georgie in position, where she was facing Con, who looked as if he wanted more than anything to rush to them and prise the knife from the other woman's hand. But the distance was too far. By the time he reached her side, Lettice could have slit Georgie's throat.

"Ah, yes," Lettice said, wrapping her left arm across Georgie's chest to hold her steady, and bringing the knife up against Georgie's throat again. "I wanted to ask you a few things before you have to dash off."

She laughed at her own joke for a moment before continuing. "But seriously, I would like to know what it is about you that makes grown men turn into slavering idiots. I've never been able to understand it. Even my own dear husband thought you were the prettiest little thing he ever saw. And let's not forget your dear husband, Robert, who still watched your every little move even while he was bedding everyone but you! Now is that fair, I ask you? I say that it is not! Then your brother-in-law, dear Malcolm, took the instructions I gave him to watch over you far too seriously. Didn't he realize that he was only supposed to watch you? There was nothing in my notes instructing him to build castles in the air about taking you away from it all.

"Men are so unutterably foolish. But none of them has been quite as foolish over you as your own dear Galahad, there, Lord Coniston. Though Galahad was pure, wasn't he? And your dear, dear Coniston is anything but. He can be a very naughty boy. Why, I suspect he had carnal desires for you while he was betrothed to your dear friend the young dowager. He is a man, isn't he?"

As she spoke, Lettice's voice became more and more strident until she reached the end of her speech when she was shouting. "I want to know what it is about you,

Georgina!" she cried through clenched teeth. "I want to know why they all love you!"

All the while Lettice was winding herself up into a towering rage, Georgie was biding her time. She could feel the other woman shaking as she allowed her anger to overtake her, until finally the hand holding the knife against her throat was so unsteady that Georgie feared she'd cut her throat accidentally. But when Lettice shouted her last words, Georgie judged the moment to be right, and her hands free, she grabbed hold of the forearm of Lettice's knife hand and pushed as hard as she could away from her neck. Then she dropped all of her weight downward and scrambled away from Lettice and toward Con.

Having her arm thrown forward then back made Lettice lose her balance, and as she scrambled to right herself, she found only air. Unable to regain her footing, she flew backward over the edge of the short wall and down to the stone-covered ground below.

"So this Lettice Stowe person was responsible for all of it?" Isabella asked from her perch on the arm of Trevor's chair. "But what on earth sent her over the edge?"

"Oh, Isabella," Perdita said with a grimace. "That was a bad pun even for you."

They were all, including Georgina and Con, who were seated next to one another on the settee, gathered in the drawing room of Perdita's house in Laura Place.

After the events of the day before they'd all been reluctant to let Georgie out of their sight. Especially Con, but Georgie could not find it in herself to resent him for it. After so many years of feeling as if she had no one to lean on in times of strife, it was a comfort to know she could lean on Con if she had to.

"Yes, to answer the question," she said, breaking into the sisterly bickering. "From what her journals revealed, she was living here in Bath when she received a summons from someone she never names. He offered to pay for her to stay in Bath if she would perform a service for him. Which was to make my life here miserable."

"And there's no way of knowing who this person was?" Trevor asked, frowning. "I am dashed tired of this fellow getting away without punishment while his minions take all the blame."

"It is rather troubling, isn't it?" Isabella asked, absently stroking his arm. "It sounds all too familiar, this delegation of dirty work."

"I didn't say that, precisely," Georgie said quickly. "Mr. McGilloway gave me a letter to examine from the person who wrote to Lettice. I'll give you one guess as to whose hand it's in."

"Never say!" Perdita gasped. "The same person who pens your threats about last season?"

"Correct," Con said. He'd been quiet through this entire exchange and Georgie could feel the tension in his body next to hers. She had tried to reassure him that she was in one piece, but that didn't seem to be enough to quell his fears.

Since Georgie knew how she would feel had their positions in the bell tower been reversed, she understood and tried not to worry him further.

"The penmanship is definitely the same," Con continued. "And the paper is similar as well. So this person, whoever he is, is determined to see to it that you three are punished in whatever way he can manage. Though it seems his preferred method is to use someone who already bears you a grudge to do the task."

"And someone we don't already see as a threat," Isabella said thoughtfully. "I must admit, it's rather clever of him. If the attack comes from a direction we don't expect then the blow is likely to be more painful."

"Exactly," Georgie said. "We aren't dealing with a weak intelligence. This person is extremely bright. And is willing to do whatever it takes to prey upon our worst fears."

"Let us hope that he doesn't like repeating himself," Perdita said in a joking tone. "For I have no wish to see the specter of Gervase mooning up at me from the back garden."

"It's not a joke, your grace," Archer said, rising from his chair by the fire to stalk over to the window. Almost as if he wished to reassure himself that there was no ghost hiding in the garden. "This man, whoever he is, has unsuccessfully attempted to arrange the deaths of your sister and your friend. And if he holds to his pattern, you will be next on his list. It is not a matter for joking. We should instead be making plans to get you away from your usual locales and find somewhere that you can lie low for a while. Until the threat passes."

"And when will that be?" Perdita asked, her face taut with annoyance. "Next year? The year after? I have spent long enough cowering in the shadows, Archer, and I do not intend to do so ever again."

"He may be right, though, Perdita," Isabella said

quietly. "If there is a way to protect yourself from this monster, then perhaps you should take advantage of it. I should hate to see you suffer as we have."

"I have twice now seen this person threaten people I love," Perdita said firmly. "I will not be the one to hide myself away when my turn comes. I will stand firm, and when he comes for me, I will be waiting."

With a muttered imprecation, Archer strode from the room and down the stairs. Faintly they heard the front door close after him as he left the house.

"Well," Perdita said, "I didn't mean to annoy him, but it is my decision to make, after all."

Suspecting that Lord Archer was more invested in keeping Perdita safe than her friend realized, Georgie kept silent. It was not her place to tell Perdita of her suspicions. And if Archer wished her to know he would have done so by now.

Changing the subject, she said brightly, "Enough of this morose talk. Let us discuss something happy." She looked pointedly at Isabella who frowned in puzzlement for a moment. Then comprehension dawning, she laughed. "Oh, that. I'd quite forgotten it was news."

"What was news?" Con asked, looking from one lady to the other.

"Only that it would appear that the house of Ormond is expecting a new addition to the fold," Georgie said with a grin. "You knew that already didn't you, Con?"

"Oh, that," he said, echoing Isabella. "Yes, I already knew that. But it is a delightful change of topic all the same."

The good news did what Georgie had hoped and infused the room with a happier atmosphere as they began to suggest possible names for the impending heir. Perdita mouthed "well done" at Georgie while the others were looking the other way. Georgie gave a slight shrug, but she was pleased with how her attempt at changing the subject had worked.

But she was somewhat puzzled when Con stood in the middle of the conversation. Georgie watched, curious, as he said, "I hope you will forgive me for doing this here and now, but I did promise Georgina a spectacle, and since we are unable to go out of doors without encountering a loathsome scandalmonger, I thought you all might serve as our audience."

"Not at all," Trevor answered with a grin.

"If this is what I think it is," Isabella said, her eyes alight with mischief, "then I wouldn't miss being privy to it for the world."

"Don't look at me," Perdita said with a broad smile, "I said you should do it days ago."

Beginning to suspect what might be afoot, Georgie felt her heart speed up within her. As she looked on, Con walked toward her, and to her astonishment, he stopped and came down on one knee before her.

She looked up into his dear face, which had become nearly as familiar to her in the past days as her own, and saw love, patience, and something else, something rare and precious, shining out at her from his eyes.

"Georgina," he began, his voice strong and sure, "I knew from the moment we met that you would be important to me, but at the time I had little knowledge of just how important you would be. Since then I have discovered so many wonderful things about you. Your patience, your kindness, your generosity, your loyalty to your friends, and your passionate nature." This last had Georgie turning rather pink in the cheeks. "I have known for a while that there is no other woman I would wish to have alongside me as I journey through this life. My darling, my partner, my most precious Georgina, please say you'll marry me and make me the happiest of men."

All through his speech, Georgie felt tears streaming down her face, and when he reached the end, she let out a sob.

His face becoming increasingly worried, by the time he finished his proposal, and Georgie sobbed aloud, Con was looking sincerely alarmed. "Georgina, dearest, I know it might be a bit sudden, but I had hoped that you might be happier upon hearing this than you seem to be. Perhaps if I—"

Before he could finish, Georgie shook her head vigorously. "No," she managed to choke out between sobs. "This is . . . because . . . I . . . am . . . happy," she said, before throwing her arms around Con's neck and sadly crushing his cravat.

Behind them, she heard the door to the drawing room open, and Con leaned back a bit to accept something from Archer, and before she could speak again, Georgie felt a ring being slipped over the knuckle of her ring finger.

"This was my grandmother's," he whispered against her hair. "I knew from the moment I saw you that I would be needing it soon. Fortunately, Archer was able to retrieve it for me yesterday. Otherwise we'd have been forced to make do with my signet ring. Which isn't nearly as pretty."

Pulling back a little, Georgie looked down at the ring on her finger. It was pretty. A sapphire surrounded by tiny winking diamonds.

Looking into Con's eyes, however, she said only, "You're prettier. And stronger. And more beloved."

At her words, his expression softened and he kissed her. "Not as beloved as you are, my dearest Georgina." He stroked her cheek with his thumb, staring at her every feature as if he were memorizing her for posterity. "I thought I'd lost you up there on that tower," he whispered.

"You didn't, though," Georgie said, looking into his eyes. "I had too much to fight for to ever let her take me."

"And I had too much to lose to let her win," Con said, leaning his forehead against hers. "I love you, Georgina," he said quietly. "I love you more than I ever thought possible."

"I had a suspicion," she said with a crooked grin. "What a lovely coincidence that I love you too."

"Promise me you'll never put yourself in danger like that again," Con said fiercely. "I don't know if I'd be able to handle it."

"I shall certainly try," Georgie said, "but you must know there are certain things that we simply cannot control. But I assure you that if it is at all in my power, I will try never to frighten you like that again. But the same goes for you."

"I think I can make that promise," Con said, giving her a hug. "Now, I suppose we'd better stop embracing and share our joy with our friends. All right?"

Georgie nodded, and turned around in his arms.

"We're betrothed!" she cried, holding up her newly beringed finger.

And their friends responded with a resounding huzzah.

"I can think of worse ways to begin life as a couple," Con said to her with a grin, "than with cheers."

Georgie heartily agreed.

Epilogue

So many lives were harmed by Lettice Stowe," Georgie said the next day as she, Perdita, and Isabella shared tea in the drawing room of Laura Place. The men had gone off in search of a prizefight that was supposedly going on in the vicinity. After the excitement of the past week, Georgie could not blame them. "It really is far too much to believe that my dear friend of so many years did all of that because she was jealous of me."

Not only was she surprised about Lettice, but also that the person who held herself, Isabella, and Perdita responsible for Gervase, Duke of Ormond's death, was still out there. "Perdita," she continued, "I know you were resistant to the subject yesterday, but I was hoping that was playacting for the sake of hiding Lord Archer's reasons for leaving the room. Please tell me that you are not as resistant to taking precautions for your own safety as you suggested yesterday."

Perdita's expression, which had been one of good humor, turned wary. "I was exaggerating a bit for the sake of drama," she said carefully. "But it is an old

argument between Archer and me. He is being a bit
old-womanish about the whole thing, really. I mean, I
know that the two of you faced some sincerely disturbing attacks, but I have no intention of running away
from the field before our mysterious last-season corre-
spondent even makes a move. Aside from the fact that I
don't wish to appear cowardly, I don't know how long I
would need to stay away. Five years, ten years, fifteen,
forever? It's a ludicrous proposition for me to leave
when there has yet to be a genuine threat to my safety."

"What of the letters you've already received from
him?" Isabella asked, her lovely face taut with worry.
"Do those not count? Or do you think that he's of no
harm until the first death threat? Or perhaps it's an attempt on your life that you see as the more legitimate
signal to let you know that the game has begun? Tell,
me, Sister, when should we begin to feel terror on your
behalf?"

"Do not be so melodramatic, Isabella," Perdita said,
waving off her sister's words. "I am not proposing to
simply place myself within target range of this person
and wait for him to shoot. I had enough of that with
Gervase, thank you. I only mean that I won't run away
from him. I cannot. It is not in my nature, but more
importantly, it hasn't done either of you any good."

"What do you mean? That we are cowards?" Georgie demanded, her voice hurt.

"No, no," Perdita rushed to assure her. "Of course I
do not. I only mean that you both removed yourselves
from the site of Gervase's death, which was London,
and this person still managed to find ways of getting to
you. So, what good would it do me to go abroad or hide

away in Scotland? He would simply find some way of getting his minions to wherever it was I chose to hide.

"No," she continued, standing and beginning to pace before the fire. "What I intend to do is go about my day-to-day life behaving as if I expect nothing untoward to happen."

"And what if it should?" Isabella asked, her brows raised in question. "What if you suddenly find yourself in the position of fighting for your life? Will you simply decide to stand your ground and fight alone?"

"Hardly," Perdita said with calm assurance. "I shall be protected by you all. And do not forget Archer. He has made it quite clear that he has no intention of letting anything happen to me. Whether I wish him to or not."

"I was about to ask what Archer thought of all this," Georgie said with a grin. "He seems to take a great interest in your health and safety these days, does he not?"

Before Perdita could respond, Isabella spoke up, "Yes, indeed, our Perdita seems to have gained a champion there. I wonder if she returns the favor or if she simply thinks of him as yet another hapless suitor."

"There is nothing hapless about Lord Archer," Perdita snapped, tiring of being the butt of their jokes. "He is simply a good friend who has promised to look after me, despite the fact that I've tried heartily to dissuade him."

"I do not doubt it," Isabella said with a grin. "Those come-hither looks you give him definitely seem the most probable means of warning a man off."

"Stop it, both of you!" Perdita said, her temper getting

the best of her. "I tell you once and for all that there is nothing between us. We are friends. Now, I wish that you would stop haranguing me over a subject which you know makes me uncomfortable."

Her words hung in the air for a few moments, as Georgie and Isabella exchanged looks, then turned back to look at Perdita.

Contrite, Georgie reached out to squeeze Perdita's hand. "My dear, we had no idea this was such a sensitive subject for you. We were only teasing."

Isabella also spoke up. "Perdita," she said, "if I thought for one moment that our teasing could possibly have brought you pain, I would never have done so. I had hoped that there might be something between the two of you, that is all."

"Well," Perdita said, rising from her chair, pulling away from both ladies, "there is nothing between us. I wish you will not speak of it again."

To Georgie and Isabella's surprise, she stalked from the room and shut the door firmly behind her.

"What on earth was that about?" Isabella asked, staring at the now closed door.

"I'm not sure," Georgie said with a shake of her head. "But I know one thing's for sure."

"What's that?"

"She's lying. There is definitely something going on between those two," she said with certainty. "I don't care what Perdita says."

Coming soon . . .

Don't miss the next novel of "emotion-packed, passionate
historical romance" (*Romance Junkies*) from
MANDA COLLINS

Why Lords Lose Their Hearts

Available in August 2014 from St. Martin's Paperbacks